The Gift of Joy

The Gift of Joy

Ian Whates

NewCon Press
England

First edition, published in the UK April 2009
by NewCon Press

NCP 011 (hardback)
NCP 012 (softback)

10 9 8 7 6 5 4 3 2 1

ISBN: 978-1-907069-00-0 (hardback)
978-1-907069-01-7 (softback)

Cover Artwork by Vincent Chong
Cover layout and design by Andy Bigwood

Invaluable editorial assistance from Ian Watson
Book layout by Storm Constantine

Printed by the MPG Books Group in the UK

'Without Whom' Department:

My sincere thanks to the members of both the Northampton SF Writers Group and the BSFA's Orbiter 1, who have read and critiqued many of these stories. Also, to the editors who have been brave enough to publish them and the friends who have been so generous with their time and wisdom; in particular: Henry Gee, George Mann, Lee Harris, Farah Mendlesohn, Eric Brown, Mark Robson, Pat Cadigan, Storm Constantine, Liz Williams, Kim Lakin-Smith, Chaz Brenchley, Heather Bradshaw and Tom Hunter. I'd also like to acknowledge the debt owed to the late Trevor Jones, proprietor and editor of *Dream Magazine*, who published my first stories back in the late 1980s.

I would especially like to thank two people: Helen, for her love, her support and for putting up with me; and Ian Watson, for his encouragement and his willingness to share such a wealth of knowledge and experience, but most of all for his friendship.

Contents

Introduction

Ian Watson

In a few brief years Ian Whates has already established himself as a great and jovial presence at conventions, rather like a latterday Bob Shaw, and also as a maker and shaker within the genre world, not least due to being a publisher of innovative and beautifully designed anthologies from his own Newcon Press; and here in his first collection he reveals himself as a master of the short story too – both SF and horror, for his range is wide.

The Gift of Joy is the sort of collection I love, where planetary escapades and vivid battle action rub shoulders with charming yet eerie rural tales and with perilous urban nightmares. Generally, chatty narrators tell these tales, narrators who may sometimes be flawed individuals. The result is an engaging sense of an intimate conversation; rather than narrators, perhaps we should say raconteurs. I'm reminded of the humanism and the science-fictional inventiveness of, yes, Bob Shaw, whose natural heir Ian Whates often seems to me to be.

Here are disappointed desires and frustrated yearnings, poignant misfortunes, hard-bitten yet tender episodes, brilliant surprises and finales, and much lovely imagery in lucid prose, grace notes abounding. Ian is a master of pacing, and he's far from averse to skilful experimenting, as in "The Sum of the Parts" which questions not only narrative but also the nature of reality, yet without flying off into metafiction. Or there's the one-sided interrogation of a naïve spoilt brat in "Piratical Sabbatical", just the twit's answers, resulting in a comic tour-de-force.

Utterly gripping is "The Final Hour", where the entire universe is at risk in a countdown from one hour to zero. Powerful, surreal and nightmarish is "The Ghost in the Machine", a Kafkaesque vision where persons who lack... no spoilers please! ...where those persons will live in my imagination for a long time, in the same way that in the film *Pan's Labyrinth*... I said no spoilers!

A nifty variation upon Dorian Gray, and much else besides, propels "Knowing How to Look" – and Ian Whates certainly knows how to do so – set in a London somewhat more familiar to us than that of the fast-paced "One Night in London". As a narrator points out, there are many Londons, just as what underlies the carpet of reality we tread upon blithely may be frighteningly different when that carpet is lifted or pulled aside; which is what the innocent narrator of "Hanging on Her Every Word" discovers to his cost. Ian does have rather a knack with titles! Expect to discover dire implications in this particular phrase, although not the most obvious one.

Whates describes one of his tales as a sugar-coated bonbon with a hot chilli centre. So I'm tempted to describe this collection of nineteen stories as an assortment box of varied delights, beautifully gift-wrapped, except that far from being just confectionery to amuse a few moments, the tastes of the centres linger long. And as for gift-wrapped, be aware that *gift* is the German word for poison, of which there are various insidious kinds, not necessarily always fatal, though for some characters it might be better if this were so.

The Gift of Joy

Conrad sauntered into Lacey's bar and took his accustomed place on one of the high stools, which settled with a disconcerting lurch. He wriggled in an effort to find a more stable base, causing the stool's feet to scrape against the mock-wood beneath with teeth-jarring effect. Roach glanced up to favour him with a sour look that bisected a smile and a grimace – his customary form of greeting.

Roach was a constant feature at Lacey's. He ate there, drank there and worked from there. For all Conrad knew, he might even have slept there.

"Another lousy day," he observed.

"Aren't they all," Conrad responded, completing a ritual that had become established between them an age ago. My-Ling materialised at the other side of the counter, armed with a coy smile and a glass of gently effervescing beer. She was not coy, as Conrad well knew; it was just part of the camouflage she presented when at work. With a grunt he fished in his pocket for some coins, forcing his fingers beneath the tight crease formed by his trousers and wishing he had thought to take the money out before sitting down.

Beer paid for, his gaze settled on the television. It sat above the bar and currently featured what was clearly a news or current affairs programme. The image switched from earnest reporter to a close-up of President Kelly; coverage of a recent speech, by the look of it. Grey-blue eyes gazed straight at the camera for an instant, integrity oozing from every pore of his craggy, near-handsome face. The volume was set too low to make out individual words – a minor mercy for which Conrad was grateful. The picture then cut to a long shot from the same event, the President shaking hands with some dignitary or other.

"Do we have to have that thing on?" Conrad complained. He had his own reasons for not wanting to look at the President more often than necessary.

My-Ling shrugged and clearly had no intention of switching the TV off. A deliberate act of perversity – she knew how much he loathed watching that man and why.

"I hate this town," Roach said to no one in particular.

No he didn't; more camouflage. Slate was not the sort of place that anyone stayed in unless they wanted to, and Roach had been there for as long as anyone could remember. The comment did not require a response and Conrad duly obliged by ignoring it.

The story went that the town's founders had called the new settlement Slate because it represented a new beginning, a chance to start again, to 'wipe the slate clean'. Conrad had his own theory. He believed the place had been called Slate because it was cold, hard and grey. Of course, not everyone shared his jaundiced view – it was all a question of perspective, with his particular perspective being from the bottom looking up.

As with any place that had been established for a while, Slate inevitably evolved its own districts and strata. There were those who had done very well for themselves – affluent types who lived in nice, upmarket suburbs. Anyone who saw only these areas might be forgiven for thinking this was a nice place to live. But that was just the icing; lift it up and you would soon find the crumbling layers of stale pastry hidden beneath.

Conrad was not a native of Slate, having arrived several years ago and knowing at once that it would do just fine. He quickly found his own level, settling somewhere towards the base of the pile, where people kept themselves to themselves and were rarely inclined to ask too many questions. Not that he had a problem with questions as such; it was the answers that could prove a little awkward.

By way of contrast, the woman who had just walked into Lacey's and was now hovering uncertainly by the door clearly belonged to the opposite end of the social spectrum; the icing. Tall, blonde, porcelain-skinned and immaculately made-up, wearing designer shoes that were perfectly matched by a bag of the most impractical sort: far too small to hold much of anything. The ensemble was completed by a long, stylishly tailored coat that had not been bought from anywhere around here… unless it had come from the back of a large anonymous vehicle, and Conrad was willing to give her the benefit of the doubt.

He looked away, continuing to watch from the corner of his eye. Beside him, Roach came alert and did the same. They were both calculating the odds. The woman stood out like a mermaid in the desert and there could only be so many explanations for her presence. The way he figured it, either she was lost or she was looking for something. If the latter, then she was probably seeking one of several illicit thrills that Roach could guide her to, or his own unique services.

She made her way hesitantly to the bar. Both he and Roach continued to feign indifference.

Further evidence that she was out of her element: she ordered an expensive cocktail that stood absolutely no chance of being made properly in a joint like this. My-Ling did her best, presenting a tall glass that held a fair approximation of the requested drink – at least to Conrad's inexperienced eye.

Then she wanted to pay electronically and was completely fazed by My-Ling's shake of the head, fumbling around in her pocket-sized bag for coins as if she had all but forgotten what real money was for.

"I was looking…" Both his and Roach's ears pricked up. "I mean, I was told that a man called Conrad sometimes drinks in here…" Roach slumped a fraction.

My-Ling's eyes flicked in Conrad's direction an instant before he turned, displaying his most engaging smile. "Then you were told wrong, madam. I *always* drink in here."

"Oh." Her nervous laugh was a delight.

He led her to a corner table, where they could talk more discretely. As he took both their drinks from the bar, he caught My-Ling watching him, her expression unreadable.

"My name's Joy," the vision before him stated.

How very appropriate.

"You were recommended to me by a friend, Anna."

He smiled and nodded, as if that explained everything. In truth he knew three women by that name, any one of whom could have been the Anna referred to. Well, any of two, he amended, discounting the under-age junkie from Sandra's massage parlour next door.

"I was told that you… That is, Anna said…" He let her flounder for a minute, taking small pleasure in watching her do so. She really was a beauty; younger than he'd first assumed, as well. The tailored clothing and expert make-up created an illusion of greater maturity and sophistication than truly existed in the woman they adorned. Nor was she entirely stupid, having evidently divested herself of all jewellery before venturing into this part of town. With one exception.

"You're married." The wearing of wedding rings had again come back in vogue in recent years.

Her cheeks reddened prettily. "Yes. So?"

Which was a fair question. What had been intended as an observation must have sounded more like an accusation and it had been a mistake to blurt that out. She was having doubts. He could see as much in her face. Presumably it took a lot of courage for her to come here and now the resolve that had carried her this far was starting to waver. He cursed himself for a fool and set about repairing the damage with reassurance, smooth words, and warm smiles, until she relaxed once more.

Then it was time to discuss payment. He had been weighing

her up throughout, balancing her obvious reservations and nervousness against her apparent affluence and the fact she was here at all. In the end he decided to raise his usual fee by fifty and blithely said, "Two hundred and fifty."

She hesitated, her eyes widening slightly. Was it too much? Was it more than he'd charged Anna, more than her friend had warned her to expect? Probably, but he trusted his instincts.

Whatever her thoughts she kept them to herself, eventually responding with a simple nod – a quick, shallow bob of the head.

"In cash," he stressed, feeling it a point worth making after her performance at the bar.

"Yes, of course. I drew out specially." She reached for her bag.

"Not here," he said, holding out a restraining hand. "That can wait until we're less public."

"Oh… right." Her hand retreated back to her lap.

When Conrad felt she was ready, he suggested they leave.

He made a point of not looking in My-Ling's direction on the way out.

His place was just around the corner. They were there in less than five minutes. Rarely had any client made him so aware of his home's short-comings. It had not seemed *this* shabby when he left it, nor as chilly.

"Sorry, it's a bit cold." He switched on the fire, conscious as he did so of how quaint this must seem. Doubtless in her own residence the heating was completely automated; perhaps she even had one of those integrated systems where temperature, humidity – the entire ambience – was constantly maintained at predetermined levels according to the time of day and the season of the year.

He turned back to Joy and found her staring at the bed. At such moments, that particular piece of furniture always seemed to dominate the room, as if it somehow swelled in stature especially for the occasion.

"Drink?"

She shook her head. A pity, it might have steadied her nerves. She had barely touched her drink back at Lacey's – not that he blamed her, My-Ling being no cocktail waitress. It was also apparent that her nervousness had increased since they left the bar and he had no intention of allowing her to back out, not with two hundred and fifty at stake.

He helped himself to a scotch. "Are you sure?" Again she declined.

"Shall I pay you now?" It was always a relief when the client offered without any further prompting. He accepted the money and tucked it away so rapidly that it must have seemed like sleight of hand.

His was not a large room and the fire was already having an effect, taking the edge off the chill.

He helped her out of the coat, fingers lingering a fraction longer than they needed to – a brief caress of shoulder and top of the arm. She must have been aware that the touch was deliberate but did not shrink away, which was a good sign.

"Now, Joy," he said, with an appropriately reassuring smile, "is there anything in particular you had in mind?" Knowing full well that there would be.

"As a matter of fact…" Her breath was coming in ragged heaves, the result of either anticipation or nerves… or both. He waited for her to continue, but the sentence seemed to have stalled permanently.

"You've not done anything like this before, have you?" It didn't take a genius to work that out.

She shook her head.

"Relax." He lifted a hand to caress her cheek. "You're supposed to be enjoying yourself."

She laughed – a nervous hiccup of released tension. "I'm sorry. It's just so… I mean, now that I'm actually here…"

He laid his hands on her shoulders. "It's okay. Take your

time."

She buried her head against his chest and for a moment they were hugging each other. He drank in her scent, which was delicate and evocative rather than over-powering; suggestive of wild meadow flowers without being cloyingly floral. He held her until she loosened her hold, before slowly stepping back. "I take it your friend Anna has told you what I do?" In response he received a confirmatory nod, with that short, shallow motion of hers – like a bird pecking for seed. "And since you came looking for me, I presume there's something specific you're after."

"Yes." Again she hesitated, but this time had obviously found the courage to complete her sentence. "This is embarrassing, but... the President."

"The President," he repeated. Not again. Why did women find that damned man so attractive?

Something of his disappointment must have shown in his voice. "Is that a problem?"

"No, not a problem at all," he assured her, while reminding himself that the customer was always right. He had just hoped for something a little more original from her, a little more challenging. He excused himself, saying, "It'll take me a few minutes to prepare." With that he slipped into the other room – the only other room his apartment boasted – a small cupboard-like space that would just accommodate a single bed but which he used as a changing room and for storage.

He took out a slim valise from a drawer and flipped it open. It looked like an old-style laptop pc, but was in fact something a great deal more specialised. His home might have been shabby, with its antiquated heating system, but this was state of the art and he was proud of it.

Sitting down on the room's only chair, he took the narrow headband from its slot in the case. 'Metal with memory' – as soon as it was unclipped, the band sprang unfailingly into shape, fitting snugly around his head. He fumbled for the thin wire that hung down one side and attached it to the jack-point tucked discretely behind his left ear.

"I thought it was all you," the girl said from the doorway. "I didn't realise you used a machine."

Swallowing his annoyance at her uninvited appearance and managing to smile, if a little indulgently, he said, "It is 'all me'. We're a very rare breed," he added, suddenly wanting to impress upon her just how lucky she was. "All this does is carry information," he tapped the headband. "The more detail I receive, the closer I can get to the original. You want the President, you'll get the President. His own mother wouldn't know the difference."

"But would his wife?" she quipped, which suggested a welcome return of spirit.

"Modesty forbids me to comment. Now, if you don't mind…" His eyes ushered her away.

"Oh, sorry," and the doorway was empty once more. He would have shut the door had there been one; something which was at the top of a long list of things he must get around to sorting out one of these days.

He took a deep breath and set about composing himself, focusing on his body and the flow of information from the headpiece, analysing the discrepancies. The small, apparently innocuous laptop he was now attached to carried detailed particulars on nearly a thousand individuals. They were all public figures. The data bank had been up-to-date at the time he… acquired it – *stole* always struck him as such an uncouth word. Sadly that had been some three or four years ago and the number of profiles that remained current were ever-dwindling as time went by.

George Arnold Kelly's election to the highest office had been a welcome stroke of good fortune. Already a prominent figure, the charismatic politician's personal details had been mapped and stored long before. It was this information that now flowed into

Conrad's brain: the man's height, weight, build and aspect, broken down to a stream of minutiae; hundreds of bits of information regarding skin pigmentation, bone and muscle density, weight distribution, hair colour, spine curvature and every other element that combined to produce Kelly's physical appearance. The data was self-modifying. The system monitored news reports and other media sources, updating its details as time progressed, adjusting to the changing appearance of the individuals whose specifics it contained.

Conrad started to change. The President was a little taller than him: his height adjusted accordingly. Everybody's spine is designed to accommodate a degree of movement – the average person is fractionally shorter at the end of the day than at the beginning, simply as a result of gravity compressing the vertebrae together. Conrad's body took this to an extreme, with his spine being a lot more flexible and adaptable than most people's. This was also a process over which he could exercise conscious control. Cartilage and muscle swelled to extend the spine, drawing substance from the stomach, which shrank to mimic Kelly's board-flat physique; elastic skin stretched to accommodate the additional height, with internal organs settling to the slightly altered body shape. His hair grew out a fraction and he boosted the levels of melanin, darkening its colour to the appropriate shade. Hundreds of tiny alterations swiftly accumulated, a transformation comfortably accommodated by his deliberately baggy clothes.

To have made each subtle change individually would have taken hours, which was where his link to the data base came in. It fed the intricate details directly to his subconscious, which instigated the necessary metamorphosis as a programmed sequence of steps rather than a random series of adjustments. In moments the transformation was complete. There was only one physical feature that he then consciously amended; and no lady had yet complained about that particular part of the body being made larger than the president's original; not that size mattered, or so they claimed.

He stepped back into the room.

"My God," she said, raising a hand to her mouth.

"Thank you, but I wasn't aiming quite that high; just the President."

"You even sound like him."

"Of course." Why were people always surprised by that? "Voice is largely shaped by physical characteristics, after all."

He was before her now, a hand lifting to undo the top button of her blouse, her bosom rising and falling in exaggerated fashion. They kissed, her mouth surprisingly cool while her breath carried the suggestion of mint. Her blouse peeled away beneath his hands, revealing shoulders that were near-white in their paleness and finely sculpted in contour, like some elegant mountain ridge coated in virgin snow, inevitably drawing the eye downward to follow the sweep of its slope, which in this case developed into full, pert breasts. Each was crowned by small areolas and nipples that stood dark and proud against alabaster skin. As he bent to cup them, kissing first one, then the other, he found himself engulfed by her subtle, pheromone-laced scent. His finger tips traced the smooth perfection of her skin – a bewitching paradox of paleness and warmth.

Clothing flaked off like blistered paint shedding at the gentlest rub and by the time they tumbled onto the bed, both were naked.

To Conrad this was a job; such encounters were what he did for a living. Generally he found himself emotionally uninvolved, mentally able to step back from the physical act and view his performance and that of his client in detached, analytical fashion. Not this time. Joy proved an active and imaginative lover, taking the lead as often as she was led, and she was so beautiful. He found himself swept up in the act of love-making, rediscovering that most precious ingredient of sex: passion.

Completion arrived far more swiftly than he was used to.

They disentangled, lying together on the bed. She favoured him with a timid, awkward smile. "Thank you."

She was thanking him?

The second time was gentler, but no less satisfying. He was more in control on this occasion, paying greater attention to her pleasure – something he had not been entirely conscious of first time around.

Far more than the stipulated hour had passed when she eventually left. "Can I come back some time?" she asked at the door as they kissed a chaste farewell.

It was all very touching, yet he knew full-well that whatever memories she carried back into her every-day life would not involve making love with him, but with President George Kelly.

He switched on a light – evening had arrived at some point while they were in bed, bringing its customary baggage of twilight – that transient state of almost-darkness – like some traveller who has partially unpacked their luggage but made it perfectly clear that there is plenty more to come.

He sat in a room made suddenly empty by Joy's departure, imagining he could detect the lingering ghost of her scent and realising that he wanted to be somewhere else… anywhere else.

With that directionless decision his only guide he finished dressing, grabbed wallet and keys and fled the claustrophobia of his home, his life.

Where to? Not back to Lacey's, that much was certain. Too great a chance of being collared by some demanding client or other, which was the last thing he wanted. Besides, Lacey's would probably mean Roach and would definitely mean My-Ling. The only company he craved just then was his own.

So he walked in the opposite direction, letting his feet carry him wherever they would. He passed unheeding through streets that were sluggishly stirring – cafés and bars welcoming the first influx of evening trade as work ended and relaxation began. He soon found himself in a district dominated by neon: pulsing banners of garish light that tore chunks out of the gathering gloom, as strip joints, gaming halls, narcotics dens and assorted clubs vied with each other for the attention of every passer-by.

He moved through as swiftly as he could, like some well-oiled body slicing through water, allowing the surroundings to wash over him without touching or sticking. Finally he was at the river – all clustered bars whose tables and chairs spewed out onto paved courtyards and crowded walkways. An ornate iron-framed footbridge spanned the water, attracting such places at either end with the irresistible force of a magnet. A ragtag assortment of skiffs, punts, rowboats and canoes bobbed at their moorings beneath, seeming vaguely sinister in the spilled light that washed over them.

He spurned the bridge as thoroughly as the bars and instead turned to the right, striding along a narrow boardwalk, the river to one side and the dark walls of over-priced waterfront apartments on the other. The crowds thinned almost at once and the staccato thud of his footsteps became audible – a hollow, muffled drum that somehow fell short of his expectations as to how shoes on wood *should* sound, but which suited his mood precisely.

The boardwalk ended and he was moving across grass; still beside the river but alone now – all others evidently sucked into the neon and noise behind him like moths to a flame. The grass in turn gave way to concrete as he crossed a road – one which stopped abruptly just short of the water's edge, as if inviting anyone so inclined to drive pell-mell off the edge and end it all in a watery grave.

After the road came a wasteland, a junkyard of abandoned cars, broken glass, battered crates and discarded machines; the mechanical effluent of an industrial society. It might have been a wasteland but it was far from deserted. If his adopted status in Slate were towards the bottom of the social pile, then those who lived here were firmly entrenched in its lowest basement; their lives as derelict as the surroundings.

This was a dangerous place to be, particularly at night. A flickering glow told of a lit fire somewhere out of sight, while concentration brought the faintest suggestion of voices, either barely heard or wholly imagined. The calculating eyes that watched him from the shadows were unquestionably real, and glimpses of movement between the car corpses bore further testament to the fact that he was not alone.

Boldly he strode between the wreckage, his very presence a statement, his attitude a challenge. He was inviting someone to notice him and respond, would welcome the opportunity to vent his seething frustration through the channel of physical violence.

Nothing happened. Perhaps those watching were unnerved by his self-assurance, perhaps they sensed in him something of what he once had been: a killer.

His return home was equally uneventful. Turning away from the river he left the scrap-land behind, walking through streets of boarded-up houses, sporadically defaced with fluorescent graffiti in a brazen cacophony of night-glow colours, as if in pale imitation of the neon nightlife that thrived just up-river. The streets here were empty, apart from the occasional burnt-out car and a single black shape that slunk belly-low across the road ahead of him at one point, to melt away between decaying houses. Conrad never had liked cats. He respected them as hunters; but never liked.

A few blocks further and the quality of the neighbourhood improved perceptibly, moving up from wrecked to vaguely habitable. The few cars he saw here were at least moving. A little further and he passed his first pedestrians since leaving the boardwalk – a young couple on their way home or doing goodness knew what. Such encounters grew increasingly frequent as the streets became better lit.

Then he was home, having burned off a little of the

aggression and frustration that afflicted him and reaffirmed just what an awful dump Slate really was. Whatever demons that walk of Brownian motion had been intended to exorcise were still hanging around, but at least they were a little more muted for now.

He poured himself another whiskey, sat down and tried hard not to reflect on emptiness – the emptiness of the apartment, and of his life... which were soon to be joined by the emptiness of the bottle.

*

He woke to the awareness of another presence in the room... on the bed.

"Did you enjoy her, your little white doll?" My-Ling whispered in his ear. "Did you screw her good?"

The whiskey must have hit him harder than he realised; he had not even heard her come in.

"Tell me," her voice commanded from somewhere in the darkness above.

The mattress moved as she changed position and he felt the bed clothes drawn down from his body.

"Tell me everything," she said, an instant before kissing his navel, an instant before the tip of her tongue traced a line downward to his groin.

His earlier gloom banished at least for the moment, he closed his eyes and went with the flow.

*

It was the next day that disaster struck.

He awoke to find My-Ling already gone – they lived their own lives. His schedule for the day was pretty full. He had a late morning booking with a regular, an elderly married woman with a fixation for a particular sports star. She had been coming to see him for over a year and never varied, never wanted him to be anybody different. His lunchtime was another matter. Young, single and not-unattractive, she *always* wanted someone different.

As things turned out, he was destined never to discover who had taken her fancy this week. For the first time he could recall, Conrad was forced to cancel an appointment.

It was all due to what happened during the first appointment; or rather, what failed to happen.

Impotence. Not something he had ever experienced before, nor something he was prepared for.

Having to refund a disgruntled client and knowing he had just waved goodbye to a regular source of income only made matters worse. Left alone, he attempted to resurrect the situation, but without success. And so he felt obliged to cancel the rest of the day rather than risk the ignominy of further failure. Even My-Ling, summoned hastily back from work by a desperate phone call, proved unable to elicit a response.

The afternoon found them both closeted in the apartment and him behaving like a bear with a sore head. There were doctors he could see – a quack My-Ling swore by who worked miracles with acupuncture and a closet of mysterious potions based on traditional oriental medicines – but he was not yet ready to share news of his misfortune with anyone else and met the suggestion with a snarl and a curse. It was with evident relief that My-Ling made her excuses and left to cover the evening shift at Lacey's. In truth he was just as glad to see her go, since this allowed him to wallow in self-pity uninterrupted.

With the approach of evening the apartment walls seemed to close in once again. He headed out, wondering whether this sense of claustrophobia in his own home was becoming an obsession.

Consciously avoiding Lacey's, he started to retrace his route of the previous evening. This time, instead of hurrying through the nightlife district he stopped at a half-empty bar, chosen at random. The first beer had barely been tasted when he was approached by an overtly glamorous girl – flashy red sequinned dress and too much lip gloss. At least, he initially assumed it was a girl. Closer inspection caused him to revise the assessment. The timbre of voice seemed just a fraction wrong to his practiced ear and the posture just a little too masculine. He made it clear he was not interested, at which point a testosterone-packed bouncer made it equally clear that his custom was no longer welcomed.

The next place proved less particular, content to leave him in peace. It was an ideal spot in which to sit and think. Sit and brood, if he were being entirely honest.

When he first came to Slate it had been an escape, an attempt to establish his own life and assert his independence; a desperate bid to preserve his sanity. He had other abilities beyond the mimicry; things he was trained to do for which there would always be a market. The trick had been to earn a living in a way that would draw the least attention – hired assassins tended to create a stir. On the other hand, accepting money to sleep with an endless variety of women seemed likely to make fewer ripples and was too tempting a proposition to resist. Of course, his new profession proved far less glamorous than it promised and the thrill of novelty soon paled. More often than not the women who sought him out were unattractive and uninspiring. Rarely did he encounter such things as beauty and passion – it was more likely to be halitosis, body odour and a fawning lust for some micro-celebrity.

It was a living, but did it really constitute a life?

Increasingly he found himself reflecting with wistful nostalgia on his former existence; at least the standard of living had been a hell of a lot better. All he had achieved in running away was to swap one form of prison for another... this time of his own making, perhaps, but a prison none the less. His abrupt disability only reinforced a feeling that had been nagging at the fringes of his awareness for a while now, crystallising it into a certainty. It was time to move on.

In fact, he rationalised, his impotence might well be a symptom of that very thing. Stress and unhappiness were doubtless the root cause – this was probably his subconscious telling him to look for pastures new. As soon as he said goodbye to Slate and the self-fashioned constraints of life here, everything would be fine again.

Much heartened, he headed back to the apartment. Only to find it already occupied.

A figure sat in his favourite chair, which had been pulled over to face the door square on. It was a man with whom he was all-too-familiar, someone he had not seen for years – except in his worst nightmares. Reynolds.

"Hello Si, long-time-no-see. Sorry, it's 'Conrad' now, isn't it."

"You found me, then." He was pleased to hear his voice sounding so steady. Inside, his heart was racing.

"Found you?" A short bark of laughter. "We knew where you were from day one. I received a call ten minutes after you first stepped into Lacey's place."

Conrad was less surprised than he might have been. Part of him had always questioned the lack of pursuit and doubted his ability to vanish so successfully, particularly carrying an expensive piece of company hardware.

With as much composure as he could muster, he strolled into the room and sat down slowly on the end of the bed. Reynolds had him feeling like an intruder in his own home. "So why…." The words trailed off, their meaning self evident.

Reynolds shrugged expansively, "This seemed as good a place as any to keep you stashed until we needed you. Besides, I reckoned you deserved a break."

A break? If he had wanted a break he would have chosen somewhere a lot more comfortable than this squalid hovel… a break-*out* perhaps – a bid for freedom – but a vacation? Hardly.

Details started to register, as his focus began to expand beyond the locked-in shock of finding Reynolds here. He saw the newly opened bottle of whisky – his last – on the table beside the intruder, and the glass that accompanied it. Then he saw the valise, his precious memory bank of identities, and any last vestige of hope crumbled.

"What are you doing here?" was all he could muster.

"We want you back. Playtime's over."

"Back? To do what?"

"What do you think? No need for gigolos, thanks all the same. Besides, I hear you're having a bit of a problem in that department of late."

The accompanying smirk spoke volumes.

"You bastard!"

Reynolds just smiled.

"What is it, a toxin? A virus?"

"Nano-virus, one we're quite proud of, actually. You can visit as many quacks as you like, pump yourself full of as many tonics and guaranteed wood-restorers as you can find – it'll nullify them all. Oh, and it'll keep on doing so until we decide to de-activate it.

"Think of it as slow-burning justice – delayed retribution. After all, you did go awol with some very expensive kit that didn't belong to you." He tapped the valise absently as he spoke. "Of course, without this, or your other... equipment, you're going to have to look for a new line of work."

Conrad ignored the barb. He ought to be seething, yet already his temper was draining away, cooling towards resignation. Mixed in with everything else was a strong sense of relief; relief that his sudden impotence had an external cause and relief too that he was being offered a way out of the dead-end his life had become. The reaction surprised him. It merited further analysis at some point, but not at that particular moment.

"And presumably you'll happily turn off your little softening agent if I come back to the fold."

"Got it in one."

"What exactly do you want me to do?"

"Nothing you haven't done before. There's been an... untimely death." He chose his words with obvious care.

"How long would it be for?" Meaning how long would he be

forced to live life as a stranger.

"Who can say? Not long; a month maybe. We should be past the vital period by then and in a position to let the death become official."

A month. It could be worse, it had been last time. Then it had been an actor, the biggest star of the age. The man's popularity and income were so great that his wealth underpinned the whole economy. His sudden death in a drug-fuelled sado-masochistic orgy spelled financial disaster. So Conrad had made him live again, even starring in his final two movies – considered by critics not to be amongst his best. The impersonation had lasted for three long years, during which time the powers-that-be had quietly gone about the business of restructuring the economy, moving funds and bolstering investments. It had given them enough time to prepare for the great man's eventual departure. Unfortunately for all concerned, Conrad had cracked a short while before the scripted exit.

Prior to that assignment his brief had invariably been to assassinate a target and replace him short-term until the relevant mission was completed. The killing he could handle; it was the living that proved beyond him. Being another person for a few days or weeks was one thing; living in somebody else's skin for three years turned out to be quite another. The complete lack of control had been part of the reason, the sense that his life was no longer his own, but there was more to it than that. While appreciating the irony that a mere celebrity's unexpected death could destabilise an economy far more than any business magnate's, the three years had been pure hell for Conrad. The fame and glamour had been enjoyable enough, particularly at first. It was everything else that went with it. The man's penchant for hedonistic debauchery went way beyond his own tastes and proved far more than he could stomach. He tried to limit his involvement, but it was too established a part of this adopted lifestyle to be toned down to any great extent, at least not without raising unwelcome questions.

The more Conrad experienced, the more he hated it and the harder the pretence became. He felt as if his soul were progressively shrivelling inside him. With each event, each sordid act, it withered a little more. Feeling himself teeter on the edge of a breakdown, he had cut and run.

Now they wanted him to do the same thing all over again. Except that no-one could be that bad. Whoever it was they needed him to become, it could never be as stressful or as impossible as before. Okay, so this might be coercion in a big way, but he knew he was probably going to accept without too much complaint.

Besides, he had a pretty good idea of who it was. For Reynolds to be here in person it had to be someone of the 'Utmost Importance'. As far as Conrad could see, there was only one likely candidate.

So he braced himself and asked, "Who is it?"

Without saying a word, the other reached into an inside pocket and produced a photograph, which he handed across.

Conrad stared at it, incredulous. For a moment he was genuinely speechless, then he managed to produce a strangled, "You're kidding."

Reynolds stared back, impassively. "You've done this sort of thing before."

"True, but..." Conrad licked his lips, nervously. "How've you kept the lid on this? I haven't even heard a whisper about it."

"Yes, well it was sudden – a heart attack. Took everyone by surprise"

"When?"

"Tomorrow."

Reynolds' gaze skewered him, prohibiting any thought of movement, so he sat there, absorbing the full implications of that single fate-laden word. At the same instant he was struck by the realisation that refusing the assignment was no longer an option, if it ever had been. Not if he wanted to live beyond this meeting.

"Why?"

"Security risk. That's all you need to know."

"Does *he* know?"

"No."

Conrad was off-balance, his thoughts reeling from one subject to another in an effort to cover too many vital issues. They settled on one: a matter that continued to bother him.

"How? Infecting me with this nano-virus, I mean… how did you do it?"

Reynolds just smiled, challenging him to figure out the answer for himself.

It could have been slipped into a drink, or food… No, that wasn't the way Reynolds' mind worked…. Sexually transmitted – it had to be. A face swam into his mind's eye and suddenly he knew.

"Joy." The name turned to ashes in his mouth.

The other's smile broadened. "See, you *can* still think when you're forced to. Good, isn't she?"

Conrad wondered briefly in what sense the comment was intended – a good actress or good in bed. Not that it mattered; either could apply and they both amounted to the same thing: good at her job.

It came unbidden; hysterical, belly-wrenching spasms of laughter that bubbled up from somewhere deep within, causing him to keel over on the bed, clutching his stomach. Somehow, the revelation of Joy's complicity was the final straw. He glanced across at Reynolds through watery eyes. The look of startled alarm on that habitually controlled face was enough to set him off again.

Eventually he regained sufficient composure to struggle back into a sitting position.

"Pass me that bottle."

Reynolds did so without comment. Before taking a long swig,

Conrad saluted his former and future boss. Then he handed back the bottle, along with the photo – the one showing the unmistakeable face of the President's wife, the First Lady.

The woman he was about to become.

***

This is the first time this particular version of *The Gift of Joy* has ever appeared in print, though it has been heard before, and the reason for that is a little embarrassing.

While the story was already submitted to TQR, an additional twist to the ending occurred to me, so I rewrote the final scenes, anticipating that TQR would reject the piece. They didn't; the story duly appeared on their webzine and I consequently forgot all about the rewrite. To my delight, *The Gift of Joy* was subsequently nominated for the BSFA Award for 'best short story' and then, amazingly, appeared on the five-strong shortlist, alongside pieces by Ken MacLeod, Ted Chiang, Al Reynolds and Chaz Brenchley. It didn't win, but then it didn't deserve to.

StarShip Sofa decided to dramatise the five shortlisted pieces as podcasts, and duly approached me for a 'clean' version of the text which I happily sent. While listening to the broadcast, I had a growing sense that something wasn't right; and only then realised that I had sent them the rewritten version, not the one on the BSFA shortlist.

So that is how there came to be two different versions of *the Gift of Joy* available at a time when it was up for a major award.

The story itself evolved from my exasperation at the cult of celebrity which seems so prevalent these days. I wondered how extreme this trend might become, how far celeb-worshipers might be willing to go in pursuit of their obsessions...

A Hint of Mystery

It was a strange feeling, knowing that the world was about to change forever and that he was the only person who knew it.

Ross had no intention of allowing the fact to detract from his own big night, however. He still took particular care in dressing. Unusually, he found himself plagued by indecision. This was the third shirt he had tried on and, after casting a critical eye over his image in the mirror yet again, finally decided it would do. Just as well. Much longer and he would have run the risk of being late – something which had never struck him as being fashionable, just irritating. Especially in himself.

His mind's eye had pictured tonight countless times and settled on exactly the image he wanted to convey, yet the first shirt selected had not even come close, despite his confidence that it would be just right. His second choice had been little better. This though, this was okay.

He stepped back and turned sideways, admiring his profile with critical approval; still flat-stomached, despite his devotion to food, and not at all unhandsome. Whoever said 'vanity, thy name is woman' knew little about 21st Century man.

It was silly really. These *were* supposed to be friends he was meeting. Yet in many ways tonight meant as much to him as the award itself. The fact that the group gathering in his honour included most of the top Asian chefs in London might just have had something to do with it – such acknowledgment from his peers made success all the sweeter. Of course, he realised that one or two of the smiles would be a little forced. Rajendra, for example, would doubtless grin through gritted teeth; but knowing that he would have to smile and offer congratulations at all made it sweeter still.

It would be an interesting evening spent with friends, friendly colleagues and tolerated rivals. Chefs were often subject to over-inflated egos – self-belief was as necessary an ingredient as any that went into the cooking – and with certain of the group there had always been an ill-concealed edge that precluded true friendship. Fortunately, friends held the balance. Cyrus for one, who had been the first to phone and congratulate him.

Rajendra, on the other hand, had yet to congratulate him at all.

He sighed. There was an arrogance to Rajendra, an assumed superiority based on his having served an apprenticeship under 'the best chef in Bombay' – as if he were the only truly 'authentic' Indian chef amongst them and all others were therefore inferior by definition. This was an attitude that made Ross instantly bristle. The award of a Michelin star to Rajendra's restaurant two years ago had only exacerbated the problem. The minor detail that Ross's own restaurant had won its second star the same year was an irrelevance, since Ross chose to 'bastardise traditional dishes by diluting them with irrelevant and inappropriate western influence' – an accusation Rajendra had once made to his face during a particularly frank exchange. Ross remembered the outburst word for word.

However, he was not about to let Rajendra or anybody else spoil this evening. His restaurant had just been awarded the much-coveted third Michelin star; the first Asian restaurant in the UK ever to be so honoured, dispelling once and for all any lingering doubts about Asian cuisine. Nobody could now fail to take it as seriously as French, Italian or any other national school of cookery. That seemed worth celebrating and tonight his fellow chefs and restaurateurs were staging an informal gathering to pay him homage. The thought caused him to smile – vanity was clearly not Rajendra's private preserve.

He had worked hard for this, centred his life around attaining the ultimate accolade: three Michelin stars. He savoured the phrase, which burned like a beacon in his mind, still not quite able to believe it. Would that his father were alive to see this day.

Ross had been born in Glasgow, where his father ran a celebrated restaurant of his own. Ross had been proud of his father, feeling that he had done much for the image of Indian cuisine in that part of the country, helping to elevate it above the cliché of the curry house and take-away.

His preparations were finally complete. He glanced around his bedroom in disbelief, as if suddenly seeing it for the first time. Open drawers, clothes strewn on the bed, a favourite silk shirt discarded on the floor – had he *really* been responsible for making this mess? It was something he would never have tolerated in his kitchen.

At that instant he felt a familiar tug on his thoughts.

Why now? Not that he truly resented the intrusion – how could he, after all the success it had brought him?

He quickly sat down, ensuring he was comfortable, and set about relaxing, both physically and mentally; slowing his breathing and calming the mind. It took only minutes and the other Ross was there.

"Hi, ready for your big night?"

"Just about to leave. You?"

"Ready as I'll ever be. God, I'm nervous."

"No need."

"I know." Their conversations were always like this – an economy of words that still conveyed full meaning, since they knew each other so well.

At first Ross had dismissed the other's presence as a figment, a dream figure – easy to do since the initial contacts had been made in his sleep. Only later did it become possible to make contact while awake. From the outset they chatted like two life-long friends, his counterpart a twin brother he had never known.

Ross came to the conclusion that this was his alter-ego, a suppressed side of his own personality which surfaced in his dreams. It took him a while to accept the truth.

"I'm a physicist, a cosmologist," which made sense – that had been Ross's ambition in his youth, what he had worked towards at university. *"My reality is different to yours,"* which was easy enough to dismiss.

With cooking and the business of running a restaurant so central in his life, cosmology had long ago been relegated to a hobby, yet it was still something he paid attention to. String theory had intrigued him; the membrane theory of multiple realities which it led to excited him and appealed to the romantic side of his nature. "As in another dimension?" had been his flippant response.

"You could view it that way."

"Right." Being excited by the concept was one thing, accepting as real night-time visits by an alternative self quite another.

Still, if that was how his alter-ego chose to manifest himself, who was he to argue? He went along with things and became fully engrossed in their conversations. They reminisced and compared notes, discovering that up to a point their recollections seemed identical. Where they veered sharply from each other was during his gap-year at university. Both had gone to Canada, but the other Ross had not gone on to Australia as he had, cancelling at the last minute and returning to the UK due his mother's involvement in a car accident, which proved fatal.

"Mum's still alive," and so he had gone on to Melbourne, where he had been taken under the wing of a brilliant young chef who was dabbling in fusions of eastern and western cuisine. He now realised that this was the point where his love of cooking finally came to take precedence over his ambitions as a physicist.

From then on, their experiences diverged considerably, as Ross came to work as a chef in London, before establishing his own restaurant and a growing reputation, while his counterpart contributed significantly to the understanding of cosmology and moved to the forefront of his chosen field. Ross marvelled at the ingenuity of his subconscious, which had taken the fragments of unrealised ambition and constructed such a detailed and plausible life story.

Then had come the moment when all that changed. *"I think I can give you something."*

"What, from your reality, to take into mine?"

"Yes."

"That's possible?"

"It should be now, in theory. I'm refining this all the time. Something small though. Physical transfer will require a lot of energy."

There followed a lengthy discussion as to what the object should be – something unique to the reality of Ross-the-physicist and unknown in the world of Ross-the-chef.

They stumbled on it almost by accident, when discussing one of Ross's signature dishes.

"What is black cumin?" the physicist had asked.

Ross was startled – the other had enjoyed the same upbringing he had, how could he not have come across black cumin? "Kala jira, kashmiri jira, cumin noir, comino negro, kalazira..." He tried every name in every language he could think of, but all were met with the same shake of the head. "Tiny dark brown granules; it's actually a long, thin fruit, only about 3mm long..." Again the shaken head. In desperation, "It's an apiaceae."

"Ah, the parsley family."

"Yes. You're familiar with the apiaceae?"

"Certainly. We have coriander, fennel, anis, caraway..."

"What about cumin, dill?" Again the shaken head.

The physicist had remained an amateur chef and it seemed unlikely this was simply a chasm in his knowledge. As the discussions continued, it emerged that the discrepancies ran both ways.

"Tarim? What is tarim?"

It appeared there were spices and herbs in both realities which had no obvious counterpart in the other. Either his imagination was working overtime, or...

"I will bring you tarim." So it was settled.

When they next met, the other produced a small cellophane packet containing a number of purplish strands.

His dream-self took and examined the proffered sachet. "This is tarim?" The other nodded. "What is it?"

"The stigma from a plant."

"Like saffron."

"A little, but it's from a member of the aster family rather than a crocus; like safflor, the bastard saffron."

Ross was only half listening, mesmerised by what he held. He awoke still clutching the packet of tiny purple strands and any thoughts that Ross-the-cosmologist was a construct of his subconscious were banished forever.

The other had given only a general idea of how tarim was used, which left him plenty of room to experiment and find out for himself. Like saffron it was highly fragrant, but when he placed a fleck on his tongue it had a sweetish, almost fruity taste, whereas saffron tended towards bitterness. A few strands soaked in a little hot water produced a violet, inky solution. Ross set to work, incorporating the tarim in this dish and that. Its inclusion in a sharbat produced a unique experience, totally unexpected from such a familiar drink. All too soon his meagre supply of the precious spice was exhausted.

"Can you get me more, much more?" he asked that night.

"Of course." The other laughed. *"In the meantime, I brought you this."* He passed over a packet containing another spice new to Ross.

"Does this transfer work both ways?"

"It should do, yes."

"What about the energy needed?"

"I can supply that from this end, as long as the budget lasts."

"Good. I brought you this," and he held out a sprig of wispy green fronds. "Fresh dill, one of the apiaceae you don't seem to have. Great with fish and in pickles."

Ross experimented continually with the new ingredients, adjusting established recipes and creating new dishes, the type that made Rajendra so hot under the collar. He was *not* a traditional chef and made no apology for the fact. True, that was his grounding, one he was proud of, and he fully recognised the rich variety available within traditional Asian cooking and knew that many excellent chefs found fulfilment in that area.

Nothing wrong with that, but it was not for him.

He found his own fulfilment in creating new and original combinations, invariably with strong Asian basis or elements, but borrowing freely from any of the different cooking styles the world had to offer. The advent of the other Ross, with his seemingly endless supply of these unfamiliar herbs and spices, enabled him to be more inventive than ever.

Ross knew he owed a great deal to his counterpart, that the unique ingredients helped his cooking to stand out and had undoubtedly contributed to his success, but it had still taken skill and flair to take advantage of the opportunity. After all, his restaurant had been awarded its second star before the two Rosses had even met. Still, their friendship had undeniably given him an edge and he wondered whether he would ever have achieved that all-important third star without it.

Of course, to maintain his restaurant's reputation and status, Ross took great pains with every aspect, not just the food. He had made a lot of false starts before achieving the ambience he sought: calming, relaxing – something that spoke of Asia without in any way making non-Asians feel excluded, but which rather invited each and every visitor to dally a while and be made welcome. The right blend of staff had been another headache, but eventually he had built a settled core of experienced and reliable individuals. The service had to be absolutely right – attentive without being intrusive, ever-helpful while only offering as much direction as a given patron required... and it all had to appear effortless. Apart from anything else, Michelin had fully justified the pride he felt in both his establishment and his team.

"I won't keep you, just wanted to say have a good time." The comment dragged his thoughts back to the here and now.

"You too." That same evening Ross-the-physicist was to be guest of honour at an important function of his own, a potentially world-changing event. The dill and other herbs passed to him by Ross-the-chef had been accepted as alien to his reality and had provided the scientific community of his world with proof more tangible than mathematics that other realities existed and could be reached. As yet, this breakthrough had been kept from the world at large, but a public announcement was planned for that evening.

"The different planes don't just sit there, always equidistant," the other Ross had once explained. *"They interrelate at slight tangents and can approach each other at one point and veer gradually away at another. I've shown that in some instances they can even touch and coincide."*

"So that's what's going on here? Our respective planes of existence, which run more-or-less parallel to each other, have touched."

"Yes."

Ross had in his mind the image of a mille feuille. Leaves of puff pastry that were stacked in parallel lines yet which bubbled and dipped to touch each other and then part. The truth was probably nothing like that – he had a feeling the different dimensions were far more regular, more structured – but it was a visualisation that worked for him.

In parting, physicist-Ross made reference to the coming announcement and the more formal and official programme of inter-dimensional contact that was bound to follow afterwards. *"There will be others,"* he warned. A masterful understatement.

Neither reality would ever be quite the same again.

"I know. It's been fun."

"It still will be. Just no longer unique to us."

"Luck."

"You too."

Ross stood, left the house and hurried to his car. Now he really was going to be late.

*

The evening went well. Rajendra seemed to go out of his way to be charming and flattering, as if determined to ensure that nobody could accuse him of being churlish, while no one else said anything to detract from the occasion, at least not in Ross's hearing.

As the meal drew to a close, Ross found himself in conversation with Kuldup, an aging but still greatly revered Indian chef whom Ross had always been fond of.

"So tell me again," Kuldup said, "your recipe for Patrani Machchi. I thought I knew all there was to know about the cooking of fish, especially in that dish, but you have added something special and I cannot for the life of me work out what it is."

Ross chuckled; this had become almost a ritual game between the two of them, with Kuldup inquiring what set his preparation of this most traditional of Parsi dishes apart. He knew his side of the ritual well: "I would never dream of presuming that I had anything of worth to impart to such a distinguished master of the culinary arts as yourself, Kuldup."

The older man wagged a finger in mock admonishment. "Don't think to evade me with flattery. I may yet have one or two secrets still to disclose that would surprise even you, but in this instance I bow to your greater knowledge. Now tell me!"

"Very well. As you yourself once taught me, the secret of turning a good recipe into a great dish is attention to detail." Despite whatever aspersions Rajendra might like to cast, in certain instances Ross had gone to great lengths to ensure authenticity. So his restaurant habitually offered two alternative forms of Patrani Machchi. For one he utilised lemon sole and for the other, which was a little more expensive, he used pomfret, a fish specially flown in from the sub-continent. He found that certain of his patrons were happy to pay the extra.

"It is important that the oven is at just the right temperature and that the banana leaves are properly wrapped around the fish." He was teasing Kuldup, part of the game, since it had been the older chef who first taught Ross how to make the dish. "I always steam the fish first, rather than fry it..." He had gone through the preparation of Patrani Machchi so often that he felt able to recite it in his sleep. While continuing to talk, his mind wandered. Ross had always believed that his life could have followed two different paths – physicist or chef. Long ago he had made the decision that determined which one, but he had always wondered how the other path would have turned out. Of course, the presence of the other Ross indicated that in actual fact his life had followed a multitude of different courses in a multitude of differing realities, yet he suspected that he would still have been either chef or physicist in most of them.

"As you know, the most important elements, after the freshness and quality of the fish, are the ingredients of the paste." He suddenly realised how privileged he was. Perhaps uniquely among all the people in the world to date, he had been granted the opportunity to see where both possible lives might have led. He was glad to see that Ross-the-physicist seemed equally as happy and fulfilled as Ross-the-chef. Also, he was glad to find that he had no regrets about choices made.

"Yes, but what do you add to the paste? You put something special in it, you must do," Kuldup insisted.

"Not really," Ross demurred. "Lemon juice, crushed coriander leaves and cumin seeds, green chillies, a hint of fresh coconut, a heavy hint of garlic and..." He left the sentence hanging, glancing to see the twinkle in his own eye reflected in the older man's. Both spoke together: "...a hint of mystery!"

They laughed, the ritual completed. Kuldup clapped him on the back. "One day... one day you must tell me exactly what this 'hint of mystery' is."

Ross wondered how far matters had progressed in the other world. Had the announcement had been made yet? Was his counterpart facing the stroboscopic barrage of paparazzi flashbulbs even now?

"You never know," and he smiled fondly at his former mentor, "one day I just might... and that day could well be here a lot sooner than you think."

Prophetic words indeed.

Even as Ross spoke, a familiar tingling touched his mind. He looked around in alarm. Surely the other Ross would not risk contacting him *now*.

Perhaps not; despite the outward similarity, this felt subtlely different from the now customary sensation and, most tellingly, there was no sign of his mirror-image. He could still clearly see the restaurant and his contemporaries chatting merrily, oblivious to the fact that anything was wrong.

Abruptly, all that changed, as a green mass materialised above the table, apparently from nowhere. The diners looked on in astonishment as the mass resolved into myriad tiny green leaves which dispersed as they fluttered down onto table and people alike.

An earthy, aromatic scent filled the air. Startled laughter sounded around the table. "Ross, what surprise is this you've arranged for us?" someone called.

Ross only wished he had.

He watched as, beside him, Kuldup wetted his fingertip and used it to dab a small leaf which had alighted on his knife and raise it to his lips. "Interesting."

Ross copied him, savouring the taste of a small flat leaf on his tongue. Already alerted by the aroma, he detected something faintly reminiscent of coriander, but deeper, more earthy and with a hint of sour. He had never tasted anything quite like it, not even among the herbs Ross-the-physicist had passed across.

Then it struck him: 'a multitude of differing realities', and this herb was unlike anything from either his plane or the other Ross's. It could only be from a *third* reality. His counterpart there, yet another Ross, must be trying to get in touch, or perhaps had deliberately opted to pull this cruel stunt at his expense.

He suddenly felt exposed and guilty at having been so secretive about physicist-Ross and his spices, duplicitous even; a particularly apt word given its implication of *double*-dealing.

Ross glanced again at Kuldup, to find the older chef looking speculatively first at him and then at a fresh leaf perched upon his fingertip.

Kuldup lent towards him and said, in a voice too low to be overheard above the hubbub that still surrounded them, "So, Ross, tell me more about this hint of mystery…"

***

This was one of the earliest stories I produced following my decision to start writing seriously again in the early naughties.

Helen and I were going out to a Chinese restaurant one evening to celebrate my birthday. At the time, I was trying to think of story ideas and I remembered the old adage 'write what you know'. As anybody who has met me and seen my girth can attest, one thing I *do* know about is food. So I determined to write a piece about food, in fact about a chef – a career I might well have followed had life not taken a different turn.

I'd encountered very little 'Asian' SF (this was shortly before the release of Ian McDonald's wonderful *River of Gods*), so basing the story in the UK's Indian community seemed original, and away I went.

The version here differs from the one which appeared previously in *Hub*, since it features a slightly extended ending with an added twist following a suggestion by Ian Watson. Many thanks, Ian!

The Key

It's amazing what a bunch of keys can say about a person. Keyrings and their contents hold hidden depths, or so Carl had always maintained.

Take his wife's, for example: keys for the front door, car, garage, and a Yale for her mother's… plus various superfluous attachments: a pink-plastic pig, a Perspex heart displaying the pseudo-word 'whateva' and a smiley-emblazoned disc designed to impersonate a coin when liberating supermarket trolleys.

His own set was far more practical. Keys for car and home, one for a suitcase and another for a young lady's flat which he trusted his wife would never notice or question. Two add-ons: a worn leather fob from his very first jalopy and a pizzel-shaped plait of woven leather which he'd been assured was a fertility symbol but probably wasn't.

Then there was the set he had recently 'acquired'. Six keys plus three attachments: a circular Mercedes emblem, matching one of the keys, a tiny plastic-encased photo of a girl's face – presumably the owner's daughter – and a small, squat figurine with blood-red crystal eyes. The latter vaguely resembled an owl and gave Carl the creeps. Quite what it said about the owner he preferred not to dwell on.

It was the keys that really intrigued him. Two differently-cut front door keys, suggesting two homes, Merc and Land Rover keys – a car for each dwelling – and two others less easily identified.

Sammy-the-Locksmith's considered opinion proved as much use as a chocolate tea-pot. "One's for a cabinet and the other a

43

Ian Whates

safety-deposit box."

"Any way of telling where it is?"

"Nope."

He wouldn't have cared, except for the small matter of the reward. A ridiculous sum, offered for the keys' return with no mention of the Gucci wallet lifted at the same time, nor of the cash and credit cards contained therein. One of these keys was clearly important to someone and therefore valuable. Carl knew which his money would've been on. It remained useless to him, however, unless he could find precisely what it opened. To his growing frustration, unlocking that particular enigma proved beyond him.

"Mightn't even be in this country," his best and final hope had concluded with a shrug.

Reluctantly he arranged a meet, at a time and place of his choosing; a bar where he was known and felt safe. His recent victim and prospective benefactor awaited – a tall, muscle-broad individual who, even in Armani suit, failed to look entirely polished or civilised. The rugged edges were still there; an uncut gem in a presentation box.

Carl would have preferred a dead-drop, an exchange without ever meeting face-to-face, but the other would have none of it. So he watched the man arrive from across the street, alert for any hint of police or other presence. Seeing none, he entered, glancing at the barman, whose shake of the head still fell short of total reassurance.

He took a deep breath and committed himself by sitting down. Eyes locked across a table. Unwavering self-confidence and steely strength couched within grey-blue irises; this was not a man to trifle with.

"You have the keys?" The voice was relaxed and casual to the point of being unnerving.

"You got the money?"

An envelope; produced from a pocket and then slid across

the table. A fat envelope.

Carl reached out but the other's hand clung to its far-edge. "The keys first."

"Not until I've counted it."

A frozen tableau that persisted for time-stretching seconds until the man abruptly let go. Carl opened the envelope and flicked through the wad of fifties, not counting with any accuracy, just checking.

Satisfied, he nodded to the barman, who left his station and came across with the keys.

To his credit, the stranger guffawed and nodded appreciation at such complicity. He looked the keys over once before pocketing them and rising to his feet. There he paused, fixing Carl with a glare – the first suggestion of either anger or menace.

"Don't cross my path again."

"Just a minute," Carl blurted out as the man turned to leave. "You've got them back now, so you can tell me, why are they so important?"

The man smiled – a malicious, satisfied expression which lacked any hint of humour. "Do you really imagine I'm going to tell *you*?"

Carl watched the retreating back until it was out the door and away. Despite earning far more than anticipated from this episode he still felt cheated, as if opportunity had somehow slipped through his grasp. What wealth or secrets had the key represented? Too late now. He would never know.

'Never' lasted a month.

Carl was watching the news. He remained sceptical and unmoved by the inescapable buzz about the first proof of ET, scoffing at the media frenzy and avoiding television's blanket-coverage; until now. He stared in disbelief at the image of what was allegedly an alien artefact. Set against a neutral background, the picture provided no sense of proportion, but Carl knew at once that it was small: a tiny, squat, owl-like effigy with blood-red eyes.

The reporter – all blonde hair, glossy lipstick and gushing exuberance – was explaining how its eccentric owner and discoverer had little faith in conventional secure repositories, so kept the priceless item on his key-ring while awaiting the vital test results, which were soon to confirm its non-terrestrial composition. Thus inspired, she dusted-down her poetic licence and waxed lyrical about the artefact's potential for unlocking new worlds, labelling it 'the Key to the Future'.

Carl switched off the TV. For long minutes he sat there, simply staring at the empty screen.

**

Driving home late one night with the radio on, I heard the show's host explain how, following a burglary, the thing she missed most was her keyring, because of the sentimental value of the various fobs it carried. That comment provided the inspiration for "the Key".

At the time, the science journal *Nature* ran a column called 'Futures', featuring a single SF story in each issue. The list of former contributors read like a 'Who's Who' of the very best genre authors. I wrote "The Key" the day after hearing the radio show, tweaking it to fall within Nature's very tight word limits (850 to 950), then sent it off and crossed my fingers, without any great hope of success. The magazine's features editor, Henry Gee, accepted the piece a week later.

This was all within a few months of my deciding to pursue a writing career seriously, and having a story appear in such a prestigious venue was an enormous fillip. To see the story subsequently selected for Tor books' 'best of' anthology *Futures From Nature* was the icing on the cake.

Gossamer

I used to know a man who was a writer. I mean a *real* writer. His books were taken seriously enough to be noted in the broadsheets and reviewed in their literary sections and I even saw him on TV a couple of times. I never actually read anything by him, at least, not all the way through. I tried once or twice, but could never get beyond the first few pages.

My most determined attempt came after I saw him speak at some literary festival or other – in Cheltenham, I think it was. The speech was excellent: intelligent, well delivered, and containing just the right amount of charm and wit. He had the audience won over from the very first sentence. I was impressed and really *wanted* to read one of his books, but failed to do so even then, giving up partway through the first chapter. Not that it was badly written – far from it. My attention simply wandered elsewhere. None of which I ever admitted to the author, of course.

His name was Jeremy Talbot and he lived in this wonderful cottage tucked away in a forgotten fold of the English countryside. It was one of those villages which, if mentioned at all, are always spoken about in terms of being between places, as if not existing in their own right but only there because they had to come up with *something* to put between this town and that.

Compton Delby is typical of the many hamlets that are to be found scattered around the Midlands and southern counties; a cluster of buildings which have somehow condensed along a stretch of road like dew gathered on spider silk and conspired to become a village. Within its boundaries can be found: a Norman church, a small village store boasting a large plate-glass window at the front and a sub-post office at the back, and a single pub – The White Horse, a coaching inn dating back to the 16th century which, according to the brass plaque by the door, was once the favoured watering hole of a highwayman I'd never heard of.

Summer Cottage is the prettiest and most charming property in a community that prides itself on such. Jeremy had lived there for as long as I'd known him. He always said that the cottage was a magical place, but I think he intended the comment in a dreamy, poetic sense, indicating that he loved his home and everything about it, without having any concept that the words might contain a literal truth.

I, on the other hand, realised from the very first that there was something extraordinary about the cottage.

Jeremy was my dad's friend really, but I always got on particularly well with him and he seemed far closer to my age than my parents ever did. There was a roguish twinkle in his eye and a sense of rebellious energy about him which I instantly warmed to. That twinkle, combined with the goatee beard he favoured, always put me in mind of mischievous Pan, even in later years when the grey frosting at its fringes spread to completely mask the dark brown it had formerly boasted.

There was nothing sexual to our relationship; I think he might have been gay, though there was never any firm evidence to support such a conclusion. It was just a feeling. He never spoke about any past loves and I don't recall hearing mention of any partners, male or female. Perhaps his generation were simply more discreet about such things, although he didn't seem discreet about much else. Jeremy possessed a wicked, irreverent sense of humour and I always had the impression that he went along with society only in as much as he was required to, while privately mocking it from within. I've no idea how he and my father ever became friends.

After Dad died we stayed in touch. I would go and see him at

Summer Cottage. The visits were not especially frequent but were always much anticipated, with the cottage proving the perfect refuge whenever the pressures of everyday life threatened to overwhelm me. To be honest, it's pretty hard to recall which I looked forward to visiting more: Jeremy, or Summer Cottage. The latter resonates with happiness in much the same way that a pleasant dream leaves you with a warm feeling and a smile on your face in the morning, even when you can't actually remember the dream itself and have no idea why you should be so happy. That's exactly how Summer Cottage has always affected me – wonderful, welcoming and just about perfect in every way.

I felt more at home there than in any of the sequence of anonymous dwellings which my family resided in over the years and referred to as 'home'. It was as if Summer Cottage were some forgotten remnant of another age, a corner of faery that had been overlooked and left behind by the fey-folk when they abandoned us to our own devices.

Fronted by a tiny strip of garden contained within a white picket fence, the building might have been lifted straight off the cover of one of those souvenir boxes of fudge that are sold in every town with a tenuous claim on history or a hope of attracting tourists. I fell in love with it the first time Dad took me there. Mum never came with us and I never really understood why, except that she didn't much care for Jeremy.

The cottage itself was beautiful: solid beams and small windows which Mum would probably have put chintz around but Jeremy never did, thank God; steep wooden stairs, a low window on the landing with a broad, unpainted, wooden sill, and irregular-shaped bedrooms – no box rooms here. Two of the bedrooms were built into the eaves and possessed floors which you were never entirely certain weren't sagging, just a little.

We tended to spend much of the time in the kitchen, which was this huge room with quarry tiled floor, dominated by a wood-burning stove and a big, solid-looking wooden table, around which Jeremy had assembled an assortment of ill-matching chairs. We always ate here and at other times would simply sit around the table, nattering while we steadily drained a pot of coffee or perhaps a coveted bottle of red wine – a souvenir from his latest trip to Italy or Spain.

Sometimes I would stay over, sleeping in the guest bedroom. In latter years there was only one, the other 'eaves-room' being cluttered with all the junk and knick-knacks that Jeremy had accumulated but not yet found a home for elsewhere.

I don't know why I woke up on that particular night. It was almost as if something called to me. Not anything that could be heard, you understand, but something that hooked onto a strand of my inner-self and pulled me awake; an invisible thread that then drew me out of bed and over to the window.

It was one of those moonless nights, when the moon is probably busy renewing itself and in any case has been wrapped away in clouds to keep it coddled and content. My window looked out over the back garden, which is on a couple of different levels. Directly outside the back door is a small stone-laid patio, from which a set of eight or nine steps, bordered by rockery on either side, leads upwards to the lawn, which is more or less flat. There's a pear tree towards the back of the lawn, in the left corner, and after that come the flower beds, which are slightly raised behind neat little stone walls. Behind them, defining the garden's border with the fields beyond, is this magnificent, bushy hedge.

Of course, I couldn't actually see any of this at the time because it was too dark, but I could make out where the hedge was. A whole section of it directly opposite my window was lit up by these tiny lights, like dimmed fairy lights on a Christmas tree. I stood there at the window, leaning on the sill and just watching them. And after watching for a while, I realised that they moved. Not much and not quickly, but unmistakeably, some of them shifted position. Childhood memories leapt to the fore and I suddenly knew what they reminded me of. The Silverkin; you know, those tiny glowing fairy-creatures in the Gossamer books.

I'm not sure how long I watched and afterwards had no recollection of climbing back into bed, but I must have done so at some point, because before long it was morning and I was waking up with my head partway down the mattress and my toes dangling off the end of the bed.

I told Jeremy about the intriguing little lights over breakfast. He was not in the least surprised, barely even looking up from the newspaper as he munched his toast.

"Oh yes, the glow worms," he said, turning the page. "We see quite a few of them at this time of the year."

"Glow worms?" I had heard of them, of course, but never expected to see any. "I didn't know there were any left in England."

"They're not as common as they used to be," he conceded, "but there are still plenty about. People rarely see them, of course – too busy rushing around the countryside in their cars with headlights blazing. Never going to see anything that way."

I told him about how they reminded me of the Silverkin. The comment seemed to puzzle him for a moment, as if the word ought to mean something but didn't; then it apparently fell into place. "Emily Mitchell," he said. "I haven't seen her in years."

"You *know* Emily Mitchell?" I gasped, after I'd managed to lift my jaw from where it had dropped to.

"Yes," he replied, oblivious. "Known her for yonks." Then he looked up and grinned, suggesting that maybe he wasn't quite so oblivious after all. "Would you like to meet her?"

"God, yes!"

So it was arranged. Dinner at Summer Cottage: me, Jeremy, and Emily Mitchell. Can you imagine? I mean, forget pop stars, actors or footballers, this is *Emily Mitchell* we're talking about.

I'd wanted to meet her for as long as I can remember, ever since I opened the very first page of the very first book she had written – the one that unveiled Gossamer to the world. When I was younger that 'wanted' had been more in the nature of a yearning; an all-consuming childhood ambition which had subsequently been filed away under the heading 'unrequited' as I grew older, but which suddenly seemed fresh and desperate again now that opportunity presented itself.

She proved to be exactly as I imagined; a little older and a little frailer than in those old interviews, but just as warm, charming and lovely as you could wish. I kept wanting to pinch myself to make certain that this was really happening.

I loved the Gossamer books when I was a kid and had read them all long before anyone thought to make them into a TV series. I used to dream of growing translucent wings in the moonlight and being able to fly, of having friends as loyal and loving as the Clockwork Monkey and the Silverkin, and foes as terrible and implacable as the Toymaker.

My favourite book in the whole series has to be the third one, in which the Clockwork Monkey gets his wheels. For anyone who hasn't read it yet, this is the one where the Toymaker kidnaps Monkey and tries to force him to spill all the secrets of Gossamer's wings. Of course, Monkey refuses to tell and is eventually rescued by Gossamer while the Maker is being led on a wild goose chase by the Silverkin, though not before he has started to dismantle Monkey in a last-ditch attempt to make him talk. Try as she might, Gossamer can't fit Monkey's hind-legs back on, but luckily there are lots of bits and pieces of broken toys lying around, and she manages to attach a discarded set of wheels from an old model train onto him instead. The Maker comes back and interrupts her at the last second and there's a scary bit where he stuns her and you think that she's going to be caught as well, but then it's Monkey's turn to save *her*, using his new wheels to carry them both away faster than the Toymaker can follow. Phew!

So there I was sitting with my childhood hero, doing my best not to come across like a gushing moron and convinced that I was failing dismally.

"It's wonderful to be back here," she said with a wistful sigh. I thought I knew exactly what she meant, because that was how I always felt about Summer Cottage. But then she surprised me. "I used to live here, you know."

"Really?"

"Oh yes," Jeremy said, as he topped up my wine glass. "I bought Summer Cottage from Emily. That's how we met. I was still a mere lecturer in those days, not the 'celebrated' author I am now." The last was said with the familiar self-mocking twinkle.

Emily was gazing around the kitchen with a far-away look in her eye and a small smile at the corners of her mouth. "I'd forgotten how much I miss this place. They were the happiest years of my life, the ones I spent here."

"Then why did you move?" I blurted out, before it occurred to me that the question might be considered impertinent.

"My husband died – cancer," she said, adding the last quickly, as if to forestall another inappropriate question, "and there were so many memories. It would have been too painful to stay, but I still sometimes regret ever leaving.

"I wrote the Gossamer books here, you know; all ten of them."

The comment tipped me over into gushing mode again, I couldn't help it.

"I *have* written other books as well," she said defensively when I paused for breath, "but people only ever seem to remember the Gossamer stories."

I did actually read one of her later books, but only the one. It lacked the magic of Gossamer, and seemed formulaic and mechanical in comparison. I would have given up on it early but for a sense of determined loyalty which caused me to persevere to the less-than-satisfying end. The same sense of loyalty stopped me from reading any further books – I didn't want to not like anything written by Gossamer's author.

"Did you write all your books here?" I asked.

"No, only the Gossamer ones. I think the muse deserted me after Jonathan died." Then she leant towards me and said in a conspiratorial stage whisper: "Just between you and me, my later books weren't really all that good, in any case." All three of us laughed. "I haven't written anything in years. I don't dream any more, you see; not about Gossamer."

That night I saw the glow worms again, or perhaps I dreamt them. This time there seemed to be a pattern within the lights. With only a little imagination, it was possible to make out the word 'Gossamer'.

*

Jeremy's death came as a terrible shock. It was like losing a favourite uncle and affected me equally as badly as when I lost my own parents.

Of course, there was a silver lining, though that sounds almost callous and isn't meant to be. In fact, I'm sure Jeremy would have been delighted with the way things turned out.

You see, after that evening we spent with Emily Mitchell I did a little digging, and discovered that Jeremy had never published a single thing before moving into Summer Cottage. Only after he moved into that wonderful place did he become a writer.

Two successful authors living consecutively in the same home and writing everything they ever wrote worth talking about while living there?

Emily had been mistaken, I realised, when she claimed that the muse deserted her after her husband died. In fact it was the other way around: *she* abandoned her muse the day she moved away from Summer Cottage.

Following Jeremy's death, his home was put up for sale. Of course, things were not that simple. He died without making a will, so probate took an age, but eventually it came on the market.

When it did, I bought it. How could I not?

Summer Cottage is now my home and I'm so excited. Even more so after the events of yesterday. You see, I've made a thrilling discovery. I'm having a lot of work done – the place needs it – rewiring and that sort of thing. It's funny how as a visitor you fail to notice details which leap out and demand attention once you're the property's owner.

In the process of doing something or other, the workmen had to lift up some of the floorboards in the second bedroom, the room I used to sleep in as a guest. Underneath, they found a toy. I've no idea how it came to be there, but I think I do know why. It was hiding, staying out of sight while waiting for the right time and the right person to discover it. It's a cheap plastic promotional toy of the sort that's given away by the fast food chains with kiddies' burger meals: a monkey, which originally had mobile back legs by the look of it. But the legs are no longer there. In their place, a short axle has been pushed through the model's hindquarters and the Monkey now has a set of free-spinning wheels.

There's a full moon tonight and the Silverkin will come, I can feel it.

I'm sleeping in that eaves-room again and I've cleared everything off the windowsill and placed Monkey at the very centre, facing out, so that the Silverkin can see him and he can see them. I'm going to bed now and can't wait for the dreams to start.

There *is* one thing that causes me slight concern, and it's to do with Jeremy.

You see, he wrote horror stories; haunting tales of insidious evil, insane obsession and creeping terror, all of them vividly realised and chillingly told. This was one of the reasons I could never read them – I found them too disturbing.

Still, I'm not Jeremy and my dreams will be different. I just know that *my* dreams will be of Gossamer, of wings, and of

Ian Whates

flying...

***

When doing the signing sheets for the limited edition anthology *Time Pieces*, I met up with authors Sarah Singleton and Ian Watson at Ian's home – a charming cottage in a picturesque Northamptonshire village with an unlikely name and fluctuating location (or so it seems when you're trying to find it). Only then did I learn that Sarah had grown up in this same cottage, and that the room Ian now uses as an office and study used to be her bedroom.

The coincidence of two award-winning genre authors having lived in the same cottage within a comparatively short period of time struck me as remarkable. It sparked thoughts of 'place' having a more than passing influence on 'art', ideas which eventually bore fruit in the story "Gossamer".

In Fear of Fog

Fog is a true triumph of nature, not simply a by-product of atmospheric conditions. It diffuses light, restricts vision, muffles sound, distorts distance, and bedevils direction. It is insidious, creeping up silently and unannounced, with none of the fanfare of storm or hurricane, yet in all the world there is nothing more alarming or disorientating. Had nature deliberately set out to create a medium for terror, an environment specifically designed to evoke primordial fears, she could have done little better than fog.

*

Jenice had written that in her diary a lifetime ago, or so it seemed, when emotions were raw and the horror still fresh. Each word resonated with echoes of the fractured mind which birthed them, while every sentence was saturated with the memory of terror. The circumstances that prompted their writing lived on in her dreams and would haunt her darkest moments ever after.

Jenice's family had moved to the coast when she was still a baby, deserting a land-locked city whose only connection to the ocean was the umbilical of a river's winding course. Her earliest memories were of sand, beach, and waves – an elemental rhythm that she would never outgrow. Jenice was bright, her affinity with all things oceanic clear from a very early age. Neither the decision to become a marine biologist nor her subsequent prominence in that field surprised anyone.

It was at school that she was first labelled a loner by her peers. Not entirely merited, but, as the only child of career-minded parents, she had learned the value of her own company.

Relationships proved difficult and her sexual experimentation was limited. Fellow girls never appealed to her and the inept fumblings of virginal boys seemed embarrassing and annoying, while the first time a man of any experience tried to seduce her turned into a disastrous farce. She was excited by his attention and enjoyed the kissing and the foreplay well enough, but the moment he tried to remove her clothes she panicked and refused to let him touch her. They never spoke again.

After that, she decided that sex was overrated and not for her. She never lacked for male attention, but reasoned that there were other aspects of life to which she was better suited, so subsumed her passion into her work and slipped into a habit of celibacy.

Until, that is, she met Jamie. With his chiselled good looks and a mind sharper than the suits he wore, Jamie was quickly installed as the pin-up boy of the department. His arrival set hearts, tongues and eyelashes fluttering in equal measure. She was surprised and flattered when he singled her out for attention rather than one of the more obvious candidates, reasoning that perhaps this was because she didn't fawn over him at every turn.

Before Jamie, the most important person in Jenice's life had been herself; not through any innate selfishness, but simply by default. Meeting him proved a personal epiphany. He opened the door to a world of emotional and physical intimacy beyond her imagining and brought a brightness and levity into her life that she had never realised it lacked.

Every new day was a joy, and Jenice devoured each moment as if she were a starved epicure presented with a feast of gourmet cuisine. Even had she appreciated how transient this period of her life would prove to be, Jenice could not have savoured it more.

The end came abruptly and painfully. It was early in the Disappearances, when people were still not fully clear about what was going on.

They had been out to a colleague's birthday party – an event for which Jenice would almost certainly have made her excuses in the past and not attended. But this was the new Jenice, who found she actually looked forward to social events and who *wanted* to be seen with her boyfriend. This was the first time that many of those attending had seen them as a couple. Everyone told her how pleased they were for her. Some of them even meant it.

In the end they had an enjoyable evening, and lingered far longer than intended. It was close to midnight when they finally said their goodbyes and stepped out into a world cloaked not only in darkness, but also in a thick blanket of fog, which had rolled in from the sea at some point without any of the partygoers noticing. They lived in a coastal town on a water-rich world, where temperatures could fluctuate dramatically. Fog was hardly a novelty. Jenice would not then have been afraid to walk home on her own, let alone with the solid presence of Jamie beside her.

"You seemed to enjoy yourself tonight," he commented as they walked.

"You noticed that, did you?," she teased, snuggling against him, still a little bewildered that the unfamiliar sensation of an arm around her should feel so comforting and so right.

"Tina's nice."

"Mmm. Glad you like her." This was the first time Jamie had met Tina, one of the few people from school Jenice stayed in touch with and probably her closest friend.

"Hope you know where we're going, I'm already lost."

The fog lent their walk a surreal aspect, the illusion that they moved in their own private world, a bubble of cotton wool privacy created just for them.

A large part of the respect and reputation that Jenice had garnered as a marine biologist had been earned in the field, after she spent a year as part of a team studying the most inaccessible reaches of the world's oceans. For much of that time she was

Captain and crew of a one-woman submersible, cocooned from the world outside; an intimate observer of the deeps – able to see everything while remaining apart. A fair reflection of her life in general, as Tina once quipped. Down there she had always felt totally isolated and quite at home. Being in fog was the reverse. Beyond their immediate sphere of reality they could see nothing, which would have made her uncomfortable in the past but now, she didn't care.

"Let's hope I can remember the way, then, or we might end up wandering around forever." Jamie was staying the night at hers, a development which still thrilled her to the core whenever she took the time to analyse it.

"Now there's a cheery thought."

There came the muffled boom of an explosion, some way off, in the direction of the harbour; an ominous, rumbling sound which rolled out of the night.

"What was that?"

"No idea, but its nothing to do with us, whatever it is."

Despite Jamie's glib dismissal, everything changed. By unspoken consent their pace quickened. The fog, which until then had seemed a boon, now took on a sinister menace. Again Jenice saw in their situation the antithesis of her experience in the sub, where she was the detached observer – watching and untouchable – protected from the environment that surrounded her. Suddenly she felt as if she were the watched rather than the watcher. Instead of cosseting them as it had seemed to previously, the fog now became a featureless barrier, hemming them in. Anything or anyone could be out there, just beyond the limit of sight, watching them, studying them. None of her senses could be trusted or relied on to warn of imminent threat. Their cocoon of privacy had somehow been transformed into a limiting enclosure.

A figure loomed out of the mist, a stooped giant which towered above them, massive and threatening, crystallising her latent dread. Jenice stumbled and slowed, causing Jamie to falter, the rhythm of their march lost.

"What's the matter?"

"Nothing," she said quickly, realising that it was simply the gnarled trunk of a tree made dangerous only by her imagination. "Sorry."

He laughed and squeezed her tightly for a second. "Come on."

She drew comfort from his closeness and the confidence of his tone. They carried on.

Without warning, shapes materialised around them. Several this time, appearing as if from nowhere and, unlike the tree, moving. Despite her shock, part of Jenice's mind studied the apparitions with the clinical eye of a trained observer. But only part; most of her was simply terrified. They were gross, misshapen figures, humanoid in general terms but alarmingly distorted. The truly unsettling thing was that these figures made no sound, no attempt to communicate either with the two of them or with each other.

She knew instantly what they were and had no doubt that Jamie did as well. Without hesitation he released her hand and threw himself at the nearest pair, yelling at her to "Run!"

She did; blindly into the fog and into the night, knowing that she was pursued. She careened into something, bruising her shoulder, but didn't stop; rushing onward to graze her shin against something else. Unseen obstacles too insignificant to note and left behind too quickly to recognise, knocks that she would only become aware of later, when it was over and the rush of adrenalin receded.

To her everlasting shame, she spared no thought for Jamie. All that mattered was to run, to escape. She could hear them, *feel* them behind her and knew that at any second they would catch her. Eventually she tripped on uneven paving and fell into someone's front garden, to lie there gasping for breath, waiting to be Taken.

After minutes in which nothing happened, she sat up, to find herself alone, the night deceptively quiet. She hauled herself to her feet and stumbled to the front door of the house whose garden she had fallen into, sobbing now, both for herself and for Jamie. She hammered on the front door, but nobody answered. She tried the neighbouring house and the next, and so on down the row, hammering on doors and pleading to be let in, but to no avail. Some of the homes had lights on behind their closed curtains, but all turned a deaf ear.

She gave up and slumped down to sit with her back against one of the doors, crying. Muffled movement sounded from within, but still no one ventured to aid her.

Eventually the sobs receded, dissolving into aching tremors, and she stood up, wandering off into the fog and the night, not overly caring where her feet carried her. For a while time lost all meaning, but as she walked, a degree of rationality returned.

Jamie had been Taken. She had read accounts of recent cases with morbid fascination, never dreaming that she might be directly affected. This was the sort of thing that happened to other people in other places, not here and certainly not to her.

Some of the reports claimed to know what happened to those who disappeared, and every such one claimed something different. The Taken were brain-washed, made to forget about their homes and those who loved them. They had implants grafted into their brains, turning them into human-robots. Their brains were surgically removed and placed into machines, to pilot warships... In short, *nobody* knew what happened to them. It was all conjecture and hearsay. All that was known for certain was that nobody Taken had ever been seen again.

Jenice found herself reviewing the mental images of those apparitions that had materialised from the fog: body armour, high-tech sensor arrays, automated weaponry and other less recognisable attachments and appendages turning them into outlandish, grotesque effigies of the human form. It was hard to believe that the perpetrators of these atrocities were men – that anything *human* could do such a terrible thing to their fellows – but they were, albeit not her breed of human.

This world, her world, had been a forgotten sapling of mankind, settled centuries ago as men first surged outward into the galaxy. As quickly as it had arrived, human influence in this area of space withered away. Only then did the settlers realise that they had colonised a world in an area already claimed by a sentient, space-faring species. They were totally alien and rarely seen. Their interest in this world was not territorial and so the colonists were allowed to remain. What little contact they had with the aliens was low-key and never hostile.

Then, after centuries, human-kind returned. Man was expanding into space once more. He encountered the aliens with predictable results. War. No one ever seemed clear as to what actually sparked the conflict, which made it no less real or vicious.

Fleet met fleet in elegant ballets of light and death. Fortunes ebbed and flowed, with the colonists largely oblivious. It was a distant war, fought in the depths of space and no real concern of theirs. Humanity gained the upper-hand, pushing the aliens back for the moment. The colonists once again fell under the dominion of their own kind.

The new arrivals were confused by the reception they received, perplexed even.

They had expected to be greeted as liberating heroes. They were not.

They had expected the colonists to rush forward and volunteer to enlist in the armed forces, to join in the crusade against the alien horde. They did not.

Initial meetings had not gone well.

The newcomers withdrew from talks, declaring that the colonists were traitors to their own species and deserved whatever happened to them. So began the raids. The colonists

Ian Whates

could not fully grasp what was happening. They wanted only to be left alone. Where was the wrong in that?

Humanity did not listen. Instead they chose to take by force what had been refused them. They came at night and in the fog; military units with a simple, indiscriminate mission. They rounded up anyone they encountered, irrespective of age, race or sex, Taking people to fight in the front line. Cannon fodder. Though what exactly became of the Taken, what purpose they actually served, no one ever offered to explain.

Despite their heritage, the colonists had no cultural reference for this aspect of human behaviour, for Man's habit of taking whatever he wanted when superior technology allowed, riding roughshod over any opposition or objection. It seemed more alien than anything the aliens themselves had ever displayed.

Jenice had never heard of anyone escaping the raiders before and had no idea why she had been allowed to. Perhaps those pursuing her had been distracted by other, less alert prey, or perhaps they had filled their quota for the night and could not be bothered. She neither knew nor cared.

Never afraid to fall back on her own resources, Jenice had always viewed isolation as any ally, and had thought she knew all there was to know about being alone, but as she walked through that night, with only her wits for company, she was forced to revise those assumptions. The fog played mind-games, cloaking objects until the very last moment and persuading her to see danger in every half-glimpsed outline. On top of which the fear, the hurt and the emerging guilt – both at Jamie's sacrifice and at her own apparent survival – brought with them an overwhelming despair, as she began to mourn her loss.

The fear at least served a purpose, keeping every sense sharpened and alert as she attempted with darting eyes to spot any hint of movement and with straining ears to catch any indication that she was not alone in this murky, grey world.

Despite her imagination occasionally suggesting otherwise,

she saw and heard no one.

Street lights reared out of the night – fuzzy yellow globes of wan illumination, struggling to make their mark. A sign materialised before her, an insubstantial shape coalescing from the gloom. Jenice squinted in an effort to read the words as she had with so many others. 'Nene Close': a name actually meant something to her. Whether by accident or subconscious design, she had stumbled into familiar streets and was now only minutes away from home.

She strode on with renewed purpose

Another street sign hove into view on its stilt-like twin supports. 'Compton Avenue' this one declared in proud black letters – almost her own back yard.

Around the corner and, mercifully, her home's familiar silhouette loomed out of the fog. Before she knew it she was standing at her front door, fiddling with the key. Then she was inside, her back pressed against the wall, shaking as the tears came again.

Jenice meant to call the authorities, but somehow her finger summoned up Tina's number instead.

"Oh, hon, I'd come if I could," said her horrified friend in a voice still muzzy with sleep, "but it's not safe out there."

"I know. That's okay."

"I'll be over first thing in the morning."

"No need, I'm fine," she lied. "Sorry to wake you."

She hung up. Then, operating in a detached, near-automatic state, she called emergency services.

As she sat there in the dark, waiting for them to arrive, Jenice found herself both hoping and praying.

She hoped that Jamie had somehow escaped the pressgang and was lost in the fog even as she had been – hoped desperately that he might appear at her door any moment.

What she prayed for, with all her heart, was that humankind would lose.

***

There was a throwaway scene in a Stephen Baxter novella (PS's *Riding the Rock,* I think) which stayed with me long after I'd read the book. The story involved mankind expanding outwards into space while waging a vicious war against a retreating alien aggressor, the Xeelee. In pursuit of victory, the human war machine ruthlessly plundered human worlds for soldiers.

It struck me that for those living with that Sword of Damocles hanging over them – the knowledge that at any moment they might be taken as cannon fodder in a war not their own – life would be truly awful. The idea joined that great mental log-jam of 'things to be explored sometime'. There it stayed, until one day I started jotting down a few observations about fog – there was no plot as such, this was simply a mood-piece involving the fear-inducing potential of shapes half-glimpsed in the murk. As so often happens, the two ideas gelled, and "In Fear of Fog" resulted.

One Night in London

Mayfair was the last place Kyle wanted to be.

Traditional pubs sandwiched between terraces of takeaways, noodle bars and plate-glassed storefronts – multi-cultural grocery shops and off-licences predominant. This part of London never slept and most of the stores were still open. All around was commotion and garish light.

As he moved further into the district the eateries and shops that granted the place a semi-respectable veneer peeled away, revealing its corrupt heart, like some faded raincoat held open by a sleazy flasher. What lay beneath was tired, naked, and unwholesome.

The days of luxury apartments, expensive hotels and exclusive restaurants were long gone. Mayfair was now clubland – every sort of club for every taste and depth of pocket. He walked unheeding through one holographic obscenity after another and the bright lights became increasingly in-your-face, as the clubs vied for prominence. All they achieved was a brash uniformity.

Doubtless the effect was intended to be welcoming, alluring even, but in contrast Kyle found it sinister and off-putting. To him these places all shouted the same thing: *We're only in it for the money. Come on in and be fleeced.*

Not that he was in any real position to pass judgement, since just such a club was his destination. The street noise vanished as soon as he stepped inside, masked by the pulsing throb of music from within. He paid entrance to the skinny, listless girl behind a recessed desk and headed down the stairs. The music grew louder with every step, reaching a crescendo as he passed through the twin doors at the bottom. The accompanying visual display was overwhelming, if entirely predictable. Swirling lights and rippling lasers accompanied the holographic dancers who took centre stage – scantily clad nymphets and Adonis-like men who oozed allure and sexuality, moving with precision to the mesmeric beat of the music.

A choice of brightly coloured pills was presented to him by the equally bright smile and cleavage fronting a young brunette. Designer narcotics: mass-produced and cheaply cut – not in any dangerous sense, just watered-down. Enough kick to give you a buzz and leave you wanting more.

Kyle shook his head and walked past.

It was early. The club was doing business but was far from packed. He brushed past a trio of lads intent on leering at the holographic dancers with lecherous glee.

Along the wall to his left hung the shimmering veils of privacy booths, which were always much the same: deeply upholstered seating on three sides, built around a central table. The fourth side, facing towards the dance floor, was fronted by a null-curtain, offering complete privacy to those within. From the occupants' perspective, both vision and sound from outside were reduced without being totally obscured.

A green light on the wall beside the first booth blinked on and off – his invitation to enter. There was no noticeable sensation as he stepped through the veil although there was transition, in as much as the noise level dropped dramatically. The thud of music became muted and flat.

The first sight that greeted him was a pair of raised buttocks, separated by a thin red line which began to develop into a thong before disappearing beneath a dishevelled black dress. The thong did very little to obscure what it covered, but doubtless it was never intended to.

Having taken in this most immediate demand on his attention, he now registered that the booth held three occupants.

One lay slumped across a section of the crescent seat and had clearly passed out, presumably as a result of drink, drugs, or a combination of both. She was a young oriental, wearing a body-hugging dress of iridescent blue. Even in her current state of collapse, she was strikingly beautiful.

Then there was Hawkes, sitting in the opposite wing of the booth, his shirt part-open. He raised his eyebrows in greeting as Kyle slipped onto the seat beside the comatose oriental.

The third occupant sported both a skimpy black dress and the shapely buttocks that had first caught his eye. Apart from the fact that she was blonde, there was little else he could tell about her at that moment, since her head was buried in Hawkes' lap.

"Won't be long," Hawkes mouthed to him, before closing his eyes.

Kyle turned his attention elsewhere, looking out toward the dance floor. The privacy booths still fascinated him; self-contained micro-worlds associated with but not fully a part of the club itself. Within their veiled areas you could indulge in an orgy, hold a business meeting, commit adultery or even carry out a murder, all in a public place while those around you were oblivious. In theory, at least.

He caught movement in the corner of his eye, glancing back across as Hawkes raised a hand, pressing against the back of the girl's head.

It was not often Kyle had an opportunity to observe a man's face during orgasm. On balance, it was an experience he decided he could live without.

Hawkes slumped and his grip on the girl's hair relaxed, allowing her to sit up. Very glamorous, Kyle noted without surprise. She was older than the oriental but still youthful. The black dress now fell to perfectly cover yet simultaneously display a voluptuous figure. The girl favoured Kyle with a smile, full of warmth and suggestion.

She reached to pick a napkin from the table and dab at her

chin. The red lipstick never smeared and still looked freshly applied, even when it had every excuse to be completely wiped away. The wonders of modern cosmetics.

"Want some?" Hawkes asked, glancing towards the girl.

Kyle shook his head. "No thanks." Any fleeting temptation withered before it was born – not because he had no idea where she might have been, but rather because he knew exactly where she'd been.

Hawkes signalled the girl to leave. "And take her with you." He indicated the still-motionless oriental.

The girl rose gracefully and came across to Kyle's side of the table. Before he gathered enough wit to fully move aside she was reaching across him in an effort to rouse her friend. Without consciously deciding to, he found himself helping the blonde with the oriental girl, who was still barely responding.

He actually felt a thrill as he first touched her, wrapping a hand around her limp arm, an effect probably boosted by pheromones in the girls' perfume. He was acutely aware of the softness of her skin, the tautness of her muscles, and the sensuous feel of the fabric that formed her designer dress.

"Is she going to be okay?" he asked.

"She'll live," the blonde assured him, her voice higher, younger than expected. As if on cue, the oriental moaned, her eyes struggling to flicker open. The blonde half-led, half-carried her from the booth.

"You liked the Chink, didn't you?"

Kyle was momentarily startled by the use of the archaic word 'Chink', especially in this era of supposed Anglo-Sino détente.

"Can't say I blame you. She's new here, caught my eye straight away. Unfortunately she passed out before she could catch hold of the rest of me." Hawkes laughed. The fact that he laughed alone did not seem to deter him in the least. "Ah well, there's always next time."

A waiter appeared, bearing a fresh bottle of champagne. He

hovered discretely outside the veil until given the green light to enter.

"Decent vintage," Hawkes commented. "It costs a fortune here, of course, but the house champagne's crap."

"Now, to business," he continued once the waiter had gone and the Champagne was settling in twin flutes. "And don't worry, I swept the place as soon as I arrived. No one's listening."

Since Kyle had no idea what was about to be discussed, he couldn't give a monkey's whether anyone listened in or not. The fact that the other man thought such precautions necessary spoke volumes.

He picked up the chilled glass and sampled the golden liquid. Hawkes had been right: it was good.

Having drained half his flute in a single gulp, Hawkes produced a photo and handed it across. "I need you to deliver a package for me, to this man." The picture was a close-up of a Chinese man, early fifties. Not someone Kyle recognised.

"Is this recent?"

"Of course."

He studied the picture for brief seconds, committing the image to memory, and then handed it back.

"Sure you won't need this?" the other joked. "They don't all look the same to you?"

"If I needed it, you wouldn't be hiring me."

"True." Hawkes slid a folded sheet of paper across the table. "Delivery is to his home."

Kyle studied the hand-written name and address. Hampstead – an area of London that still boasted some greenery thanks to the sacrosanct status of the Heath. Not just Hampstead, but The Bishop's Avenue, no less. The wealth and power embodied by the residents of that particular street was the primary reason why Hampstead Heath had remained inviolate to planners and developers alike.

Hawkes took back the paper and placed both it and the

photograph carefully into a slim metal wallet. "Acid spray," he explained. "Burns off the ink and photographic image then takes care of the paper itself. The best forensics in the world couldn't reconstruct anything after this." He beamed a conspiratorial smile and topped up their glasses.

Kyle was familiar with Hawkes' penchant for melodrama, but this seemed over-the-top even by his standards.

He sipped at his glass before asking, "When?"

"Tonight. Straight from here."

No hurry then. "Am I expected?"

"You will be."

Kyle stared at Hawkes for long seconds, liking the sound of this less and less. "What else?"

The other smiled. "I don't pay you to be curious."

"But it does pay me to check exactly what I'm getting involved in."

"It's a simple courier job, that's all."

"Then why do you need me? Why not just give it to a kid on a bike?"

"Because certain parties would prefer the delivery isn't made and I know I can count on you to ensure that it is."

Kyle digested that. His anticipated fee was rising by the second. "So I might meet with some opposition."

"Oh, I doubt it."

So it was a possibility. "Are we talking professionals, or just amateurs?"

Hawkes said nothing, but instead handed across a credit chip, which Kyle slotted into his wallet. The amount that came up on the display was sufficiently impressive to raise his eyebrows. For this amount he would not have argued, no matter what the opposition. "There's a locked section on the chip," he observed.

Hawkes smiled, "Carrying the same amount again. When I have confirmation that the package has been successfully delivered, I'll give you the release code."

One very serious package, it would seem.

It proved to be a sealed envelope. Really sealed, with microchipped tamper-proof tags laid carefully along each join; none of which gave any clue as to what it might contain. Kyle slipped it away with his wallet.

"I'll be in touch."

He rose and left. The club was busier. He glanced towards the crowded bar on his way to the exit, stopping as one face in particular registered. He looked again, without success. Not that it mattered; it was unlikely to have been the same girl, at least not judging by the state she had been in when he last saw her. He was seeing things. She must have made one hell of an impression.

He dismissed the thought and headed for the stairs, triggering dormant systems on the way. His augmentations were extensive. Not just muscles, nerves and tendons, but organs, blood vessels, limb joints – all had been modified. The human body is a balanced system. In order to obtain higher performance from some elements of that system, you have to enhance the capabilities of every other part, or the whole thing will be out of kilter and fail. All the necessary upgrades had been taken care of free of charge, courtesy of the military.

Ideally the authorities would have loved to remove every trace of the costly hardware when he resigned his commission. In practice, the alterations were too extensive. Removal would have killed him. So instead inhibitors were put in place – designed to block access to the upgrades and so prevent a veteran from becoming a 'menace to society'. The army would have you believe that such inhibitors were state-of-the-art and impossible to circumvent.

Not for the first time, the army was full of shit.

Removing the blocks proved expensive, painful, and not without associated risk, but far from impossible.

Kyle was under no illusions. He knew just how rare his level of body-tech was and how valuable an asset that made him. His fees reflected the fact.

Due to the inherent energy demands, he tended to leave the systems dormant until required. But Hawkes' paranoia had disturbed him and he decided to run with everything active until the package was safely delivered, just in case.

He reached the top of the stairs. Outside, Mayfair had come fully awake. The air itself danced with impermanent neon graffiti. In the split-second it took his systems to compensate, he was invited to try:

Black Diamond for the trip of a life-time — feel your veins burn and your mind soar...

The Chiang twins. Each more beautiful than the other, both expertly trained in the ancient erotic arts of the orient. They will take you to heaven and back...

The Virtual National – the race of the century! The 40 best horses of the last 100 years pitted against each other over the legendary Aintree fences. You can be there...

The best screw of your life. Hannah the stunning hermaphrodite – have her do to you everything you want to do to her...

His systems came to terms with the visual assault and reduced it to mere background, easily ignored.

If he thought the streets had been crowded before, now they were even more so, as locals and tourists alike poured into Mayfair to sample the thrills on offer in London's hottest district.

He passed VR games stations, slot-machine arcades and the doorways to members-only casinos, as well as strip-joints, sex clubs, designer drug bars, virtual booth parlours where you could gamble on mud wrestling and dog racing or take part in sexual acts that would have you thrown in prison with the key flushed away, were they anything other than virtual. *"If it's not real, it can't be illegal."* That argument had been won in a high profile court case a long time ago. It made no difference how real to every sense the experience might seem.

Kyle hated it. A vast, gaudy money-making machine designed

to strip the gullible of their credit by pandering to their basest desires.

Maybe he was just getting old.

As soon as possible, he cut away from the busiest streets by ducking down alleyways and side roads. Even here, every other doorway seemed to lead to a narcotics bar, a model's flat or some other questionable delight.

He finally escaped Mayfair and was able to make good progress. After a slight bottleneck caused by Regent Street and the retro-chic of Carnaby Street, he was skirting the slums of Soho to his right. Only at that point did it occur to him that he was being followed.

Whoever they were, they were good. For him not to have spotted them until now, they were very good.

Rotating tail, he realised, as one pursuer faded from the scene and another took up the pursuit – a man who had been casually loitering outside a bar. That and the crowds explained how they had managed to stay anonymous for so long. It also suggested they had no shortage of manpower.

Would they try to take him, or were they simply on a watching brief? He was nearly at the car. Did they know that? If they intended to jump him, it was now or never.

Now, it would seem.

A large, hulking figure stepped out and blocked his way, not walking towards him, just waiting. Until this point those tailing him had gone to great lengths to remain unnoticed. Now they closed in behind him; two of them.

Two behind and one in front, doubtless intending to converge together... Not a chance. He sprinted forward, straight towards the new arrival.

He was a big man. Put him in a black suit and any Mayfair club would have been proud to have him standing at their door. Nor was he as ponderous as his size might suggest. Anyone with slower reflexes would have been flattened by the first punch. As it was, Kyle leant away from the ham-sized fist. At the same time he struck a heavy blow of his own, straight into the man-mountain's kidneys. His other hand was already in motion, to chop at the neck. It proved a less effective strike, both because his target was already convulsing forward and because bunched neck and shoulder muscles absorbed much of the impact. Still, the combination had the other almost doubled over. Kyle connected with a swinging upper-cut to the chin. Crude, but effective: snapping the head back despite the thick muscles. The big man toppled. Just in time, as his two associates closed in.

They approached warily, the stance of one suggesting martial arts training, while the other moved with a fluid gait that spoke of augmentation, a body-system similar to his own. They tried to circle him, one to either side, but he stepped carefully backward, keeping them both in sight. Realising this, they abandoned the attempt and attacked anyway, from as wide an angle as possible. It was timed to be simultaneous, but Kyle stepped towards the Kung-fu kid, enabling him to block his strike a fraction ahead of the other.

Yes, martial arts to one side, body-system to the other, but it was comparatively crude, not in the same league as his own. The Kung-fu kid danced back out of reach. His friend was a fraction slower to respond. Kyle pressed his attack in that direction, unleashing a sequence of blows far too quick for the lower grade system to react to. One landed heavily on the shoulder, numbing if not breaking it.

The Kung-fu kid was back, aiming a kick in text-book style, body leant back as counter-balance. Again, Kyle was simply too fast. He dropped to one knee, allowing the foot to sail over his shoulder, and launched a counter-blow. Just as the kick reached full extension, his fist slammed into the lad's genitals. With a sound that struggled between a scream and a gasp, the kid collapsed, writhing.

To his credit, the remaining attacker still attempted to fight, even with one arm useless, but it was no contest. Within seconds he rested against the alley wall, unconscious. The Kung-fu kid was too busy trying to crawl away while maintaining a semi-foetal position to offer any further threat.

At that point, Kyle's systems went crazy in a manner all-too-familiar. Someone had just locked onto him with laser targeting. He whipped around. Two figures at the mouth of the alley. One slender – a girl – but it was the other who held the rifle.

There was a shouted "No!" and the girl whipped out an arm, striking the gun so that the bullet went high and wide, ricocheting off the wall somewhere above him. Kyle was already moving. As the gun swung back he was on them, operating in full adrenalin-pumped combat mode. He lashed out with trained precision, too swift for his own mind to consciously follow, landing a series of blows on both the gunman and the girl.

Only when both were down did he relent. Only then did he slowly regain normal awareness and fully register what was going on. Only then was he able to acknowledge that the girl who lay unconscious at his feet was the Chinese girl from the privacy booth at the club.

On impulse he scooped her up. A few people had started to gather, drawn by the sounds of violence and now gawping at its aftermath. Not yet a crowd, but the beginnings of one. He ignored them and strode swiftly past, turning a deaf ear to their whispered mutterings. A dozen strides and he was into Soho square, ringed as ever by its defensive wall of slant-parked cars, one of them his own.

He poured the girl into the back seat, leapt in, and drove off.

Not Hampstead, not yet. Home.

He must have hit her hard at some point, because she was still out when he put her down on the settee. By the time the smelling salts had been located there were signs of returning life, but he broke a capsule under her nose anyway.

Eyelids shot wide and a hand came up to try and push away

the offending source of ammonia. "God, I hate that stuff." Her cut-crystal accent was pure southern England, the sort only acquired at the best, the most expensive, of schools. "You don't hold back when you hit someone, do you?"

"Not when they're trying to shoot me, no."

"Me? I was the one who saved you."

"Why?"

"Not sure. Seemed like a good idea at the time. Shit!" The last was accompanied by a hand lifting towards her cheek. The pain had started to kick in. "Do you have any ice?"

He held out a bag of frozen peas, wrapped in a tea towel, both of which had been grabbed while he searched for the smelling salts.

She glanced inside the towel before lifting it gingerly to the side of her face. "Peas?"

"Ancient British tradition."

"Shit, shit, shit... I think you've broken my jaw."

"Couldn't have," he assured her. "You wouldn't be able to swear so much. Now, let's begin with you telling me who you are, shall we?"

After a slight pause, "Helen."

"That's a start, I suppose. Helen what?"

"Just Helen."

Okay, he could always come back to that later.

Before he was able to continue, she asked, "Ex-military?"

He nodded.

"Special forces, I presume." He made no response. "Thought so. How recent is your bio-tech?" Which was something he had no intention of commenting on. "Not that it really matters; it's obviously pretty up-to-date. We've got nothing to match military-tech like that, few people would have. Do you have any idea how unusual that makes you, how valuable?"

Not liking the way she had seized the initiative, Kyle ploughed on with a question of his own: "Why did you jump me?"

"For the package, of course, the one that Hawkes gave you."

Of course, but it was nice to have it confirmed.

"You had the booth bugged," he suddenly realised. She smiled. "Hawkes assured me the place was clean, so you must have planted and activated the bug after he'd done his sweep."

Her smile broadened, "Brains *and* brawn."

Her unconsciousness had obviously been feigned in the hope that Hawkes would discount her, but she had the bug there as insurance in case he threw her out anyway.

She seemed to guess the train of his thoughts. "Thanks for being so gentle with me, by the way." Her words and coy half-smile brought back the memory of the thrill experienced as he had first touched her. Even now, despite the angry bruise that was starting to show on her cheek, she was disconcertingly beautiful.

He determined not to be distracted. "The fact that someone's done their homework on Hawkes well enough to plant you at that particular club speaks of quite an organisation. I repeat my first question: who the hell are you?"

She looked at him, as if searching his face for something, "You really have no idea what you're carrying, do you?"

"No. Not my business." Since she had the booth bugged, she must have been confident of that answer in any case.

She took a seep breath. "Where do you stand on the government cozying up to the Chinese?"

Politics? Was Hawkes getting involved in politics? Surely the man had more sense than that.

In an age that had seen a growing rift develop between the USA and continental Europe, the UK's attempts to keep a foot in both camps had misfired badly, leaving her trusted by neither.

Conveniently, this all coincided with China's true emergence on the world stage.

China had been quietly going through its own upheavals,

drifting away from communism and doing much to address human rights issues, events that had gone all but unnoticed in the prevailing turmoil and anxiety of world politics. The UK needed a strong ally, while China needed the international knowledge, connections and experience that Britain could provide. Common links through Hong Kong and Singapore were emphasised and suddenly Britain developed a growing political warmth towards the cleaner, more palatable China.

Not everyone was happy with the situation, including Kyle himself to a certain extent. Nothing against the Chinese as such, but he simply couldn't see such an unlikely alliance working in the long term. More than a few people were concerned that China might end up swallowing Britain whole.

"You'll know that not everyone is convinced by the current alliance," Helen continued. "What you may not know is that even people within the government are having second thoughts about the direction we're headed in.

"There have been negotiations, very sensitive and very hush-hush, intended to build bridges with both the EU and the USA. Of course, publicly we're still committed to a program that ties us ever closer to China, but behind the scenes the groundwork's being laid for a move back towards more traditional alliances."

He felt increasingly uncomfortable, wondering again exactly who he the girl represented; was she part of a radical action group as implied, or something more official?

"And Hawkes is involved in all of this?"

"Somewhere along the line papers have come into his possession." Papers, he noted, it was always paper. Ironic that in such a hi-tech age, all the really sensitive stuff was still being committed to paper, because it was so readily destroyed and left the least traceable trail.

Helen continued. "We understand they contain details of meetings, transcripts of conversations, possibly even photographs, we're not sure. Enough to sabotage the whole process at this early stage, in any case."

"And you think Hawkes is selling all this to the Chinese?" He would of course, were he ever to obtain such high-level and sensitive intelligence.

"Yes. If you're taking it to the address in Hampstead we think you are the information will be in Beijing-King by the morning. That will give them enough ammunition to quash the negotiations and bind us even more tightly to the Chinese cause."

So they knew enough to know his destination, as well.

Did he believe her? It certainly explained his unprecedented fee. Of course, Hawkes would never involve himself directly in such a situation; no, he would employ a go-between, a mule. Someone like him. "You keep referring to 'we'," he said. "Who exactly is this 'we'?"

"We're a group of committed patriots," she said cautiously, "working in the interests of the British people."

He shook his head, still uncertain what to believe. A smile played at the corners of his mouth.

"You find this amusing?" she nettled.

"No, it's just that…" What was it exactly: the fact that she looked so obviously Chinese and he had always believed the Chinese to be loyal to their own culture? Or was it the fact that she seemed so young?

"You're wondering what a nice Chinese girl is doing mixed up in all this and why I'm so concerned about Britain," she said, raising her voice as she second-guessed with commendable accuracy. "I was born in Britain. I was educated in Britain. I've never even *been* to China. I am *British*." The last was virtually shouted.

"Okay, I'm convinced." He held up his hands, realising he'd hit a nerve. So much for judging by appearances.

"I'm not just some wet-behind-the-ears half-wit rebelling against a privileged up-bringing. I went into this with my eyes open. I know exactly what I'm doing."

"If you say so."

"Fuck you!"

He couldn't help it, he grinned.

Instead of the anticipated outburst of rage, her anger seemed to melt away and she responded with a reluctant smile of her own. "That wasn't a statement of intent."

"Pity."

"Look," she implored, the smile vanishing but her voice now softer, "can't you see how important it is that the package never arrives?"

"I've been paid to ensure that it does."

"And you still intend to deliver it, even knowing what it contains?"

He hesitated. The truth was that if the package were all that she claimed, he *would* prefer it never arrived. "I'll need some more persuading, if you expect me to renege on a commission."

"Then we'll have to see what I can do." With a smile, she rose to her feet.

Only a few steps separated them, but she managed to turn those steps into a parade as she flowed towards him. It would have been impossible to look anywhere else.

"Are you still wearing that scent from the club?" a small corner of him wondered, surprised by the intensity of his reaction.

"Does it matter?"

No, it did not.

Her lips were soft, cool. He was conscious of not hurting her, of the bruise to her face, but such concerns almost instantly melted away. His hand caressed her slender back as they kissed, moving up to stroke her neck, all the while aware of the gentle pressure where her breasts pressed against him. They came up for air, her smile reflecting a combination of triumph and invitation.

They kissed again, his fingertips tracing the detail of her neck, her chin. This time, as they separated, he wondered if his own smile mirrored regret. "I'm sorry," he assured her, pressing the ampoule he had palmed to her throat.

At the base of the neck, the carotid artery is deeply buried and protected, but as it travels up the throat it ventures closer to the surface and becomes more accessible. The ampoule released a fine spray of chemicals which shot through the skin and into the carotid, to be delivered directly to the brain.

Her beautiful face just had time to register puzzlement before it slackened into unconsciousness. He caught her as she wilted and carried her through into the bedroom, to be placed tenderly on the bed. She would be unconscious for several hours, more than enough time for him to drive to Hampstead and back.

As he drove, he took the opportunity to reflect on things. What it boiled down to was that he only had her word for any of this. Beautiful, charming and bewitching though she was, he knew nothing about her except what she had volunteered, which might or might not be true. Everything she had said could be complete bullshit; probably was. Of course, he could settle matters by opening the envelope and seeing what it contained, but that in itself would involve making the choice, since he hardly dared deliver a package that had been tampered with.

No, the only decision facing him was whether he trusted her word enough to abort the delivery. Logically, he had no solid reason to... which did not prevent him from being tempted.

However, at the end of the day, he simply could not imagine Hawkes being involved in anything so crucial. Hawkes, with the fate of nations in his hands? No, the man was strictly small time, whatever pretensions he might nurture.

Kyle only hoped he could make Helen understand his point of view when he returned. Unlikely, but a man had a right to dream.

The high iron gates fronting the Hampstead house opened automatically once he had identified himself. Slick-haired, shades-toting security opened the imposing front doors. He was immediately confronted by a neat, short man, fifty or so, immaculately clad in suit and tie even at this hour. He recognised the face from the photo Hawkes had shown him.

"You're late."

"There were complications," Kyle explained, immediately bristling at the man's air of assumed authority. He reached into his pocket and drew out an envelope. In the act of passing it across, he froze.

"Is there a problem?"

"Yes." His voice turned leaden by realisation. "This is not the envelope I was given to deliver."

Similar, so similar that the bug placed in the privacy booth must have provided visual as well as audio, but not the same.

The kiss. What had her hands been doing while he concentrated on exploring her throat and tracing the artery? Clearly the lady had hidden talents, and he had grossly underestimated her.

Extricating himself from the house on The Bishop's Avenue without resorting to violence proved as difficult as expected, but eventually he succeeded. The hardest part was persuading them to let him leave unaccompanied, but he managed that as well – largely by assuring them that he knew where the envelope was and could return with it, if they let him go quickly and alone.

All of which proved to be overly optimistic.

She was gone, of course.

The bed's only occupant was a torn, empty envelope – the original given to him by Hawkes. A brief message was scrawled across it. Three words followed by a kiss.

He forgot about the envelope for a moment and activated the computer. When first moving in here he had routinely hacked into the building's security systems. He now used that access to scan the security tapes.

There she was, leaving by the front door, timed at less than ten minutes after his own departure. So much for 'unconscious for hours'. No apparent accomplices, she was alone, so her body must have been primed with a cocktail of counter-drugs. Over two hours. No chance of finding her now.

He turned from the computer and wondered who to call first. Hawkes. Would the man want his money back – the half that had already been paid via the open part of the credit chip? Probably not, but Kyle would return it anyway. Maybe at some point in the future Hawkes would trust him enough to put some work his way again... Maybe.

So, had the girl spoken the truth about what the envelope contained? World events would likely provide the only clue.

He picked up the envelope, rereading its brief message. What did those three words and the kiss mean to her as she wrote them? Were they intended as a threat, a promise, or were they just flippant farewell?

Be seeing you X

He knew exactly what they meant to him. Prophecy.

***

I went to school in central London and have been visiting the place throughout my life. As a result, I've seen it in all manner of moods, seasons and circumstance. This probably explains why London features in a number of my stories.

Various snippets and factors went into this one, including a recent lunchtime visit to the wonderfully indulgent *Le Gavroche* restaurant in Mayfair, memories of an intimidating walk through Soho during a time when sex clubs were deploying pavement hawkers to entice passers-by into their parlours, marvelling at the houses along 'The Bishops Avenue', Hampstead, while en-route to the Kenwood music festival, the prevailing political climate in the wake of the 2003 invasion of Iraq

– the growing strain the invasion was putting on US and British relations with the rest of Europe – not to mention the rise in prominence of China as an international presence... and, of course, the desire to write a story featuring an explicit sex scene for a change.

Ghosts in the Machine

I woke up with a truly foul taste in my mouth – which was my first awareness... that and the fact that my tongue seemed overly large and to be coated with an unpleasant, slimy deposit. Oh, and my head was throbbing, as if playing host to a full drum kit complete with enthusiastic drummer who was intent on beating out a percussive refrain to every pump of my heart.

There was real resistance from my eyelids. They wanted to stay shut, thank you very much, finally opening only with the greatest reluctance.

Where the hell was I? The phrasing of that self-query seemed particularly apt. It was dark, dingy and oppressively warm – all qualities that I tended to associate with the devil's abode. I pushed myself up; which sounds misleadingly dynamic. In fact, I dragged and bullied a rebellious body from prone into a shambolic semblance of sitting.

Thoughts were arriving in disjointed shards rather than as a continuous stream: drinking, joining, the lads, Gella; revisited scraps of the recent past. It was as if no two memories were in any way related. Even those that felt as if they ought to fit together were fragmented and isolated, repelling their near-neighbours with the stubbornness of similarly-charged magnetic poles.

I gave up, trusting that if ignored, the images would settle into a coherent progression of their own accord. Eventually.

Clearly I had drunk far more than my mental processes could handle. In short, I was hammered, which made sorting out where I was and how I came to be here... difficult, to say the least.

Mind you, even sober I might have had a problem with that one.

Something smelt like a brewery. Me, I realised. Dampness: the side of my jacket, where I had been lying, was soaked. As I took the jacket off, the shattered remnants of a bottle tumbled from a pocket. Scotch whisky. Where on earth had I picked up a genuine *glass* bottle of whisky? Decent stuff too, by the look of the label.

I staggered to my feet, rubbed my eyes, and peered around.

Some sort of basement, perhaps... Underground, I felt certain. It seemed vast, not to mention filthy. Strip lights were mounted at intervals along the ceiling. Somehow, they had an air of antiquity about them, as if they had burned here unseen for centuries. They gave out far less light than might have been expected. Lines of them stretched into the distance in all directions, though my view was curtailed by large, anonymous blocks which hemmed me in. Were they storage containers, or perhaps machines? All were covered with the accumulated dust of ages. Which might also explain the dimness of the lighting – each tube was similarly laden with filth and grime.

If this *was* machinery, what was it for? And was it still working? Something seemed to be, at least to judge by the background thrum; not simply a sound but a vibration that pervaded everything. At first I had dismissed it as going on inside my own head – an after effect of over-indulgence – but now I realised that the source was external. This was a sound that spoke of energy being used, but for what purpose?

The heat was stifling and there seemed little or no movement of air.

I started to walk/shuffle, choosing a direction at random, with no clear objective in mind, just a desire to be somewhere else.

Slowly thoughts were filtering through the alcohol, taking on a semblance of meaning as my subconscious sought to interpret what was going on.

I wasn't scared, you understand, just... befuddled.

Gella. That name became a centre, the seed around which structured thought began to crystallise.

Gella and I were joining this weekend, signing contracts in a couple of days. Now that was scary. I had never lived with anyone before. Well, my parents, of course, but that didn't count. This would be my first joining, a big step.

Girls had come and gone before – a few days at mine, a week or two at theirs – but they were just transient things, short-term conveniences for all concerned. There was always our own place to go back to when the relationship cooled... fizzled out... or we became bored.

Joining, that was different: a mutual acceptance that we wanted to share the same place and space.

Originally the custom of joining was intended to be a casual thing, nothing too formal, but formality had crept in over the years. It was inevitable, I suppose. I mean, if you just moved in together without any contracts it would be a nightmare. The legal implications of the inevitable separation would be horrendous – I brought this into the relationship with me, but she uses it most of the time; she brought that with her but I've adopted it as my own... and what about the stuff acquired after a couple are together? *You* try figuring out who should have rights over how much of what. Impossible, unless you agree such details beforehand; hence the existence of contracts.

This was progress, although I still had no idea where I was and just continued to follow the course of two old pipes that ran along above my head, their outline broken at intervals by bulky brackets clasping them to the ceiling. A seemingly endless mass of hulking shapes slipped by to be replaced by the next in line, each indistinguishable from the last. Machinery, I grew increasingly convinced, though of unfathomable purpose and all covered in a uniform layer of muck, too filthy to investigate... at least, for me to investigate. I still wasn't scared.

Welcome to the Machine... a snatch of song drifted through my mind. It had been a hit a month or two ago. Pilfered, of course, from a previous age; dusted down, tweaked, copied by some anonymous hopeful and presented as if it were new.

Originality? Who needs it?

My mind was wandering. I really must have had a skinful.

The joining was important, though. That was the reason I was out celebrating... getting drunk... getting plastered. With friends, naturally; friends who might just think it funny to do this to me, to dump me somewhere unexpected and see how I reacted.

Ha, ha.

"Hello." I tried calling. Maybe I expected an echo but there wasn't one. The sound just seemed to be swallowed by the silence, by the vastness of the place.

I was feeling increasingly irritated; still not scared, just, well... bored.

I could see how to my friends this might all seem a bit of a laugh, fun even. To me it was simply tedious. Wandering around in the semi-dark, with no idea where I was going, not knowing if this was the right or wrong direction or even if it made any difference... and I was beginning to sober up. *Fun* did not even begin to come into it.

"Jezz? Alan?" Again, no response.

"Come on, I'm getting thirsty down here. Let's all hit another bar."

They were doing it on purpose, letting me stew. Doubtless this was all hilarious for them, but not for me, not any more.

I stopped walking and decided to try shouting again. "Jezz? All right guys, enough is enough."

"Who are you calling to?" The voice, at my elbow, made me jump.

An old man stood behind me. "What the... where did you come from?"

He was about my height and dressed in a featureless brown garment – a sort of all-enveloping smock. Definitely not the latest in cutting-edge fashion; in fact I very much doubted it ever had been. He reminded me of… a monk. I dredged the ancient comparison up from somewhere.

"Here," he said simply. "I live here."

"And where exactly is 'here'? Where are we?"

"Below, within, and between."

Oh great – old, mysterious *and* cryptic.

"Huh?" This was not destined to go down as one of my more inspired conversational moments.

"Below the surface, within the Machine and between the forgotten and the present," he said patiently, as if addressing a child. Was that supposed to explain something? "You must be from Above."

"Well… I suppose…"

"From the City: Above."

"Yes."

"What are you doing here?"

What indeed. "Long story. Who are you?"

"I'm the Caretaker, of course."

Of course. "What do you take care of?"

"Why, all of this," he gestured expansively.

"And this is?"

"The Machine." I must have looked blank. "You do know about the Machine, about the way it provides for the City Above?" I shook my head. "Running hot and cold water, air conditioning, communication, transport, power for lighting, synthesis, recreation, food… have you never wondered where it all comes from?"

Had I? "Not really." I had just assumed.

"The Machine *is* the city and the city is the Machine. What do they teach you these days?"

Not enough, it would seem. "So this Machine supports the

whole city?"

"Of course," he snapped, as if losing patience. "Have you ever seen a factory, or industry of any kind for that matter, in your precious city?"

Again I shook my head. What on Earth was a factory, anyway?

"No, you haven't. It can recreate anything, you know – the Machine – manufacture a perfect copy of any and every thing that's stored in its data banks; which is virtually everything that has ever been."

He focused on me with renewed intensity. "You don't belong here."

No argument from me.

"Come."

With that abrupt command he was off, walking with purpose and at a deceptively rapid pace, forcing me to hurry in order to keep up.

An uncomfortable silence enveloped us. I felt that I should be asking him things but had no idea what to say. "Have you been down here long?" Lame, I know, on a par with *do you come here often*, but it was better than the silence.

"Longer than you can imagine."

I abandoned conversation as a lost cause and concentrated on following him, hoping that he could soon get me back to the surface, where the company was a little warmer. It was then that I noticed something odd about my reticent guide. Every step I took disturbed the layer of dust that carpeted the floor, resulting in a clear trail of footprints, whereas the Caretaker's passage left no mark at all.

I was saved from having to ponder the implications too deeply by our apparent arrival. The Caretaker abruptly stopped.

"Here we are," he said with a small smile.

The spot he had chosen seemed indistinguishable from any other. We had not reached a wall or any sort of structure, there was no flight of stairs or elevator, not even a ladder. I gazed up at the ceiling, which was unbroken and provided no clue. It made no sense.

"How am I supposed to return to the surface from here?" I asked.

"The surface? Who said anything about the surface? I told you this place is 'between'. People do occasionally travel through, but only ever in one direction. Nobody goes up."

"What do you..." I started to ask, when suddenly the floor parted beneath my feet.

So unexpected was the fall that I may have screamed. I struck a metallic surface, a slide or chute of some sort – a shiny, steep slope which I shot down with no chance of slowing or stopping. I began to turn sideways and fought to bring my feet around beneath me.

The pell-mell journey ended as suddenly as it had begun, but not before I had picked up some stomach-churning momentum and was convinced I was about to die. Abruptly there was a sense of space as I shot out the mouth of the chute, landing on something soft, which I half bounced, half slid off of, tumbling onto hard pavement and slamming against a wall with bruising force.

For long seconds I simply lay there, regaining my breath and thankful to be alive.

Then I began to take stock of my surroundings. My fingers clawed at the wall as I struggled to sit. They found eroded bricks and mortar that was flaking and powdery to the touch. Water seeped slowly from the wall opposite, which was slick and green with slime. Beside me was a pile of rubbish – a towering mass of black bags, garbage cans and overflowing detritus – which must have been what I landed on. Several of the bags had split, bearing witness to my impact. A single headlight and a grill of rusted chrome that might once have belonged to some vehicle or other protruded from the mound at about head height.

Unwholesome, nose-wrinkling smells surrounded me: the stench of dampness, of stagnant water, the acrid tang of oil and other things even more unsavoury. They hung in the still air, layered one upon the other, and combined to produce an all-pervading backdrop, like rancid olfactory wallpaper.

Something scuttled within the trash mountain, not seen but heard, and water dripped out a ponderous rhythm somewhere nearby. Sounds here were warped and dulled. By the time they reached me, it seemed I was hearing only their echo and not the actual sounds at all.

It was night time, although I could never imagine it being anything else in this strange, subterranean world. The only sources of light in what appeared to be a blind alley were two lamps fastened to the wall behind me, which provided insipid and inadequate illumination.

I climbed to my feet, aching everywhere, but not badly enough to suggest anything broken, and started to limp away from the garbage pile.

A ground-hugging shadow scurried away as I moved, to vanish down what might have been a stairwell. I had no idea what type of animal it was, nor had any wish to find out. I felt rather than saw eyes upon me and quickened my pace as much as the assorted aches and pains would allow.

The background hum of machinery seemed louder here than it had been even in the level of the Caretaker, and as I turned a corner and saw what appeared to be a street beyond the mouth of the alley, it grew louder still, acquiring a harsh, grinding tone.

There was more light too in the street beyond the alley. It was cast by lines of streetlamps that stood sentry beside the road, many flickering and some not lit at all. Their erratic amber glare did nothing to reduce the surreal nature of the surroundings.

I stopped at the mouth of the alley and peered cautiously around the corner. A little way down the street there were people, lots of people. I saw men and women but no children. They stood on both sides of the road, lined up two or three deep, as if waiting for something.

This was the most chilling sight I have ever seen. All were dressed in similar style, in shapeless functional trousers, shirts and tops, all in greys and white and black and browns – no bright colours anywhere. Yet the most disturbing aspect of the scene was their conversation. There wasn't any.

No talking, no laughter, no gestures, no apparent communication of any sort. Perhaps a hundred or more people who just stood there in complete silence; the occasional shifting of weight or movement of heads the only things to belie the illusion that they were statues and not alive at all.

I became aware of a new sound, a distant vibration that seemed to be growing nearer. I shrank back from the corner, crouching down to make myself as small as possible.

The sound built rapidly now, as if something were rushing towards me. There were clicks and clacks, the shriek of metal scraping across metal, the deep rumble of something monumental being rolled along, all accompanied by hisses and grinding – a chaotic symphony of mechanical menace. I almost broke and ran back down the alley, but was curious to see the source of this inconceivable sound and so stayed.

It shot into sight, charging past me towards the crowd of people: a giant metal snake. A train or tram that ran along twin tracks in the road which I hadn't even spotted until its passage. It was divided into three articulated segments, presumably carriages, and was a uniform dull metallic grey, without any livery or adornments. It was also caked in dirt; not the dustiness of neglect such as I'd seen in the Caretaker's level, but rather with the spattered muck of frequent use and infrequent cleaning.

The tram juddered to a halt, wheezing and hissing as if catching its breath. Doors opened simultaneously along its length. The waiting people all stepped inside, moving in unison, as if at some unheard signal. No one emerged. The doors closed again and the great grey serpent began to move, groaning and protesting as it steadily picked up speed. Everything seemed eerily clinical and efficient, the whole process taking seconds rather than minutes.

The tram continued straight down the street away from me, towards a huge, hulking building that I could just make out in the distance. The only reason I could see it at all was because the place seemed to generate its own nimbus of light, emanating from windows and orifices. Tall chimney stacks bracketed the building and from their tops rose wisps of smoke or steam, visible due to the flickering glow that accompanied them, suggestive of flames at the chimneys' hearts. I sensed that this was the tram's destination, where it was taking its dour human cargo. A word the caretaker had used sprang to mind: factory; although I have no idea why.

Just then something touched me on the shoulder. So unexpected was the contact that I sprang forward into the street, turning around to find myself confronted by a slouched and ragged man. I registered tattered clothes and unkempt hair and a beard framing a wizened face, all of which was in total contrast to the meticulous drabness of the people who had boarded the tram moments earlier, as was the animation that showed in his actions. Only after noting all this did I take in the eyes. There weren't any. In their place, the skin continued seamlessly from cheekbone to forehead.

Instinctively, I recoiled.

Then I remembered my manners. "I'm sorry, you startled me." I felt absurd even as I spoke.

He said nothing, though his face remained unerringly pointed towards me, as if looking directly at me – a blank-faced stare if ever there was one. His nostrils expanded and contracted unnervingly. Was he scenting me? Hearing me? Or did he utilise a combination of both?

Disturbed by this strange parody of humanity far more than I cared to admit, I chose to move on, striding down the street in the wake of the tram with as much dignity as I could muster; only to falter and come to a halt after a few steps.

Ahead of me more people were appearing. In ones and twos they slunk out into the open, emerging from between buildings or from sunken stairways. It was as if they had been in hiding, waiting for their sighted and more sombre brethren to go before they dared show themselves.

All were like the old man: dressed in rags, moving with a cautious, furtive manner, and all were eyeless.

One of them had been disturbing enough; being surrounded by a mob of these strange, feral people was too much for me. I felt as if I had stumbled into somebody else's nightmare, one in which I had no reference points and no control.

They were appearing in every direction. The only possible sanctuary seemed to be back into the alley, so I turned and retraced my steps, hurrying on legs suddenly weak and unstable as fear rose within me.

The old man was still there. His face lifted as I approached, his lip curling in what seemed to be a snarl rather than a smile. As I drew level, he grabbed at me, reaching for my arm with long-nailed fingers. More on edge, more scared than I had ever been in my life, I was ready for him. I twisted as he lunged, so that his grasp found only my shirt sleeve, which ripped as I pulled away. His talons left gouges on my arm, drawing blood, but I was past him and running.

From behind came an ululating cry. This was the first sound I had heard issue from a human throat since I arrived here and it sounded anything *but* human. Truly terrified now, I ran for all I was worth, all aches and pains abruptly forgotten.

Around the corner, and I arrived at the garbage heap, the end of the blind alley. Spurred on by the sound of running feet behind me, I didn't hesitate but leapt onto the mound, climbing, pulling and clawing my way to the top, oblivious to the ripping bags, the rotting filth and stench that surrounded me.

Mercifully I came to the summit, only to find myself confronted by a brick wall. But by stretching, I could reach its top edge. I felt the unstable heap beneath me shifting and knew that I was in danger of sinking into the supporting detritus, so clung desperately onto the rim with both hands and tried to pull and scramble my way up, finding purchase in the crumbling wall.

Panting and terrified, I lay on the flat roof, gazing down at the dozen or so creatures gathered below. They might walk like men, but I could no longer find it within me to think of them as human. Like a pack of hunting animals they jostled and prowled around the edge of the trash mound, as if seeking a clear way through. All the while, their blind faces stared up at me.

"Look, I'm a stranger," I called. "All I want to do is get back home."

My words only seemed to goad them. Two leapt into the rubbish and started to wade and clamber towards me.

In desperation I looked around for a means of escape. The first thing I saw was the gaping mouth of the chute which had spewed me forth so little time ago. It emerged from a rock wall that had been hidden from view at street level. It was completely out of reach and, in any case, memory told me that its surface had been far too smooth and steep to ever dream of climbing up.

Only then did I notice the ladder: a narrow strip of grey metal that clung to the rock face and was all but invisible in the gloom. I rushed over, finding that it came down to the very roof top I was on, extending past the mouth of the chute and disappearing into the darkness beyond.

Great. Where were all the elevators when you needed them? I was already tired and my knees felt weak just thinking about the climb ahead.

Sounds of scrabbling gave me new heart and without glancing backwards, I started to climb.

I have no idea how long that climb took. After a while it all blurred into one interminable effort. Initially I kept expecting to feel the ladder vibrate to the clambering presence of others, and strained to hear the sounds of pursuit, but none came. When I did eventually summon the courage to glance down it proved to be a mistake, as I realised just how far above the ground and even the rooftops I had climbed. At this point I was well past the chute and above even the rim of the distant chimney stacks, gaining a clearer sense of the raging fires they contained: angry, red, pulsing in the darkness like bleeding hearts.

Higher still and I was climbing near total darkness as the light from below receded. Yet as my eyes adjusted, I realised that even here it was not completely dark. Some growths on the rock-face around me, which later research suggested were probably lichen, glowed faintly with their own wan luminescence. The world was limned in narrowly defined shades of black and grey.

I rested several times and may even have dozed once or twice, clinging to the ladder which had become my whole world. Not for long, mind you; I was determined to reach the top before my strength failed entirely.

The end came almost as a surprise. Suddenly there were no more rungs to climb and I was collapsing forward to lie on a flat surface, muscles cramping with complaint at such abuse. It was tempting to lie there and slip into genuine sleep, but I remained terrified of being caught by those feral humans of the City Below and after a few moments forced myself to stand and look back. I was on a platform built into the rock-face, the distant city stretched out beneath me, etched in orange and red, as if it were on fire.

Before me stood a door, bizarre in its normality after so much strangeness. It sprung open at my touch and I stumbled through into the oppressive warmth of the Caretaker's domain.

When I first woke up here it had seemed to me like hell, but it was nothing of the sort. I now realised that this was in-between, this was purgatory: a limbo that separated the unsuspecting City

Above from the hell that lay beneath our feet.

What remained of the adventure was pretty straightforward. I shuffled along, all the while watching the ceiling, confident that somewhere up there would be a way back to the world I knew.

Finally I saw something; a barely perceptible seam above one of the anonymous blocks that surrounded me. After scrambling through rotting food and rubbish, the grime no longer held any fears and I soon climbed up the block in question to examine the possible crack more closely. Only then could I be certain: here was a hatch of some sort and I wondered how many similar irregularities I had blundered past without seeing.

Frustrating minutes passed as I stood there, pressing and prodding at the doorway, trying to find the release. By chance, I eventually pushed a spot at its very centre and the hatch started to slide open. The movement triggered a shower of dust which caused me to cough and splutter as it drifted down onto my upturned face.

I almost lost my balance as a platform beneath my feet started to rise, lifting me up through the newly exposed opening. The temperature dropped abruptly as I emerged, causing me to shiver. The cold and the sudden daylight made my eyes water. I was home. Well, almost.

I called Jezz, reckoning the very least he could do was pick me up and take me back to my apartment. He brought the whole crowd with him and within minutes I was surrounded by familiar faces, all of whom were talking at once.

It emerged that, after spiking my drink, my 'friends' had dumped me down in the Machine basement, which Jezz, naturally, knew all about. Jezz took pride in knowing about everything. Apparently there had been a door directly above my head, at the very spot I woke up. They then went back to the club for another drink, with the intention of coming back a little later and following me once I awoke. But by the time they did, I had already gone.

"We tried to find you, but it's huge down there."

"Tell me about it."

"How did you get out, anyway?"

So I told them about the Caretaker and about the City Below.

Jezz shook his head, "There's no one down there. The Machine is self-repairing, self-perpetuating; has been for centuries. It doesn't need anybody."

"How do you explain all that I saw then?"

Alan laughed. "After the amount you were putting away? Nothing you saw would surprise me."

Jezz was more pragmatic. "It may have been the Machine. It can reproduce anything, you know."

"Yes, but why would it?"

He shrugged. "Who knows? But trust me, all you saw down there were ghosts in the Machine."

None of them believed me and I began to wonder whether they were right not to. Already the emotions were receding and everything that had happened was assuming a distant, dream-like quality. Had I really dropped down through different layers of the city, or through different layers of delusion, or even insanity?

I went home to collapse into bed for a long-overdue sleep, but in the process of drifting off I was struck by a thought which brought me wide awake again. The Caretaker had claimed that people only ever travelled through his realm in one direction, that nobody ever went up. If true, was it only because nobody Below had ever thought to do so? Had I just shown them the way?

What would happen if those awful, feral, eyeless creatures should find a way up to the surface?

On that terrible day, years later, when death erupted out of the sewers and the manholes, from the trapdoors in the streets and from the forgotten gaps in existence, I think I was the only person who failed to be surprised. And even I had almost forgotten, right up until that final, fateful moment when the machine stopped and the two Cities merged.

Ian Whates

***

I'd never written a dystopian tale, something we Brits are supposedly renowned for, so I set out to produce one. What emerged was a story in which the protagonist accidentally sees beneath the surface of the apparently utopian society he lives in and glimpses a reality far darker.

In an effort to create a distinct contrast, I made the utopian element snappy, trendy and superficial, while the darker underbelly is intended to be grim, gritty and deliberately old-fashioned – Wells' Morlocks as seen by the protagonist of Butler's *Erewhon* in a Dickensian industrial setting, with a sprinkling of added 'bizarre' for good measure.

Hopefully, the result has a nostalgic feel with a surprisingly dark aftertaste – a sugar coated bonbon with a hot chilli centre.

Knowing How to Look

Have you ever been to London?

If so, which one?

Was it tourist London, with its over-priced cafés and tacky souvenirs – models of red buses and phone boxes, cuddly bears dressed in union jacks and uniforms parodying the Beefeaters that stand duty at the Tower? Or perhaps it was the London of Shopping – Knightsbridge, Chelsea, Regent Street and Oxford Street, proud department stores, designer boutiques and restaurants bearing the badge of the latest celebrity chefs, or maybe Financial London with its futures, stocks and shares, its bankers and city financiers frequenting their various bars of oyster, wine and tapas. It might conceivably have been the London of Government – the Houses of Parliament and Whitehall, pin-stripe suits and gentlemen's clubs, or that of Pageantry – the Royal Family, Buckingham Palace, St. Paul's Cathedral, the changing of the guard and trooping of the colour. Perhaps you were even lucky enough to stumble on a remnant of Old London, the city that survived the plague, the great fire of 1666 and the blitz of WWII – the London of jellied eels, pie and mash, cockney humour and barrow-boy brashness. It *is* becoming harder to find these days, but it's still there if you know how to look.

You see, there are many cities called London, all co-existing at the same geographic location. Between them they contain people of every race, religion and culture, some of whom call London home, while others are just passing through.

On occasion amidst all this rich diversity, in certain places where the different Londons meet and overlap, the strangest things can slip in, unnoticed…

*

I like Jamie on the whole. Just as well, really, since he is married to my sister. Sure, I know there is no rule that says you *have* to like your in-laws, but it certainly helps.

When he phoned and suggested we should go out for a drink, I knew that something was up. As I say, I like him well enough, but we're hardly bosom-buddies – different circles, different friends. No, he wanted to talk about something. I didn't ask what, assuming it was something to do with him and Sue. Of course, at that point I had no idea about Dawn Jenkins' suicide.

Predictably, the real reason he wanted to see me was the very last thing we spoke about. There were the formalities to be observed first. So we each listened politely as the other talked about what was going on at work, though I am sure he had as little interest in mine as I did in his, then gave proper mention to the weather (a hell of a lot of rain for this time of the year), before falling back to the safety of a common interest: football; dissecting the latest rumours and transfer speculation with relish.

Only after a lot of hot air had been expelled and much alcohol absorbed did we turn our attention to the real meat of the conversation.

"Chris, I'm worried."

Ah, this was it. I dragged back that part of my mind which had wandered to the far side of the bar, where a pretty young blonde with a tight top, long legs and a short skirt sat laughing with friends. My full attention was again focused on Jamie and whatever he was intending to reveal. "What about?"

"Me, mostly… and Susan." My sister.

"Are the two of you having problems?"

"No. Well, sort of… God, this is difficult."

It always is. "Take your time," I encouraged.

"You met Dawn, didn't you? Dawn Jenkins, my P.A."

I remembered Dawn. A tall, slender woman in her fifties;

thin-lipped, grey-haired and immaculate, projecting an air of confidence and competence. Jamie always spoke of her in glowing terms – the type of secretary everyone wanted and so few were ever able to find.

I nodded, "How is she?"

"Not so good. She committed suicide last month."

"My God, I'm sorry."

"You can't imagine a more balanced and dependable person, solid as a rock. She'd been with the company for years, even longer than I have."

"You never can tell what's going on inside someone's head…"

"Until a couple of months ago, that is," he continued, as if I hadn't spoken. "She suddenly started to become, I don't know, reticent, sullen even. Not like her at all. Then I came into the office one morning to find her crying. Dawn Jenkins, crying? It was unthinkable. I tried to find out what was wrong and she just cried harder and retreated to the ladies. Came out after a while and apologised, got on with her work. Wouldn't talk about it, wouldn't take the day off, just put her head down and carried on.

"Huge mood swings after that – it felt as if I was treading on egg shells all the time. Then she went off sick. Anne, one of my colleagues, well, a friend really, called round to see her. Depression. A week later Dawn was dead; an overdose."

All this was said with Jamie simply staring at an empty chair opposite. I sat silent, letting it simply pour out of him.

"I can't help feeling responsible."

Which was only natural, under the circumstances. Something like that happening to someone you have been close to, a person you worked with every day, it would be enough to affect anyone. "I'm sure there was nothing you could've done," I said.

"Then Anne started to act the same way."

"This is your friend at work, right?"

He nodded. "Mood swings, tears… and she won't talk about

it to me or anyone. I mean, first Dawn, then Anne, it's almost as if depression has become infectious."

"Don't be daft. Coincidence; something in her private life has probably gone to pot and unsettled her…"

"And now Susan."

"Susan?" That startled me out of meaningless-platitude mode.

"Yes. Tears, tantrums over the most trivial things, bouts of depression… She's stopped talking to me and she's not eating. We go through whole evenings without her saying a word, just staring at the TV."

Not my sister. She was the last person in the world to suffer from anything like depression. "Has she been to see a doctor?"

He shook his head, "Refuses to, she won't even discuss the subject." He rubbed his eyes, as if to wipe away sleep, or tears. "Dawn and Anne were bad enough, but Susan… Chris, these are the three women I spend most of my time with, the three women in the world I'm closest to since my mother passed away. What's going on?"

He was right, of course. One was a tragedy, two might be a dreadful run of bad luck, but three was pushing coincidence way too far.

"If depression is infectious, I guess I must be the carrier."

"Only women…."

"Pardon?"

"You said it yourself: the three women you're closest to. Have any of the men at work shown symptoms of anything like this?"

He thought for a second and shook his head, "No, not that I know of."

"Neighbours, friends?"

"No."

There was something here, just out of reach. I turned it all over in my mind, furiously sifting through what he had said, and knew that there was a gap, a missing piece.

"What else?" I asked.

"How do you mean?"

"There's something you're not telling me."

"God, isn't this enough?"

"Not quite. There's more, isn't there."

He glared at me, and I saw in his eyes the shadow of desperation, like a small boy caught with his hand in the cookie jar and knowing there was no escape. For a moment he contemplated lying, I could see that in his eyes as well, but then his shoulders slumped and I watched the defiance drain away. A deep breath and, "You mustn't tell anyone about this, Chris, not even Susan – especially not Susan."

"Okay, I won't. You have my word."

"I don't see how this has anything to do with it."

"Even so…"

He shuddered. Then he told me. "It was when Dawn took her holiday. I brought in a temp to cover – Natalia, from the Ukraine originally. She was really something – late twenties, a bit feisty but good at her job, and gorgeous. I mean, all the lads in the office were talking about her and most of them tried it on – bees to a honey pot. Friday night we all went out for a drink, someone's birthday I think. Anyway, I had one too many and…"

"You ended up sleeping with her," I concluded for him, not particularly wanting to hear the full sordid details of how they ended up in bed together, not having the stomach for it.

He nodded, clearly dreading my reaction. "Please, don't tell Susan."

For long seconds I simply stared, battening down the urge to either throttle or punch him, which would have achieved little of value for anyone but me. At length I said simply, "I won't," and meant it. I had no intention of being the bearer of such tidings, of possibly wrecking their marriage and my sister's happiness. All of which seemed moot under the circumstances.

"I swear it was just the once," Jamie continued. "Don't know what got into me and I haven't been able to forgive myself since. Natalia wanted more, but I told her that I was married and that I loved my wife."

"How did she react?"

"Stormed out. I had to cope for a whole week without a secretary."

Poor him. "You don't think Susan's found out about your…" betrayal, adultery, infidelity, "indiscretion?"

"No,"

Nor did I, not really – just clutching at straws. "And this 'Natalia' was at the office long enough to know about your friendship with Anne?"

"Well yes, I suppose so, but what does that have to do with anything?"

A woman spurned. This had the potential to be nasty, very nasty.

It was Saturday night, nothing I could do just then, but there was no time to lose. I thought furiously, putting together a strategy on-the-hoof. "Could you leave work early on Monday?"

"If I had to, if it would help, yes."

"Good. Meet me at Covent Garden tube station."

Sunday was torture. I wanted desperately to go and visit Sue but at the same time shied away from seeing her like that. Besides which, Jamie had urged me not to go round, saying that it would only lead to a scene. So instead I spent the day scouring reference books and surfing the net, researching a few things. It only confirmed what I knew already.

How did I feel about Jamie? Intellectually, I knew that this was one of those rare occasions when the straying husband really was *not* to blame, at least not in the usual sense, assuming my suspicions were accurate. But this was my sister's husband we were talking about and he should have been stronger, no matter what the mitigation. At that particular point in time I was furious with him, perhaps even hated him, and was only willing to help for Sue's sake. Jamie could go hang.

Monday morning arrived and I headed into London, stepping off the tube at Leicester Square. From there it was just a few minute's walk to Soho, Berwick Street to be precise. I needed to talk to Claire.

Berwick Street pierces the heart of London's West End. It runs from theatreland at its bottom end up into Soho, with its rash of strip clubs and 'adult' shops. Here it parallels Wardour Street, where the offices of media companies and the music biz hold sway, before emerging into Oxford Street, that golden Mecca for shoppers.

Towards its top end, a host of CD and record stores now flourish, speciality shops offering urban, dance, or rock. Just below this, a timeless bit of Old London still persists: Berwick Street market, with its mounds of fresh vegetables and succulent fruit, terraces of luxury chocolate from Switzerland and Belgium at knock-down prices, mouth-watering displays of finest fresh fish glistening moistly in the sun and swathes of cloth from Turkey, India and beyond. People will deliberately divert via Berwick Street when walking from one area of the West End to another, just to sample the market's atmosphere and to be tempted by its wares.

Claire's shop is tucked away behind the stalls, just before the market peters out. As I entered she was serving a middle-aged lady who was fussing over the selection of rings.

"Chris!" she called out on seeing me, before dancing a couple of steps down the counter and leaning across to plant a kiss on my cheek. "Where have you been?"

"About," I assured her.

She wore a purple top, laced at the shoulders, and her auburn hair hung loose in a cascade of waves. A miniature representation of a flying-V guitar fashioned in silver hung from one ear. She looked about 19 or 20 and probably was, but acted with the self-confidence of someone twice her years. Quite how she came to own a shop in Berwick Street at such an age I have no idea, nor would I ever dream of asking.

"Sorry, a friend," Claire explained with a broad smile as she returned to the lady and the jewellery. The customer seemed unperturbed and soon narrowed her choice down to two rings. "That one's lovely," Claire assured her as she tried it on for the third time. "What do you think, Chris?"

I had to agree that it was, but then jewellery was one of Claire's passions and it all tended to be lovely. There was not a hint of yellow or gold anywhere in the shop. Every piece was in delicately wrought silver, because "silver is the metal of moonlight and magic," as she had once explained.

The lady ended up buying both rings.

Claire hates labels. If pushed, I would describe her as a new-age hippie-punk, but never within her hearing. Apart from jewellery, her major passion is music and she plays rock guitar in a group called 'Quiet Catastrophe'. I once heard someone ask her to describe their music. "Somewhere between the Slits and Soft Machine," she replied. This prompted the questioner to wonder how anyone her age had ever even *heard* of Soft Machine.

Good question; life is full of mysteries.

"So, how've you been?" she wanted to know, now that we had the shop to ourselves for a brief moment.

"Can't complain."

"Are you in town on business or pleasure?"

"Meeting a friend for a drink this evening – a man with a few problems."

"A lot of them about," she said. "Are we talking problems in a general sense, or something more specific?"

"Pretty specific, I'd say. Women around him keep falling ill; dying even."

"Yeah," she gave a wry smile, "I can see how that would be a downer. Where are you meeting him?"

"Covent Garden. I thought I'd take him to the Dragoon."

She nodded. "Covent Garden's as good a place as any right now." Which was my own feeling as well, but nice to have it confirmed. "And the Dragoon's always lively."

Two Japanese tourists entered. I stood back, enabling them to squeeze past – it was a narrow shop and Claire had taken advantage of every available space to cram in all sorts of esoteric oddities. She called them 'stock'.

It seemed an opportune moment to leave. We hugged across the counter and I headed for the door. "Sometime, when you're not rescuing troubled souls..." she called after me.

"Yeah, it would be good to see you, too. When's your next gig?"

"A week on Wednesday, at Ronnie's."

"I'll be there."

"Let me get those down for you," I heard her saying as I exited into the bustle of London.

It was nearly lunchtime. I followed the market's course to where it broke as the street narrowed into an alley of revue bars, opaque-windowed shop fronts and cramped cafés. Across Brewer Street and it emerged as a proper road again, reborn as Rupert Street. Straight over Shaftesbury Avenue with its impatient growl of courier bikes and thunder of black cabs held back by a wall of red lights. When the lights changed they would all desperately race the few yards to the next set, only to be stopped short again.

Then I headed left into China Town.

Christi runs a small noodle bar, just off of Gerard Street.

"Hi Charlie, you hungry?" she asked as I came in.

"Always," I assured her.

Christi has never asked me my name, anymore than I have hers. I am simply Charlie, while she is Christi because she remind of someone I used to know. It works for us.

"Good. Then you eat," she ushered me to a table at the back, near to the kitchen. No menu was offered. Within minutes a steaming plate of noodles appeared in front of me, laced with strips of chicken, tiger prawns and vegetables and fragrant with the aromas of ginger, garlic and soy. "Busy, busy, busy," Christi told me, before hurrying off to serve another customer.

Somewhere, about half way through the mound of noodles, a lull must have occurred, because Christi reappeared. "You have trouble?" she asked.

"No, I'm okay. Meeting a friend a bit later, though, at Covent Garden."

"He have trouble." She made it a statement rather than a question.

"Perhaps," I conceded.

Then she was gone, to deal with some catastrophe in the kitchen, which she was told about in franticly delivered machine-gun Cantonese, far too quick for me to follow.

When it came time to leave, she refused to let me pay. Again.

"Come on Christi, if you keep doing this I'm going to have to find somewhere else to eat." It was an old argument. I helped her out of a tight spot a year or so back and she had refused to take my money ever since.

"No!" she insisted. "You eat here life-time, no pay."

Despite my threat, I would be back and we both knew it. I hated taking liberties, but the food here was just so damned good.

I spent the next couple of hours meandering towards Covent Garden, which takes some doing, since it's only about ten minutes brisk walk, but I was in no hurry. I window-shopped, bought a couple of gel-pens, browsed my way down Neal Street with its trendy boutiques and eateries, and called in on a few old friends, passing the time of day and spreading the word.

By late afternoon I was relaxing in the courtyard of a wine bar at the heart of Covent Garden's basement level, listening to a talented string quartet and sipping chilled bucks fizz from a pewter goblet. Pure indulgence, but what the heck?

The day had gone well. I'd reached everyone I was hoping to

and the word was out. Now all that remained was to wait and see who answered.

Covent Garden, redeveloped in the 1970s, has become a very special place. Street artists and performers, new-age arcades and upmarket shops combine with cafés and pubs to provide a vibrant melting pot, a magnet for tourists and Londoners alike, where different cultures and different Londons seamlessly meet and merge.

This was a good day for things to happen. I could feel it.

Jamie arrived a little early, but even so the flow of people around the station reduced all movement to a sort of constipated shuffle. We edged free of the bottle-neck and I led the way to the Dragoon, a traditional London pub on the corner of Bow Street.

It was already pretty busy. Jamie tapped me on the shoulder. "There's a table free, over there."

Of course there was, but how could I explain that to him? "You go and grab it," I suggested, "I'll get the drinks in."

I made my way to the bar, squeezing in beside a tall, stick-thin woman wearing a moss green hoodie and a Burberry headband, which held back lank, dark hair. Her features suggested Zulu origin, although she was too pale to be pure-blood. She had a gaunt, haunted expression. An addict, probably heroin, although I felt no inclination to delve. There was no need to ask what she was seeking tonight.

"Yes, mate?" the barman had reached me already. Tall, with dark hair and a small goatee beard that might have made him look a little like Satan, but instead suggested Pan. He wore a black T-shirt embroidered with the brewery's logo at the breast.

"Two pints of Special." I nodded towards one of the three hand-pumps.

"You look like a beer drinker," said a slightly slurred voice beside me.

I wondered what gave it away. The paunch perhaps?

The speaker wore designer blue shirt with button-down

collar, open at the neck. A redundant tie had been pulled down to hang limply at near chest-level. His glazed expression suggested that the bar stool had been his home for most of the afternoon.

"I enjoy the odd pint," I admitted.

"What do you reckon is London's best bitter, then?"

A seeker. The question about beer was merely an excuse, an opening gambit. He wanted something, *needed* something, and sensed at a subconscious level that I was a likely source of answers. Unfortunately for him, I had other concerns.

"Whatever they happen to serve at whichever pub I'm in at the time," I replied.

He stared at me, as if trying to decide whether I was taking the piss or not, then grunted and turned back to the half-drained glass before him, apparently deciding to look elsewhere. I paid for the drinks and took them across to where Jamie waited.

"What exactly are we doing here?" he asked after a while. "I mean, it can't be just for the beer, good though it is. We don't need to come all the way into the centre of town just to share a pint or two, so..."

"Looking for a solution," I replied, evasively.

"I presume we're here to meet someone," he persisted.

"Hopefully," I agreed.

"So are you going to tell me who?"

"Jamie, just be patient." Now seemed as good a time as any to brief him. "Listen. Follow my lead here, okay. Whatever happens, however strange it may seem, don't question anything. It's important that you go with the flow, all right?"

He laughed. "Yes, Oh Man of Mystery."

"I'm serious Jamie."

"Okay, understood."

I think he would have asked more, but just then we both became aware that someone had approached the table. "Excuse me."

This was quick, by anyone's standards. She was petite, with

bold Eastern European features, too irregular to be considered pretty, but there was something about her... The eyes, I decided; deep, piercing almonds.

"Is this seat taken?" she asked in English accented just enough to sound exotic and interesting. "May I sit here?"

She was dressed in maroon top and slacks, so dark they were almost burgundy, over which had been pulled a powder-blue cardigan, fastened by a single large button. It made no effort to either match or contrast with the maroon. The body beneath was slender and apparently shapeless, almost boyish. Her face was framed by a neat bob of dark brown, near-black, hair.

Jamie's eyes flickered back and forth between the girl and me, seeking a lead, which was a good start. I smiled and indicated the vacant chair. "Please, be our guest."

Her smile in return was dazzling, making me wonder how I had ever considered her plain.

"Thank you." She sat, placing a miniature plastic carrier bag on the table beside her, presumably containing a recent purchase. "It is busy, this pub."

"Good beer and a good location for a pub," I supplied.

"I think so, too. Many people, yes?" She laughed, lighting up her face once more.

"Have you been in England long?"

"No, I arrive now, today."

Jamie drained his glass, clearly uncomfortable. "My round, I think."

I finished mine and passed him the empty glass. "Perhaps the lady would care for a drink?"

He raised an eyebrow, which he turned into an enquiring look in the girl's direction, though not with any great warmth.

"Yes, thank you. Could I try some of your English beer, please?"

Jamie nodded and made his way towards the bar.

"He is not happy, I think, your friend."

"Sorry," I said quickly, knowing how touchy they could be sometimes and not wanting her to take offence. "Jamie's having a rough time of it at the moment. He's married and has indulged in an unfortunate, isolated infidelity."

"Foolish, very foolish."

"I know. So does he. The other party involved wanted more and he refused, angering her greatly. He's suffered from a guilty conscience ever since."

"A guilty conscience, this is all he suffers from?"

"No, not quite. All his female acquaintances are falling ill."

"What sort of ill?"

"An illness of the soul: depression. One has even killed herself." She said nothing, waiting for me to say more. "Now it has started to affect his wife, my sister."

"I see. This is not good, not good at all."

A sentiment I was hardly about to argue with.

I had to tread carefully here, not wanting to crack the eggshells scattered beneath my feet. I couldn't afford to blow this, not with Susan's health, sanity, and possibly even her life in the balance. So far so good. After all, my newfound friend had heard the unadorned facts and was still here.

At which point Jamie returned with the drinks, and the conversation took a lighter turn. After a little more of both time and beer had been consumed, Jamie started to relax and fully join in. The three of us ended up having an enjoyable evening.

The girl told us she was from Romania. She had been brought up on a farm and described her childhood in great detail. It all sounded very rustic, like something from another age, and was completely fascinating – a total contrast to anything either Jamie or I had ever experienced.

The evening wore on. The girl was the first to leave. Hugs and kisses all around, like old friends, with the hope that we would meet again sometime. The pub door was swinging shut behind her when Jamie started, "Hey, she left her bag." He grabbed the miniature carrier which still sat on the table where the girl had put it and went to stand, to follow her.

I placed a restraining hand on his arm, "Stay there."

"But…."

"Stay there," I reiterated.

He stared at me, trying to understand.

"See what's in the bag," I told him calmly.

"What? I can't do that, it's not mine."

"Open it." Our eyes locked. "Open it," I repeated, my voice quiet but insistent. His gaze dropped to the bag and he reached inside, to hesitantly draw forth a hinged box. It resembled a jewellery box. His eyes flicked up to me again, questioning.

"Go on," I urged. "It's intended for you."

He lifted the lid, to reveal a crystal cube.

There is a store in Covent Garden that sells cubes like this. You go in and part with a tidy sum, only to walk out a short while later, clutching just such a crystal cube in which a 3-D image of your own face now resides.

This cube contained just such an image — the perfect representation of a face. Jamie's face.

"My God, how…?"

"Don't ask," I advised. "It's a gift. Don't question it, just accept it." I took advantage of the fact he was still gaping and continued, "Take it home with you and put it on display in the bedroom." Having seen the crystal, I now knew what was required.

"How do I explain it to Susan?"

"That's easy. You bought it as a present for her. Why else would a man have his own image set into a piece of crystal?"

"Okay, but what if she doesn't want it in the bedroom?"

"Insist." It had to be in a room where Susan would spend long periods of time.

"Easy for you to say. You know Susan…"

"Jamie, insist. And another thing: if you see any change in the crystal, anything at all, let me know immediately."

*

Wednesday evening, two days later; I was relaxing at home when there came a knock at the door. It was Jamie. Ashen faced, he said nothing, just held out a plastic bag. I took him into the lounge and we emptied it onto the coffee table. Out fell the crystal.

The image it showed was still Jamie's face but it was now deformed, twisted almost beyond recognition – a visage that seemed to be snarling, or perhaps screaming. It looked evil, demonic.

"What are you going to do with it?" he asked.

"Melt it."

"How?"

"In my chimenea."

"Pardon?"

"A sort of front-loading Mexican barbecue… does it really matter what it is?"

"No. But will a barbecue be hot enough to melt something like this?"

"Mine will."

That was more or less the end of the matter, at least as far as Jamie was concerned. Nothing could be done to bring back poor Dawn Jenkins, but both Sue and Anne, Jamie's work colleague, recovered quickly and were able to put their depression behind them.

As for 'Natalia', I asked about her in all the right places but with little result, apart from one or two rumours that something of her darkness had been in the area for a while but had since moved on.

Jamie and I have never spoken about any of this since. I can guess what has gone through his mind, though. Of course there is no such thing as a Succubus. Whatever happened, it had nothing to do with curses or spells, with possession or obsession. After all, such things have no place in the real world, do they?

Who am I to argue?

From my point of view, I know that this is not quite the end of things. There is no such thing as a free lunch. Even Christi's noodles are her way of paying me back for services rendered.

At some time in the future someone will call on me seeking a favour. They might look like a girl from Eastern Europe, they might not. I'll know them when I see them. The eyes will give it away – deep, beautiful almonds. Whatever it is they want, I'm sure I will be able to help, or at least, know where to find someone who can.

As I said, there are many places called London. Almost anything can be found in them somewhere, providing you know how to look.

***

Although also set in the UK's capital, this story is very different from "One Night in London".

Most of the characters and situations depicted here are pretty much true to life. My tolerance for shopping is a lot lower than my partner's, so after spending the best part of a day in the West End I bailed out when we arrived at Covent Garden late one afternoon, choosing to take refuge in a pub on the corner of Bow Street, *The Marquess of Anglesey,* while Helen continued with her retail therapy.

I spent the following hour and a half supping *Young's Special* and jotting down observations and fancies built around the places we had visited and the various people we had encountered in passing during that day. By the time Helen returned, the framework for "Knowing How to Look" had been written.

The Sum of the Past

They say a man is the sum of his past experiences. If true, what does that make me?

When I was eight, I stumbled upon my mother in bed with my father's boss. I allowed myself to be persuaded by her pleading, her cajoling, and never told; but silence came at a price. I ruled my mother totally thereafter and always got what I wanted, irrespective of cost.

So am I a blackmailer?

In my teens I was accepted into pilot training, to the envy of my friends. We all dreamed of being pilots – the pin-up boys of the age – but due to the expense most never even made the attempt. Others failed the aptitude tests. Only one of us went forward. Me.

So am I exceptional?

Suddenly I was a celebrity; my social status was enhanced beyond all recognition. Friends were still friends but the nature of relationships had subtly altered. I became the centre, the star around which the group orbited, without anyone acknowledging the change.

Local businessmen and self-important want-to-be dignitaries, who in the past would have dismissed me as an irrelevance, were falling over themselves simply to be seen with me. I was invited to parties and functions I would never have had a sniff of before. Glamorous women and beautiful girls hung on my every word where previously they would not have given me the time of day.

I loved every minute of it.

So am I a social climber?

Then there was Hannah, whom I had been in lust with forever. She only had eyes for one man – Carl, my best fiend. Even with her, things changed; we grew closer and she confided in me more. Needless to say this was not a development I discouraged.

Funny really; a moment that should have broken my heart did anything but. It was a sticky-hot midsummer morning, one of those when even the flies can't be bothered to move in anything other than slow motion.

Hannah came bursting into the kitchen. "Oh God, I can't believe it." Her cheeks were flushed, her eyes held tears, but she was smiling. "We've set a date." She was in front of me by then, clasping my arms. "Carl's asked me to marry him."

"I... I'm really pleased for you," I lied.

We hugged. "I'm so excited."

In her excitement, she kissed me. Just intended as a brush of lips on cheek, I'm sure, but I seized the moment and pressed my lips to hers, pushing my tongue into her mouth. There was surprise, but no real resistance.

We pulled back, both a little shocked by what had happened – I know I hadn't planned it. Then we kissed again; both of us this time.

I will never forget my first view of Hannah naked, as she coyly dropped the last vestige of clothing to the floor. To my passion-tinted vision she was extraordinarily beautiful.

"Am I... am I a disappointment?" she wanted to know.

"Never," I said as I pulled her to the bed, and meant it at the time.

I actually trembled as I first kissed her breasts. The whole experience had a surreal, other-worldly quality. I came far too quickly – the accumulation of years of imagining, unfettered at last and bursting forth inside her.

Afterwards we lay there, holding each other, while I floated down from whichever cloud I had been catapulted to. Then we made love again, more slowly and tenderly this time.

A month later I was best man at her wedding.

Three days after the honeymoon we introduced each other to the thrill of adultery.

We never slept together again. My decision; partly the result of belated guilt – Carl was my closest friend, after all. Mostly though, it was because I had finally cured myself of that particular obsession.

Hannah represented the first step on the path which that aspect of my life was to follow thereafter.

The next was Gemma.

I was coming back from the gents at some glitzy function, when this vision in a figure-hugging dress approached. I'd noticed her earlier, at a table with her husband and friends. She was older than me, perhaps ten years or so. She was also drop-dead gorgeous. Tall, with close-cropped titian hair, a willowy figure and a way of moving that drew a man's gaze and fastened it like Velcro.

She walked up and without hesitation, kissed me. It was a simple, chaste pressing of her lips to mine. I was too startled to react.

I found an image-chip pressed into my hand and then she was gone. Neither of us had spoken a word.

For the rest of the evening she ignored me, never even looked in my direction, though I tried to catch her eye several times.

The chip, viewed as soon as I arrived home, projected a 3-D image of her in bed, apparently asleep. She was lying on her front, naked except for the silk sheet which partially covered her. She rolled over as if restless, revealing pert and glorious breasts – too perfect to be wholly natural, but the enhancement was expertly done. Then her hands started to snake slowly down either side of her body, catching the sheet and carrying it with them. Just as it looked set to reveal everything a man might want to see, she seemed to waken and realise for the first time that there was an audience. She clutched the sheet defensively to her, and smiled. The image zoomed in, focusing on her face as she mimed a kiss. Then the scene faded, leaving behind a sequence of red digits suspended in the air: her contact number.

As a calling card, it was spectacular.

I played the chip over and over before going to bed. I still have it, somewhere.

I called her the next day.

So, am I a serial adulterer?

Gemma was happy with her life on the whole. It was just that her husband was a busy man and had so many other priorities.

I was to discover that she was far from unique.

As a commercial pilot I travelled to and fro between the stars, following the dictates of my employer; a situation not conducive to a monogamous, long-term relationship. On the other hand, a series of impermanent, casual affairs seemed ideal. I concentrated on married women, realising they were less likely to cause a fuss when the time came to move on.

I never quite recaptured the initial thrill of that first time with Hannah, but came mighty close a few times.

So am I a cad?

I came to see my homeworld for the backwater it was. Only at the spaceport, where I'd trained, did technology approach an advanced level, though still far from cutting-edge when compared with what other worlds had to offer.

Even its moral attitudes were quaint and outdated, it seemed.

This became apparent during my maiden trip, a term I've always been fond of, while I was being entertained by the chairman of a client company and his wife. Also present were two other couples. I had already accepted the invite to stay the night on the advice of our local agent, who informed me it would be an insult to refuse.

The evening was drawing to a conclusion when the chairman

casually asked me which of the ladies I would care to spend the night with.

Totally unprepared for such an offer, I had no idea how to react. My attempts to demur failed dismally, since it led to him asking whether I preferred men.

"If so..." the chairman began, before I assured him to the contrary. This only caused a more determined repeat of the original offer.

In the end I relented and chose the chairman's wife. She was neither the youngest present nor the prettiest, but she had warm, laughing eyes.

My choice was entirely appropriate, I later learned, since it demonstrated appreciation of my hosts' hospitality and conveyed honour on their house. Our local agent explained this as he laughed heartily and asked whether it had been an enjoyable evening.

Actually no, it hadn't been; at least not entirely. Embarrassingly, I found it difficult to relax. To a young lad from a world where marriage was sacrosanct (for the majority, at least), taking a married woman to bed in her own home with the full knowledge and blessing of her husband proved too much. My mind, my moral centre, rebelled. In the end I managed some sort of performance but only because of the patience and skill of the lady concerned. It was hardly my finest hour.

So despite everything, am I a prude at heart?

My life has contained ingredients other than sex. There was the time I diverted the ship in response to a distress beacon, risking the ruin of our perishable cargo. In doing so I saved the lives of five people – the only survivors of a meteor strike on a cruise ship. We reached them barely in time, scant moments before their oxygen ran out.

So am I a hero?

During the next trip I secured a valuable shipment by ensuring, through bribery, that a rival captain was arrested on trumped-up charges. He was eventually cleared but lost his job. As a consequence, his wife left him, leading to the poor man taking his own life.

So am I a villain?

I mustn't forget New Ankara, where we were caught up in a military coup. The ship and its cargo were impounded. At the time the company was going through a difficult period and the cargo in question was worth a small fortune. I led the daring raid which saw us liberate the ship and blast our way to freedom, so securing the financial stability of our employer.

So am I a loyal company man?

Apparently not. They fired me soon after, though not entirely without reason. I broke from my normal pattern – she wasn't married, you see, wasn't even old enough to be married. She had an elfin figure and the face of a fairy princess – all youth and dazzling beauty – and a confident, self-assured sexuality that belied her years. To me, that combination of innocence and worldliness proved irresistible. Don't get me wrong, this was not a case of heartless rogue seducing a naive and gullible young girl. She manoeuvred me into bed. Though in truth, I didn't put up much of a fight.

We were caught in the act.

She was my boss's daughter, the apple of his eye.

Although she had instigated things and knew exactly what she was doing, she was only in her early teens. At least, I'm pretty sure she was a teen.

Does that make me a pervert?

Fortunately I had some money behind me by this point. So in disgrace but by no means down-hearted, I headed for the rim in search of adventure and fortune. After all, it was one of the few places I would still be allowed to pilot a ship.

Of course, the word 'pilot' is misleading. In fact I am little more than a cog meshing with the ship's systems; a small but vital component of the symbiotic entity – part organic but mostly inorganic – which directs and commands every aspect of the vessel. Few people have what it takes to mesh successfully. Very few.

So am I gifted, or perhaps just lucky?

After you disengage, after you've seen the universe as part of a cybernetic ship, everything seems mundane. Except for sex.

Perhaps the act of sex helps reaffirm our humanity. Certainly a high sex drive is common among us pilots. In fact our sexual appetite is legendary, which doubtless contributes to our appeal.

I arrived on the rim with enough money to buy a ship. Not huge and not new, but she was a jewel, with solid, reliable engine and a big enough cargo bay to suit me. I bought her from a feisty little trader called Cherry, all spiked hair and attitude. She was upgrading to a larger vessel. Naturally, we sealed the deal in bed.

I then set about hustling for business.

Running a ship is costly and time-consuming. While I might be able to locate problems when meshed with the ship's systems, that doesn't necessarily mean I know how to fix them. So I hooked up with Brendan. He was a genius; knew everything there was to know about computers, A.I.s and the ship-human link.

I lived it. He understood it.

We were opposites in many ways. For example, if I were to point out some lady's ample mammaries for his appreciation, he would probably want to explain to me exactly why her breasts heaved so every time she took a deep breath, while I was just grateful that they did.

Despite our differences, we worked well together and had one all-important thing in common: we both saw our partnership as the means to becoming rich.

We nearly made it too, more than once. Take Largos: a small, dense world hugged close by a giant sun, its surface constantly bombarded by savage radiation. Nothing lived anywhere in the whole system except on this tiny, half-roasted planet. A less hospitable hell-hole would be hard to imagine. Nonetheless, people did live there, buried deep in a labyrinth of tunnels and shafts, shielded from the lethal radiation by layers of rock: miners.

Conditions were extreme, which resulted in the creation of an incredibly rare mineral. The planetoid's sub-strata were riddled with the stuff. To call it a gold mine did not even come close.

Now, I would never dream of ripping off poor, hard-working miners, but these guys were anything but poor. They were digging up ship-loads of the most valuable substances in the galaxy. Needless to say, they were very protective of the planet's co-ordinates and attention was the last thing they wanted, so there was little chance of their squealing about our fees or advertising for alternative suppliers. We charged them an exorbitant rate and were quickly raking it in.

So am I a greedy exploiter?

Predictably, things fell apart. A competitor turned up and undercut us, stealing the trade. Then a vital part of the ship's engine blew, which dug a deep hole in the near-fortune we had amassed.

They were heady days. We had more close shaves and near-fatal encounters than anyone could wish for, accumulating and then losing more money than I care to remember.

So am I a swashbuckling buccaneer of the space-ways?

If so, Brendan's death cured me of that.

It was one adventure too many, one cargo we should not have bothered fighting for. My ship-mate, my partner and my friend died in my arms that night.

But I'm still here.

So am I a survivor, or just stubborn?

If you were to gather up all these demonstrated traits and mix them together, would the result define me?

Why this introspection, this self-analysis, you may wonder. It's all due to this man I met last night; at least, I think he was a man. He's caused me to question everything I know about myself.

I'd already had a few but not enough to be drunk. 'Merry' would be the technical term. Certainly nowhere near enough to explain the way he distorted and wavered like an image suffering interference.

"Sorry about that," he said. "I'm under attack. I've beaten them off for now."

"Attack, what attack?" I queried, looking around quickly, concerned that I might be next.

"Anti-virals," he said. "Nothing for you to worry about."

"Anti-virals?" I laughed. "What does that make you?"

"A virus, of course."

"Biggest dammed virus I ever saw." I slapped him on the back, "Come and have a drink."

We sat and talked. I liked him; not sure why, but I did. At length he sat back and proclaimed, "It's one hell of a life you've had. All the gorgeous girls and all the adventures..."

"No more than the next man," I demurred, modestly.

"Are you kidding? Think about it. As a kid you walk in on your mum screwing a complete stranger..."

"Hey, I never told you that bit."

"...then in your teens you become the first person in your town ever to qualify as a pilot," he went on unheeding. "You realise your greatest fantasy and get to fuck the girl of your dreams, your best buddy's fiancée... Now come on, you think 'the next man' gets to do all that before he's even out of his teens?"

"I never told you those things," I mumbled, trying to remember desperately whether in fact I had, wondering if I were drunker than I realised.

"And since then – all those women, each of them more beautiful than the last, most of them married and all of them desperate to tumble into bed with you, culminating in your boss's precious Lolita, so innocent but so gagging for it."

I definitely had not told him that part.

"Does this sound like real life to you, or like someone's fantasy?" he asked. "Fantasy, now there's a thought." He clicked his fingers, as if struck by inspiration. "They could make a story out of your life, maybe turn it into a series and beam it into every home in the galaxy.

"Now what sort of man would we want for a hero in a series like that?

"He'd have to be good looking, for starters, charming when he wanted to be. Maybe we should give him humble beginnings which he can overcome, going on to better things. He'd need to have a glamorous job, something out of the ordinary. He'd have to possess a roguish quality – everyone loves a rogue, after all. Naturally he'd be a hero, but also have a dark side, an unpredictable edge to make him more interesting. Of course, he'd have to be a hit with the ladies. I mean sex sells, so plenty of sex, and if that sex can be a little illicit from time to time, so much the better. Last but not least, he'd have to encounter more hold-onto-your-pants adventures, more life and death scrapes than you could shake a stick at.

"Hey," he stabbed a finger in my direction, "that is you, isn't it. I've just described your life. If I could create a fantasy hero... I'd create you."

Without warning, he distorted again. I was looking right at him, so saw it clearly – eyes to the left, chin to the right, and so on down the body, with everything else stretched in-between. Then he snapped back to normal.

"They've got me now," he gasped. "There's not much time. Listen, think about it, about your life, and think..."

He was gone. No distortion this time, just an absence.

Suddenly stone cold sober, I left the bar and went home.

I couldn't sleep, so instead I've done as he suggested: spent the night thinking about my life. In the light of what he said, the questions he posed, I find myself examining all of it.

The problem is that when I'm in ship-link I become very

conscious, perhaps more so than anyone who has never merged can appreciate, that fundamentally we're all just a sequence of code. Of numbers, if you will. At the most basic level, that's all that any of us are.

I find myself wondering whether that sequence is entirely natural, or whether it could be deliberately pre-programmed.

They say that at any given time we are the sum total of our past experiences. How would you define a sum? It's just an organised sequence of numbers – of code – isn't it? Like us.

So am I nothing more than a program, run for purposes of entertainment? Am I just a construct, designed by some unknowable 'other' to do all that I have done, to be all that I am?

It doesn't feel that way to me, but how relevant is that?

Then I think about the stranger from last night. Okay, so he knew a lot about me, so he could create some pretty fancy visual effects and vanish into thin air. Weird, very weird, but it's hardly proof positive of anything.

I can't get it out of my mind, though. Am I an individual, the independent entity I have always believed myself to be, or am I something else entirely?

Don't suppose I can ever be certain one way or the other; and I'm not sure what I could do about it even if I *did* know... But you have to wonder, don't you.

***

"*The* Sum of the Past" grew out of several things: in part, my cynicism of the standard 'hero' figure, in part the desire to write a story which has a rhythmic thread running through it from start to finish, surfacing like stitches throughout the narrative, and, in part, late-night musings on the nature of reality. But probably the single biggest motivation was the desire to write a story themed around the question of 'condition or nature'? Are we genetically programmed to be who we are or is it upbringing, environment, and experience that shape our personalities, that determine whether we're sinner or saint?

I wanted the central character to have more dislikeable traits than likeable and the more I wrote the more his darker side came to the fore, so I ended up with a protagonist who is capable of noble deeds, but even these are invariably tainted with self-interest. Of course, all his adventures and experiences had to be larger than life.... After all, that's what makes good television, isn't it?

Flesh and Metal

Cullen hit the streets a couple of hours after dark, a couple of hours after the last police unit had slunk away to safer districts, abandoning this part of town to other, more basic laws.

Neon dominated the main streets, rippling and pulsing its inducements, broadcasting banalities to the night with careless abandon. Every building seemed to bear its own dressing of artificial brightness, pushing the night back into tattered shadows and brooding corners.

Music blared forth from clubs, bars and arcades; thumping rhythms that assaulted the senses and strummed the chords of the soul with dark intent. Hawkers stood in front of sinister doorways, keen to guide you towards the depths of depravity... at a price. Occasionally, a scantily clad girl could be glimpsed somewhere in the background, looks as faded as the décor and body emaciated by the ravages of addiction. Those with any true allure would never be seen dead around here but would be working Uptown, where the real money was to be found.

A stream of bikes tore down the street, the roar of their engines briefly smothering the omnipresent mish-mash of music. Open-topped cars cruised the kerb, with dudes lounging at the wheel, preening and posing solely for each other's benefit, like cartfuls of pompous peacocks. People were everywhere; talking, drinking, arguing and pulling, or simply hanging around.

Cullen had been raised on the streets. Perhaps no longer his home, this was still the environment in which he felt the most comfortable. Just walking the walk sent his heart racing and his blood singing. He felt free again, liberated from the polite behaviour and complicated etiquette required Uptown. Despite choices made, there was still a part of him that would always believe this was where he belonged.

Somewhere, a girl screamed. As he walked past the mouth of a darkened alley, the scream was repeated, choking off into a sobbing, desperate plea. There, at the very edge of neon's reach, three youths were clustered in various positions around the prostate form of a girl. The light shone from the exposed buttocks of one, his trousers pulled down about his calves as he thrust forcefully in and out of the weakly struggling girl, his hips working like a piston. From what Cullen could see and hear, this was a girl out of her element. Even distraught, the accent was too crisp, while the clothes – now ripped and dishevelled – looked to be tailored; the right kind of clothing but too well made. A dead give-away. This was a thrill seeker, a girl from Uptown out for a night's excitement and getting far more than she had bargained for.

Stupid cow. She'd certainly have something to tell her friends in the morning. If she lived to see it.

One or the youths looked up and glared at Cullen, warning him off. A predator staking claim to its prey.

He walked on.

A gang, half a dozen or so strong, were gathering outside a bar; all black synthetics, slicked-back hair, studs, knives and stun clubs – a pack tanking up before setting out on the prowl. Cullen strode through them as if oblivious. Confidence and bluff were lessons he had learned early. There were times when attitude alone could make the difference between life and death here. He passed between them without being noticed.

Not so with the two youths lounging by the next corner a little further down the street. They certainly noticed him, and one at least looked set to follow as Cullen strode past, but the other held his companion back, whispering urgently in his ear. Had the second youth recognised him? It was possible. Cullen might have been away for a while, but reputations lingered.

Of course, there were occasions when that could prove more of a liability than an asset, a goad to eager young punks who wanted to test themselves against that reputation in the hope of making one for themselves. If these were the ambitious sort, best to take care of the situation now. He had no intention of spending the rest of the night looking over his shoulder.

He turned left into a dark alley mouth, just beyond the pair, offering them the perfect opportunity. If they didn't jump him now, they weren't likely to.

He maintained the same unhurried stride; outwardly casual, inwardly alert – straining to hear the faintest sound from behind which might indicate the pair had followed him into the alley.

Nothing. Perhaps they really had chosen to let him pass and seek out a different target.

Against the opposite wall, an assortment of black bags, sacks and boxes were heaped together. Refuse which would never be collected. Something among the junk started to move, causing cardboard and rotted matter to shift and tumble from the haphazard pile. Too much disturbance to be a rat or any of nature's other vermin.

Cullen stood tensed and ready as a figure stood up and stepped forward in one fluid motion, making the action seem graceful despite the surroundings.

It was shaped like a man but was a good head taller than Cullen who was tall himself, and its silvery, polished skin dispelled any doubts.

An Andrass: one of the android assassins.

Cullen didn't stop to confirm that this thing was here for him, nor to ponder why he might have attracted such expensive and lethal attention – time for such musings later. Hesitation now would almost certainly exclude the possibility of there *being* a later. Instead, he reacted, charging towards the frail-looking door in the building to his right the instant he identified precisely what confronted him.

The door shattered beneath his assault, the rotted timbers splintering as his shoulder struck them. He reached through, unlocked the latch and pushed. He was inside. A smell of damp and of too many unwashed people assailed his nostrils as he sprinted down a dark and messy corridor, kicking up papers as he went. The corridor turned to the right. He slammed into the facing wall, bouncing off and continuing. Noise surrounded him: voices, footfalls, the enraged shriek and roar of a couple arguing, the slamming of a door somewhere above. A tenement block. Without breaking stride he drew from his pocket the small compact blaster he always carried and brandished it before him. Limited but lethal; none of the scum who would inevitably live here were likely to mess with a man carrying a blaster, whatever its shortcomings.

The front door loomed ahead, blocking his way and likely more solid than the one he had entered by. The weapon in his hand spoke and the area of door around the lock disintegrated. Ducking his head, he shoulder charged through what remained, the door flying open before him.

A kaleidoscope of neon. Two faces, obviously startled by his sudden eruption from the building, stared at Cullen in amazement. The same two youths whose attention had caused him to enter the alley in the first place. Coincidence? Maybe; or perhaps someone had set them there deliberately, anticipating his reaction. If so, that someone had presumably gone to the trouble of having a psyche-profile of him drawn up, which wasn't cheap, though it was when compared with the cost of hiring an Andrass.

He glared at the pair, focussing every ounce of menace he could muster into that gaze. They melted away, fading to the far side of the street as quickly as their legs could carry them.

The two youths were out the game, assuming they were ever in it, while the Andrass had yet to follow him out into the street and he doubted it would – too exposed, too public. He had won this round, but he knew it was only the first and that to survive he would have to win them all. The Andrass, of course, only needed to win one.

*

Cullen knocked impatiently at the door. It looked little different from any of its neighbours – peeling paint and planks nailed across a glassless window towards the top – though, knowing who lived there, he expected it to be reinforced on the inside, steel-plated at the very least. The locking mechanism had been smashed long ago, the door now secured by a thick and rusty iron chain which seemed to be looped through a hole drilled into the wall itself. A typical door in a typical tenement, at an address that Cullen hadn't recognised but which had been provided by the message left on his phone.

Almost, he hadn't come. His finger had hovered over the delete button, as if to erase the message from both his phone and his mind. Almost. But memories ran deep. There were people he owed, and this was one of them.

The muffled sound of footfalls came from within, then a pause as he was doubtless examined via some hidden peephole. Next the rattle of chains and the click of a padlock being released, before the links fell free from the door, to disappear through the hole in the wall like some retreating serpent.

The door opened a crack and a face peered out at him. Angular, with thinning hair, shrewd pinprick eyes, and ginger stubble flecked with grey. Older and gaunter than Cullen remembered, but he would have known that face anywhere.

"Hello, Ryan."

"Cul, you came!" The door opened fully. "Come in, come in."

The man, this ghost from his past, led the way through a dimly lit hallway into a surprisingly well maintained living room, although a peculiar stale smell suggested the place was not as well maintained as it appeared.

"It's good to see you again, Cul."

"You too." Had he really once lived like this? It felt claustrophobic and squalid now, but a few years ago he would undoubtedly have felt completely at home in such a place. He avoided sitting down. "Your call sounded urgent."

"It is. Thought you'd better know that there's a contract out on you."

Which certainly explained the Andrass. "And you brought me over here to tell me that?"

The other shrugged. "Seemed like a good excuse to see you, and besides, didn't want to trust something like that to a phone messaging service. Way I heard it, this contract's a heavy one."

"That figures. I just had a run-in with an Andrass."

Ryan grunted. "Doesn't come much heavier than that. You should feel honoured."

"I'll try and remember that while it tears my head from my shoulders. Thanks for the heads up, in any case. Have you got a gun I can use?" The three sentences tumbled out one after the other.

"Sure." Without hesitation, Ryan produced a pocket blaster and held it out to his visitor, cradling the compact weapon in the palm of his hand.

Cullen stared at it. "Come on, what would that do to an Andrass? I mean a *real* gun."

A frozen moment. No sound, no movement. Then Ryan crossed to the door and left the room, only to reappear soon after bearing a veritable cannon. A half metre length of sleek, death-dealing metal.

Cullen slowly nodded his approval. *Now* he could face an Andrass.

"You know what'll happen to you if you're caught on the streets carrying this, don't you?"

"I know." He reached a hand out to take the gun, and, after a brief hesitation, Ryan passed it to him. "Thank you."

With that, he slipped the gun under his coat in an inadequate concession towards concealment, and headed for the door.

"Where do you think you're going?" Ryan said.

"To face it; to finish this."

"Not without me you don't."

Cullen stopped and stared at his former lieutenant, who looked suddenly self-conscious.

The shorter man shrugged. "You'll need someone to cover your back."

Cullen's turn to hesitate, and then he felt his cheeks lifting as his mouth formed a smile – a rarity. "Sounds reasonable."

"So, where are we headed?"

"The old football ground."

Ryan laughed. "Of course; where else?"

*

Cullen led the way via a narrow passage in the rubble that surrounded the long deserted stadium. This was a route he had helped to clear long ago, one which he expected to find again choked with weeds and vines and tumbled-down rocks and concrete, but it wasn't, which made him wonder who else might be coming here these days.

He was determined that when he next faced death, it would not be in some anonymous dark alley with a backdrop of neon but in a place of his choosing. Here, to be precise. A vast open space, ignored by the gangs who preferred the crowds and the noise, the glare and the energy of the streets, where the next potential victim was never far away, and forgotten about by those living Uptown, who had long ago settled for sports of a more sanitised and virtual nature.

This relic from another age had been a part of Cullen's life ever since his youth. He had played here and then trained here. He and others of the mercenary cadre.

He could think of nowhere more fitting to face prospective death: home territory, in as much as he felt at home anywhere.

"Brings back memories, doesn't it?" Ryan muttered from behind him as they picked their way through the final twists of the convoluted path they were following to stand at the edge of the arena proper.

"That it does," Cullen could only agree.

They headed into the north stand, which remained largely intact, its concrete frame withstanding the worst ravages of time, and climbed towards the top. From there they should be able to see anything approach.

Cullen had witnessed Andrasses in action before and knew how deadly they were, but this was the first time he had been called upon to face one himself. With Ryan's gun he stood a chance; without it... little to none.

He had no doubt the creature would find him. Once unleashed, an Andrass invariably completed its task as rapidly as possible. Only by killing him tonight would the thing maximise the commission earned by its masters. Once he had dealt with the assassin, Cullen intended to hunt down those masters and persuade them of their error in accepting this commission; after which he would turn his attention to whoever had paid them.

"So, who do you reckon sent it?" Ryan asked, as if reading his mind.

"I've been wondering that myself. Pissed a few people off in my time, no argument, but I reckon there are only two who might go this far: Chrysler and Vaughn."

"I remember Chrysler. He's the one whose legs you blew off."

"That's the one. We needed the information. He survived to become a big cheese in the armaments trade. I've kept tabs on him over the years, just in case. I understand the artificial legs work fine, but I know for a fact he's never forgiven me."

"Some people; no sense of proportion. Why would he leave it until now to come after you, though?"

"Who knows?"

"All right, so that's Chrysler; who's this Vaughn?"

"More recent. A wheeler-dealer Uptown."

"What have you done to piss him off?"

"It's complicated."

"Ah, you mean there's a woman involved."

Suzanne, to be precise. "Something like that."

Ryan seemed to have run out of questions for the moment. There were probably a few Cullen ought to be asking him, but they could wait; his thoughts were monopolised by his current predicament. As the silence stretched out, the sounds of the city, of the streets, drifted to them seemingly from a great distance. It was as if they eavesdropped on another world.

His eyes well adjusted to the dark, Cullen scanned the great stadium for signs of movement. Beside him, Ryan presumably did the same. Certainly it was his old friend who saw it first, slowly moving a hand to squeeze Cullen's arm, drawing his attention to a glint of silver below them.

A stray beam of light glistened briefly on the creature's hide as it stood there, turning its head slowly from side to side, giving Cullen the ludicrous impression that it was trying to catch his scent. Whatever it was actually doing seemed to be effective enough, because when it stopped, the thing stood facing directly towards them.

Then it moved.

Fast. Incredibly fast. If not for the fact that it charged directly towards them, Cullen doubted he could have taken accurate aim. He forced himself to hold his finger off the trigger, to wait and let the thing draw nearer. He had to shoot first and that shot had to count – there would not be time for a second.

There was no guile in the Andrass's approach, it simply charged straight at him, presumably confident that speed and armour would be enough to cope with anything Cullen threw at it. The thing's mistake was to believe that he would only be carrying the type of weapon tolerated by the laws of both the land and the streets.

Cullen fired, holding the trigger down. This was no neat, factory-produced handgun but a brutal cannon of a weapon, cobbled together to bypass every safety feature going. The insulated handle grew warm beneath his fingers and he wondered if the gun was about to overload before doing its job, but after a few seconds of pouring lethal energies into the synthetic creature, the gun triumphed.

The Andrass exploded, a spectacular blast which dazzled Cullen and caused him to flinch away as heat washed over him. Something stung his arm, marking its passage in blood, but when he looked up again, the Andrass was gone.

He was shaking – that thing had really got to him. He put the gun down and drew a long, deep breath.

"Nice shooting," Ryan said from beside him. "Finished with this?" He picked up the gun.

Cullen nodded. "Thanks. Now all I have to do is sort out who sent it."

"My guess would be Vaughn."

"Why do you say that?"

"Process of elimination. Remember I told you there was a contract out on you? Well, it's from Chrysler and I took it."

Cullen suddenly realised that the gun, that cannon which had just blown away an Andrass, was now pointing directly towards him. As he watched, the weapon rotated through 360 degrees. The hand and wrist holding it did likewise. A cold smile twisted the corners of 'Ryan's' mouth.

Cullen had heard rumour of something like this without entirely believing it: an Andrass that could take human form and mimic human behaviour, even to the point of duplicating an individual's mannerisms and personality. The process had to take months to perfect, if not years. To go to such lengths someone would have to possess a vast amount of money, near infinite patience, and a burning desire to see somebody else dead.

Chrysler would seem to tick all the boxes.

Cullen spared a fleeting thought for the real Ryan, doubtless dead in a back alley somewhere. Cullen knew that he was exceptionally quick – over the years he had needed to be – but this was an Andrass. Jumping such a killing machine was next to impossible. He also realised that he was out of options.

Even as he threw himself at the creature, Cullen knew that he was not going to be quick enough.

***

Written in the post Blade Runner days of the 1980s, this was my first ever published story, appearing in March 1987. The old adage about a story never being finished is particularly appropriate here. With no electronic version of "Flesh and Metal" existing, I've had the opportunity to rewrite the piece line by line, restructuring entire paragraphs while being careful not to disrupt the essence of the narrative. It's fascinating to revisit a piece for the first time after so many years and see how far my writing has developed. I would like to think that, were I to come back to some of my more recent stories twenty-odd years from now, the required rewrites would be far less extensive, but who knows?

Hanging on Her Every Word

When Paul arrived home Laura was in the conservatory. As soon as he opened the door he knew that something had changed, and that it could only be a change for the better.

Music; she was listening to music. Afterwards, he couldn't have said for certain exactly what it was: something light and classical, Dvořák's *New World*, perhaps? He didn't pay that much attention. The fact that she was listening to anything at all was enough. Gone was the oppressive, cathedral-like silence that had greeted him so often, gone were the flat dronings of TV-channelled voices – their home's intermittent soundtrack and, of late, the only alternative to the silence. Instead, the vibrant sound of an orchestra drifted through the rooms once more. He kicked off his shoes and hurried inward, drawn by the music.

She looked up as he came across the lounge, favouring him with a dazzling smile that caused the words of intended greeting to congeal in his throat and emerge as a still-born sob, daring him to hope that all the darkness of recent weeks was past.

He wanted to hug her, wanted to sweep her up in his arms, but was afraid of overdoing it, afraid of shattering this precious prospect, of disturbing the moment in any way.

"Hello, love," she said as if nothing was wrong, as if nothing had ever been wrong.

"Hello," he replied inadequately. He hovered on the threshold of the two rooms, worried that if he came any closer the fragile semblance of normality might disintegrate before his eyes.

She looked at him querulously and then smiled again, before returning her attention to the objects scattered upon the table.

The late afternoon sunlight slanted in through broad conservatory windows, catching the extremities of her fine hair and igniting the dark blonde so that her head appeared framed by a golden nimbus. He drank her in as she sat huddled over the table: the snub, slightly upturned nose, the full lips, the elegant contours of chin and throat, and the gracefully curling eyelashes – each individually highlighted in tender detail by the sunlight. Tears threatened the corners of his eyes as he smiled; an expression of joy and relief. He had not seen her this animated since... since it happened.

Laura always played classical music when she was doing something creative, claiming it helped her to focus without being invasive. To find her here, at the table, tinkering with something or other, was so typical and yet so unexpected. More than he could have hoped for. His gaze naturally slid downward from her profile to what her hands were doing.

She was bending fine silver wire strands and weaving them to create the figures of animals. Tools lay close at hand: pliers and wire cutters, casually discarded beside the already completed form of a small bird, perhaps three or four inches long. The bird winked silver fire at him from outspread wings, reflecting the sun's illumination, which fell on it intermittently as the leaves of the maple tree beyond the window were caressed by the gentle breeze, first one way then the other.

Laura was currently working on what was obviously destined to be a cat, about the same size as the bird.

Uncertainty forgotten, he stepped fully into the room to stand beside her.

"They're beautiful," he exclaimed in wonder.

"Thank you," she responded, glancing up and smiling again,

sending his heart soaring a few degrees higher.

"What are they for?"

She didn't look up this time, but continued her delicate work. "They're for the baby. I'm making him a mobile."

The words struck like a physical blow, causing his hopes to wither and his heart to plummet back to earth once more.

"Laura..." he said slowly, every word ashen, "you know that Aaron's..."

She looked up sharply. "Oh, I know. Don't worry, I know he's gone." She stopped working, put down the cat and turned to face him, reaching out to clasp his hands. A gesture that once would have seemed so natural now almost startled him, causing him to flinch for a fraction of a second. She seemed oblivious, thank God.

"It's something that Greg wanted me to try." Dr. 'call me Greg' Santini, her therapist. "He thought that making something *for* Aaron might help to channel my grief." The smile wavered, one corner of her mouth trembled and he was afraid that everything was about to come crashing down again. "And it's working," she continued, moisture welling in her eyes. "I really *feel* that I'm doing something constructive; for him... for love."

A single tear crested the bottom of her right eye and trickled down her cheek, but the smile returned, delicate and brave.

He did hug her then, pressing his cheek to the crown of her sun-warmed head, a tear of his own welling up to disappear into her hair.

Importantly, wonderfully, she hugged him back.

Paul went out to water the plants while Laura returned to her work. Theirs was a corner plot, with a deceptively large garden that wrapped around to cradle the building. Laura was out of sight but not out of mind as he began, training the hose at the base of the broad-leafed Gunnera which stood by the pond but was unable to access the moisture it craved due to the pond's plastic lining. He shuffled around the borders, methodically administering a heavy spray to plants and shrubs, habit stepping in to guide his actions whenever distracted thought failed to.

The grass needed cutting, he noted, but it could wait another day or two. A brown mound in the centre of the lawn caught his eye. It proved to be the body of a female blackbird, doubtless abandoned there by Felix or one of the neighbourhood's other feline residents. Clearing the small body away brought him into view of the conservatory, where Laura still sat, head down, concentrating on her wire figures. He glanced in at her, half-fearing that she might abandon her work at any moment, signalling a return to the dark reticence of recent times.

He still didn't trust this abrupt transformation, this apparent healing, didn't dare believe in it; but at least he now had reason to hope.

As he brought the hose around the corner, she came into view once more. On impulse he directed a stream of water at her. It spattered against the window, drumming an irregular refrain. She looked up, startled for an instant, and he was afraid that he had overstepped some ill-defined mark, but then she smiled and poked her tongue out at him – an echo of the carefree woman he used to know.

Hope gained new strength.

That evening was the best they had shared since losing Aaron. Laura even snuggled up to him on the sofa and didn't object or shrink away when he snaked an arm along the seat's back, behind her head, his hand resting lightly on her shoulder.

*

The next morning she was up before him, moving with genuine purpose; the old Laura, getting dressed with hurried efficiency.

"Going somewhere?" he asked from the bed.

"Hmm? An appointment with Greg," she responded without pausing.

"On a Saturday?"

"Yes. He feels we're making real progress at last and doesn't want to lose the momentum. He works the occasional Saturdays, for special cases."

"And you're a special case?"

"Guess so." She flashed him a quick smile.

By the time she left he had managed to rouse himself, leaving the sanctuary of the bed and reaching as far as the kitchen and the kettle.

"Have you seen Felix?" he wondered as she blurred past him.

"No, can't say I have. He's probably making the most of the good weather. Either that or he's got himself locked inside next door's garage again."

She kissed him on the way out; a quick peck on the lips, so ordinary, yet so magical. "Won't be long," and she was out the door.

As he dressed, gazing at the bed still resonant with Laura's presence even as the house was emptied by her absence, his eyes fell upon the book by her bedside. He hadn't noticed her reading it, hadn't noticed her reading *anything*, yet there it was; a paperback with brown, textured cover, the corners slightly dog-eared. A small sepia photograph formed the cover's centrepiece – the portrait of a distinguished-looking Edwardian gentleman.

He picked it up, reading the title: *The Spirit in Perpetuity* by Edward L. Leary. Curious, he flipped the book over and read the back-blurb, finding there reference to mysticism, travels in Africa, and the Makonde people.

That last sounded vaguely familiar, but he couldn't think why.

His reveries were interrupted by the doorbell. He put the book down with a guilty start and, realising he was only half-dressed, pulled on the first top that came to hand, before hurrying down the stairs, thinking it must be Laura. Perhaps 'Greg' had not been at his office after all, so she was back early and had forgotten her key.

But it was only the plump and freckled girl from two doors

away, wanting to know if he had seen her dog, which had managed to escape. Again.

After getting rid of her, he went on the internet, referencing Edward L. Leary. The presence of the book played upon his mind and he wanted to know more about the author.

There was disappointingly little about the man, although one site did carry a brief biography, which expanded slightly on the book's tantalising blurb. Apparently Leary *had* spent a long period in Africa, principally in areas that now formed parts of modern day Tanzania and Mozambique, where he had studied the Makonde, a tribal group still resident in both countries. He evidently developed a particular interest in their religious beliefs, becoming involved with an extreme sect who were feared or perhaps revered (the account was a little hazy on the detail) even by other Makonde. There had been some sort of scandal, possibly involving this sect, which resulted in Leary leaving Africa and returning to England in something of a hurry. Again, frustratingly scant detail was provided.

Other sites added nothing new, rehashing snippets of the same biographical information. Nor could he find anything more about Leary's mysterious sect, although there was plenty of information about the Makonde's beliefs in general. It transpired that they practiced a form of ancestor worship, holding that ancestors were capable of influencing the world, affecting such practical matters as the weather and harvests. As far as Paul could make out, the whole thing centred around the concept that our own ancestors live on inside us all, their personalities submerged but always there. He wondered what extreme variety of this tenet Leary's elusive sect had adhered to.

An aside caught his attention as he followed yet another line of research to its inevitable dead end: the name Leary was generally believed to have derived from the Irish O'Leary, a name that cropped up in his own family background, none of which shed any further light on Edward L. Leary himself.

At least he solved the puzzle of why the Makonde had sounded so familiar. They were renowned for their wood-carving, a practice developed as a manifestation of their religion. A typical Makonde carving would be a mask or statuette depicting a number of faces and part-bodies emerging and blending, supposedly in representation of the multiple ancestors dwelling within us.

The statuette that stood on a bookshelf in the bedroom was a Makonde carving, he now recalled. Laura had brought it home from some craft or antique fair a while ago, enchanted by its intricacy and detail. Paul found the way that the various depicted forms melted into each other vaguely unsettling, but he tolerated it for her sake and had come to barely notice the thing.

By the time his wife returned, the computer was switched off and Paul was in the lounge, reading the newspaper. She popped her head around the door.

"Did it go okay?" he asked.

"Fine, thanks. Greg seems really pleased with everything."

"Good." He endeavoured to ensure that his voice betrayed no suggestion of disapproval.

"Just popping upstairs for a shower."

"A shower?"

"Yes," she called out, already halfway up the stairs, "I didn't have time for one before I went out this morning."

He shook his head and smiled, then tried to recall if she had ever *not* found time to shower before. Not as far as he could recall. But, of course, that was the old Laura.

Paul waited until he heard the shower and then waited a little longer, until he felt certain that she would have stepped within the umbrella of water and its isolating cloak of noise. Only then did he pick up the phone and call Dr. Santini's number.

He had met Santini once, at the initial consultation after Laura had first been referred to him. There was no doubt that the good doctor cut an imposing figure, though he was somewhat older than Paul had envisaged, surely not far from retirement.

A large part of him resented the fact that this man, this stranger, had been able to get through to his wife when he could not, but that part vied with his overwhelming relief that she could be reached at all.

Santini answered the phone himself. Perhaps he didn't expect his secretaries to work on a Saturday even when he chose to. Or perhaps he was simply too mean to pay the overtime. His rich, reassuring voice gave no clue to his advancing years.

"Dr. Santini? It's Paul Mellor, Laura's husband."

"Paul! Yes, of course, and please, call me Greg…"

So he asked about Laura's progress and about the wire animals she was working on with such fervour.

"You understand that I can't speak about specifics, even to you, but the indications are very promising…"

Of course Paul understood. He expressed his gratitude for the recent transformation, and then mentioned the book, which was so very different from the thrillers and escapist novels Laura usually favoured.

"Ah yes, the Leary. That was my idea," Santini explained. "I lent it to Laura. Something different, you see, something to kick-start things and engage her brain, to make her think."

"Yes, yes I see," Paul said, even though he didn't.

"I hope you didn't mind me dragging her away from you this morning."

"No of course not," Paul lied.

"But it's vital that I monitor Laura's response closely at this early stage."

What was it about Santini that he took such exception to? Was he really jealous of this man, old enough to be Laura's father and then some?

Paul ended the conversation when he heard the flow of water cease upstairs. The brief chat left him no more reassured than before.

Laura joined him in the lounge, sitting opposite and flicking through the newspaper supplements.

"Interesting book you're reading," he said after a while.

"What?"

"The paperback by your bedside. I couldn't help but notice it."

"Oh, that. Yes, Greg gave it to me. Not my usual sort of thing, but I'm rather enjoying it."

Despite the casual words there was a tension in the air, as if the mundane took an effort that it had never needed before, or was it just him? He almost spoke about things then, almost broached the subject of her illness and asked what she was feeling with regard to Aaron's loss, with regard to him, to them, their relationship and their marriage, but he shied away. Even the illusion of normality was too precious to jeopardise.

After lunch, Laura returned to the conservatory and her wire figures. The cat was finished, and she was now working on what promised to be a dog. He left her to it.

By mid-afternoon, when he interrupted her with a drink, the dog was completed and had taken its place at the far edge of the table beside the bird and the cat. Laura was just starting the head of a fourth figure; too early to tell what it was going to be as yet. A frame had appeared from somewhere – or had it always been there and he'd simply failed to notice? A four-spoked bracket of gleaming chrome, the spokes gathering at a central point from which a slender chain emerged. Currently redundant, the short length of chain snaked limply and haphazardly beside the frame. Four spokes; so presumably this latest figure was to be the last.

He finished his drink and decided to mow the lawn. Every other stripe he trod, the three blank-faced wire animals were in plain view. By some trick of design or light they seemed to be looking at him through the conservatory window whenever he glanced up, even when Laura wasn't.

That evening Laura surprised him again, by insisting on

cooking. Not that she *couldn't* cook, it was simply that she *hadn't*, not for a long while.

He was banished from the kitchen and told to relax, to leave everything to her. Not averse to being pampered, he did as instructed, uncertain whether to feel proud, delighted, or amused. In the end he settled for simply feeling happy.

Left to his own devices, he wandered into the conservatory to view Laura's handiwork. The fourth figure was completed: a man, made to the same scale as the animals. He found *this* figure vaguely disturbing, without being certain why, but was more than happy to let it pass without comment, if it furthered Laura's return to him.

She went the whole hog with the meal: candles, soft music and all the trimmings.

"My way of saying thank you," she explained, coyly.

"What for?"

She looked him in the eye and said, "For putting up with me."

He loved her more than ever.

One bottle of red wine evaporated as they ate and he opened a second, which was well on the way to joining the first before they left the table and retreated to the sofa. Paul felt more relaxed and happy than he could remember. Laura went to clear up, again refusing his help. Naturally he protested, though not with any great conviction. The wine had gone to his head and he drifted gently into contented sleep in front of the TV, dimly aware of the sounds of washing-up in the background.

*

He returned to consciousness slowly and confusedly – one of those awakenings that leaves you disorientated and groping for tangible referents. The world seemed to be swaying.

He knew this was the bedroom but had no recollection of how he came to be there. His perspective was skewed, puzzlingly elevated. Had something in the meal disagreed with him?

Everything seemed out of kilter. His head hurt: a tight, nagging pain.

The room was strangely lit – a subdued amber glow, constantly roiling and flickering; a light that had nothing to do with electricity. Candles, he realised. Dozens of them spread throughout the room. Squat tea lights arrayed along bookshelves and the dressing table's top alongside taller, phallic columns of wax that thrust upward from every available surface.

Then he saw her: Laura.

She was wearing the yukata that he had brought back from Japan, which she still insisted on referring to as a kimono. Red dragon emblazoned on black silk, its sinuous form snaking sensuously across the wearer's back, a single taloned foot reaching around to caress her stomach.

Her hair was worn loose and somehow conveyed a sense of wantonness. Perhaps it was not the hair but rather her posture, the way she stood, with silk wrapped around skin, or the way she held her head. Never had she looked more beautiful, more desirable.

He thought his eyes were locked on his wife, yet apparent movement behind her drew his attention to where the Makonde statuette stood, now surrounded by candles. In the uneven light it seemed to have come alive. The entire stunted column rippled, as if the myriad partial figures that coated its skin were writhing, struggling against each other and fighting to maintain their place on the totem's carved surface.

Only then did he become aware of another presence in the room; a figure standing in the doorway – a man, naked and relaxed.

Recognition brought horror, with bitterness swirling in its wake. Greg Santini.

As he watched, the figure moved, and the motion broke the illusion. Not Santini after all, but a much younger man, although the realisation brought no joy.

He was looking down upon himself, Paul Mellor.

Confusion threatened to overwhelm him, as he struggled to make sense of what he was seeing, only to realise that that he couldn't, not yet.

He had never noticed how similar Santini's features were to his own. The fickle candlelight had briefly blurred the distinctions of time's passage and revealed the close resemblance. Santini could almost be an older version of himself.

Beyond any doubt, this was his own body he was watching, yet something in the movement struck him as fundamentally wrong, as if it were not of him but rather echoed Santini's assured and fluid grace.

Paul tried to turn his head, then lift an arm, but couldn't.

The man stepped into his wife, grasping her around the waist and bending to kiss her neck, while she leaned back, melting into him, lifting an arm to caress the back of his head, running fingers through his hair and pulling him closer.

Paul recalled bitterly her self-imposed isolation, her unwillingness to let him touch her in recent weeks and the distance that had grown between them as a result. All of which was in total contrast to the way she yielded so completely to this other. She turned her head, craning backwards.

For an instant, just before their lips met, she looked towards the point from which he watched. What was that he could he see in her eyes? Triumph? Amusement? Regret? Then the lids closed and she lost herself within the kiss with this stranger, this man who had usurped his place.

A hand snaked inside the yukata, pushing the silk to one side, to cup and then massage the milky mound of Laura's exposed breast. She pulled free of the kiss, though not of his arms, moaning – a deep, animal sound – then she twisted around within his embrace. The garment, catching on her lover's forearm, came completely undone. With a single shrug of her shoulders it dropped from her body, sliding to the ground. She clung to

Paul/Greg, answering his need with her own, pulling him into another kiss as she rubbed herself against him, his hands kneading her buttocks, then lifting to rake nails down the length of her back.

This time her moan when the kiss ended, when he dropped his mouth to her breast, was a cry of need, of want, of anticipation; it was also a word, a name: "Edward," which she gasped with more heat and demand than Paul had ever heard her voice before.

Paul to Greg to Paul, the man's face flickered and danced in the fickle light, as the mouth slid across his wife's flesh, from breast to breast, nipple to nipple.

The wine had been drugged, a part of his mind grudgingly accepted, recalling how he had slipped into sleep so easily. What else had been done to him?

Strands of thought began to collide and gel, giving birth to insight. An obscure sect of ancestor worshipers, whose practices made them feared and revered even among their own people... Paul, Greg... common ancestors buried in the both. One ancestor in particular. For that ancestor to surface, to claim control, to be resurrected, the resident spirit had been deposed, the dominant personality transferred elsewhere. It must have happened to the now-aging Santini at some point in the past, in his youth, and now it had happened to Paul, with his own wife the instrument, the accomplice to this ultimate betrayal.

Laura was far more than mere accomplice, he realised, as one leg snaked up to circle her lover's hips, pulling herself onto him and him into her. Rather she was co-conspirator, willing collaborator, having doubtless been beguiled and seduced by the Svengali-like Santini.

Was his own ancestral memory now animating his body, or had the essence of Edward/Greg also been transferred, moving into the vacancy left by his eviction?

The two bodies melded, entwined, moving inexorably

towards the bed. Paul/Greg/Edward lifted her and propelled her backwards, the pair collapsing out of Paul's line of sight.

If he was no longer in his own body then what was he, some sort of nebulous spirit? If so, why did he feel so restricted, so stiff and limited in movement?

Something intruded on the periphery of vision. A silvery figure swayed gently in and out of view, catching and reflecting the dull light of the candles. Instinctively he tried to turn his head again but had to be content with moving his eyes. The bird; Laura's wire bird, but made suddenly huge, as big as he was.

Realisation hit home; he remembered Laura's four wire figures, then thought of the dead blackbird on the lawn, the absent Felix and the neighbours' missing dog, wondering what purpose their sacrifice had served. Part of the ritual, necessary preparation, or merely practice?

Despair and horror welled up within him.

Although he could no longer see Laura and Edward, he could still hear them; the creak of protesting bedsprings, the rub of frame against wall, and above all else the moans and gasps of his wife.

Only *he* could hear his own scream.

Paul knew that Laura's voice, transformed by such raw and unsuspected passion, would haunt him for however long his spirit was destined to linger here. He knew too that in that time he would die a thousand deaths, hanging on her every word, tormented by her every sound.

***

In late 2007 I deliberately started experimenting with different forms and styles of horror, a type of writing which does not come as readily to me as science fiction or fantasy, both of which I've been reading avidly since my early teens. I wrote three pieces which could loosely be described as 'horror', without any confidence that they were much good. Presumably they must have been, since all three found a home soon enough.

This is probably my favourite of these pieces – I had great fun writing it and felt the piece achieved pretty much what I'd intended. I could almost hear the theme tune to the old *Tales of the Unexpected* series playing as the words formed.

The Final Hour

For several seconds I simply stood there, trying to come to terms with this new body. First impressions suggested it was no different, but didn't they always? It pays to be cautious. The temptation to simply assume that everything is more or less the same and get on with things is always there, but I've learned the hard way. Assumptions can be deadly.

I stretched fingers, flexed biceps, clenched calf muscles, rocked eyes up, down, and from right to left, breathed deeply and exhaled, all without making any extravagant movements.

I knew that as soon as I did, the countdown would begin.

Muscles appeared to be well toned, lung capacity good and there were no obvious deficiencies in vision. Just as importantly, I felt normal, comfortable.

Satisfied that everything had been covered that could be covered without actually moving from the spot, I stepped out.

The instant my weight transferred to that forward stretching foot, a voice spoke in my head.

"One hour until the end of time."

Androgynous aural wallpaper, which I knew would haunt me throughout the sixty minutes I was destined to be here. One hour, that was all I had. That was all anyone here had, but I was the only one who knew as much. Unlike everyone else in this world, this simulation, this pocket universe or whatever the hell it was, I was actually aiming to achieve something. I had sixty minutes in which to find two specific individuals and, once I'd found them, decide what the hell to do with them.

Tiny red digits in the bottom left corner of my field of vision were counting down the time: 59.55. The analytical corner of my mind wanted to calculate what percentage of the allotted hour had already been eaten up, but I quashed that urge. Concentrate.

Find two people in a pocket? That sounds simple enough, right? After all, it's what I'm trained for. Except that these two were not your common or garden sort of people, not by a long shot. One was Tom Bryce – my colleague and my friend, as well-trained and resourceful as I was – and the other was Professor Aaron West. Yes, *that* Aaron West: darling of the chat show circuit and designer of this particular pocket universe and countless others. Doubtless he knew more about the place than anyone; certainly enough to block the A.I.'s monitoring access and so help Tom Bryce vanish.

The central question, which it was my job to answer, was: *why* had West blocked the monitors? What was he up to in here that he didn't want the A.I. to see?

The first thing I did after stepping off the entry plate was check my weapons. I quick-drew the hand gun, to make sure the easy release holster lived up to its name, and then inspected the charge level, reserve packs and other equipment. Only when satisfied that everything was as it should be did I continue towards the Hub.

You've seen Aaron West on the TV shows, everyone has. You've heard him explain how he helped develop the mathematics behind the pocket universes, or at least helped to program the computers that built the A.I. that did, and you've heard him fielding the questions about what they really are.

"Professor, these pocket universes, are they real or are they just simulation?"

"Well, Brad, that's an interesting question, and the answer depends on your definition of 'reality'. The pockets exist – we know that because people go to them... So does that make them real? You tell me."

And so on. The truth is, I very much doubt whether even he knew to what extent the pockets are real. I've seen the governing equations and they're way beyond the limits of my math degree. Even those who do claim to follow them admit they're unsure exactly what the math represents. All we know for certain is that the A.I. opens the door. Quite what that door opens *to* is still a matter of conjecture and debate. Designers working in conjunction with the A.I. map out the mathematical foundations for specific realities, after which everything is taken out of human hands. The A.I. works its magic and 'hey presto', a pocket universe is born. The jury's still out on whether the A.I. builds, simulates or simply locates the required pocket.

But what do people care? Like the Professor says, they can go there; that's all that counts.

Movement, caught in the corner of my eye. At least this body's peripheral vision appeared to be up to scratch. I dropped instinctively, whipping out my gun as I fell. An energy beam bisected the space I had occupied a split second earlier. Chameleonware: the shooter was all but invisible until he moved. Fortunately, in firing at me he gave himself away. Still lying prone, I fired back at the point of origin, scoring a hit. The figure of a man was limned in flickering energy as his chameleon suit short-circuited. It returned to its default matt black before he hit the ground.

For long seconds I lay there, scanning the corridor ahead, straining to catch any hint of blurred movement that might prelude further attack. Something nagged at my memory, a detail absorbed during the cramming undertaken for this mission. Then I had it: Chameleon-Ninjas could climb walls.

I frantically rolled over, firing at the ceiling, and continued to roll. An answering beam of energy sizzled into the ground at my elbow, so close that I could feel the heat through my clothes. That gave me all the bearing I needed and my second shot nailed him. His suit turned black and he dropped to the ground directly onto the spot I had originally lain in.

I stood up, brushing myself down. These two didn't belong

here or anywhere near the entryway. Ninjas were from the 'Action' level. They must have been put in place deliberately, waiting for somebody; waiting for me. About the only person who might be able to pull off something like that aside from the A.I. itself was West.

I continued on, knowing I was getting closer by the growing hubbub of voices ahead. Sure enough, I turned a corner and was at the Hub: a large circular chamber, encircled by doors. This was it: the very centre of the pocket. From here, each different section could be accessed.

People were everywhere, sporting a plethora of different costumes, crossing from one side to the other, laughing, gaily chatting, having a ball. Each and every one of them was determined to make the most of whatever time they had left. That was the whole point of this pocket, you see. Everyone who paid to come to 'The End of Time' knew that the pocket was destined to collapse at some point soon. The clever part was that none of them had been told precisely when. 'Live each Moment as if it's Your Last' was the tag line, and every conceivable pleasure, thrill and luxury had been crammed into the place to enable people to do just that. Each door opened onto a different level, each of which emphasised a different temptation. From 'The Sensual Palace', which speaks for itself, to 'Gastronomy', where the finest dishes from the world's various cuisines were available, from 'Adventure', where extreme sports such as cloud hopping, astro-gliding and wind riding proliferated, to 'Action', where mobsters and their molls fought gangland wars, platoons of marines stormed gun emplacements and Chameleon-Ninjas prowled shadowed streets

Doors were constantly opening and closing as people came and went, sated with one pleasure and anxious to sample the next.

55.54: no time to hang around. I determined to go after Tom first – reasoning that West could prove the more awkward and that Tom might know where to find him, having been here longer.

Where to start, though? I rejected 'Gastronomy' – Tom was not a foodie – and likewise discounted 'African Safari', 'Ocean Cruise', 'Vegas', 'Oriental Luxury' and 'Zero-G Frolics', settling for 'Dance'.

In quick succession I looked in at a dancehall where Glen Miller soundalikes had the place in full swing – a swathe of khaki uniforms, full length skirts and stilettos – a disco where fright wigs, platform shoes and flares predominated, and a rave – all thudding bass and dance loops, while lasers pierced the night.

Somewhere during this a voice whispered, "Fifty minutes until the end of time." As if I needed reminding.

'Dance' was a bust – no sign of Tom.

I had to pick up the pace, and skimmed swiftly through several other levels, taking in along the way such delights as a swish cocktail bar in which elegant drinks were quaffed to the gentle, muted sounds of a piano, while a vast picture window provided views out over a truly spectacular underseascape, where sharks and manta rays swam, a Roman orgy – all heaving buttocks, disarrayed togas and spilling wine – and a bizarre scene where richly-clad partygoers were systematically burning down a stand of trees with flame throwers, apparently in homage to a long-ago movie.

"Forty minutes until the end of time," whispered my conscience.

At an Elizabethan masked ball, a girl tried to kiss me. In an opium den that could have been lifted straight from the pages of Sherlock Holmes or Fu Man Chu, a man tried to kiss me.

Nothing.

"Thirty minutes until the end of time."

The opulence of Singapore's Raffles Hotel from the 1940's – predating the Japanese invasion – proved fruitless, as did an uncomfortably accurate recreation of Patpong – Bangkok's notorious red light district, where it was often impossible to tell glamorous lady-boy from elfin Thai nymphet until the strip routine was complete.

Things were growing desperate. I had thought my knowledge of Tom would enable me to target those levels where the on-tap pleasures reflected his likes and preferences and so find him with ease, but it was not working out that way.

Back at the Hub once more, considering my options, that smooth, emotionless voice informed me, "Twenty minutes until the end of time." As if I needed to be told.

I was conscious of the fact that since the ambush by the two Ninjas, there'd been no direct opposition. At first I figured this was down to logistics, supposing that only so many resources could be lifted out of their normal routine and left on standby, that it would take West a while to marshal other forces from 'Action' or wherever else they were, but as time passed I began to suspect that the absence of opponents was an indication of what a lousy job I was doing. After all, why bother trying to stop someone if they're not even posing a threat?

A rethink was needed, a radically different approach... assuming I could come up with one.

Okay, what if Tom's sudden disappearance had not been voluntary as everyone had assumed? What if his vanishing from the A.I.'s sensors was not evidence of collusion with West but rather was the result of his being a victim? We knew he hadn't been 'killed' here in the pocket, because he hadn't re-emerged into the 'real' world. So perhaps he was being restrained somewhere, held captive. Bizarre perhaps, but feasible. It also fitted with what I knew of Tom Bryce and was certainly easier to reconcile than the assumption that Tom had gone maverick.

I consulted the schematic for this pocket – imprinted on my mind as part of the standard mission prep – with particular reference to rooms or areas that could be sealed off or locked. There were several possibilities, although not as many as you might think. After all, it had hardly been a priority when the pocket was designed.

One of the levels where possibilities proliferated was 'Gastronomy'.

"You look lost, Snugglepup," a voice said, a female voice. I looked around, to find myself staring at an apparition from an old Hollywood movie: a flapper, straight out of the 1920s, complete with bobbed hair and cloche hat. Cherry red lips smiled at me from a white-powdered face, and she was beautiful.

The image, the dress, everything was perfect. It always amazes me the lengths that some people will go to in order to immerse themselves in the fantasy. You come through wearing one outfit of your choice, but if you want to fully enter into the spirit of things and change into the appropriate attire for a given level, you can buy a change of costume at modest cost. Plastic works here, you see; linked directly through to your bank account in the 'real' world – never let it be said that an opportunity to part people from their money was being overlooked.

The girl held a martini glass out towards me. "Fancy some hooch?"

Instantly I was on my guard, concerned that this might be West's next attempt to bump me off, using the local Mata Hari and a poisoned martini. Certainly the flapper slang seemed a little overdone, but perhaps that was just her idea of showing off.

I hoped that my answering smile reflected some of the regret I genuinely felt. "Sorry, but I have to meet someone, and I'm already running late."

"Shame."

With a slight bow of my head in farewell, I walked on towards the door for 'Gastronomy'. She made no move to stop me, so perhaps it was just an innocent encounter after all.

'Gastronomy' announced itself with a stroll through a long avenue of hawker's stalls – the aroma of sizzling meats and spices filled the air, reminding me of Malaysia, Penang, and time spent in Bangkok. I began to feel a stirring at the back of my mind as I left the hawkers behind and stepped into a square offering the best of Parisian café culture; a stirring which lifted my spirits considerably. It confirmed I was finally on the right track.

The monitoring A.I. had theorised that whatever method Tom was using to hide himself from its perceptions would be less effective against a more local detector. So I'd been fitted with one before entering the pocket.

Tom's tracer and comms software could not be removed – at least, not without killing him – they were implanted, same as mine. However, they could in theory be dampened. The A.I. calculated that no dampening would be perfect and that a mobile receptor moving through the same level of a pocket would pick up some degree of tell-tale leakage, which was precisely what I had just begun to sense. At last.

I checked the little red digits, which continued their relentless countdown to doom: 12.17.

I began to hurry, nearly colliding with a white-jacketed waiter who was presenting an ice-heaped platter of Fruits de Mer to a customer with a flourish. The blind eyes of langoustine stared back at me blankly. Crossing the square, I found myself rushing through a section of London's Mayfair, with a condensation of celebrity chef's restaurants on every side, then it was another street offering wall to wall Greek tavernas, where I had to slow due to the narrowness of the thoroughfare and the crowds that thronged it.

"Ten minutes until the end of time."

The stirring at the back of my skull had developed into an insistent itch. I was getting closer. So much for my dismissing 'Gastronomy' with casual disdain at the outset.

Finally I arrived at a swish, very upmarket restaurant – the sort of place that serves only haute cuisine at its very hautest. The Maître d' showed me to a table, which I left the instant his back was turned, walking resolutely through the swing doors next to the potted palm and so into the kitchen. There were a few startled looks from white garbed chefs and a shouted "Hey" from somebody, but I didn't pause to give anyone time to react. Instead I marched straight to a large, solid-looking metal door built into the far wall – store cupboard, freezer? Presumably not the latter, or Tom would have frozen to death long ago.

Without breaking stride, I took out a small, pliable cube from its belt pouch. A white-jacketed girl scurried out of my way, evidently warned off by my determined manner or perhaps the look on my face. I slammed the explosive onto the metal surface, where the lock had to be, and yelled out, "Stand back from the door," for the benefit of both Tom and the kitchen staff, before following my own advice.

There was a sharp 'whumpf' – although the explosive was designed to implode rather than explode, so there was surprisingly little collateral damage. The door gave a small jump and then slowly swung halfway open.

As I went to step towards it, I heard a sound behind me, reminiscent of a gas fire being lit. Turning around, I found one of the Sous Chefs advancing towards me brandishing a souped-up blow torch. From the corner of my eye I spotted another white-coated figure trying to creep around on the other side. I drew the gun and shot the first in one movement – his torch clattering to the floor, still burning. Then I swivelled and shot the second point blank, as he charged towards me with meat cleaver raised. No one else seemed inclined to interfere.

"Five minutes until the end of time," whispered a voice in my head.

I raced into the store room. Tom was on a chair, tied and gagged. I freed him in seconds.

He looked at me searchingly. "Carl?"

I nodded. "Good to see you." Having viewed images from before the A.I. lost its full monitoring access to this pocket, I had no trouble recognising him.

"We've got to stop West," he said, shaking his hands to restore lost circulation.

"That's my next port of call; always assuming you know where he is."

His turn to nod. "He's here, in this restaurant. I can take you straight to him."

Perhaps I should have spent more time studying Aaron West's profile rather than relying on my knowledge of Tom – I could have saved myself a lot of time.

"Can you reach the A.I.?" Tom asked.

I shook my head, having tried but encountered only silence. The digital countdown and the soporiphic bulletins continued, but they were automated, preset systems built into my software. Communication with the A.I. had been impossible since I arrived.

We left the cupboard cautiously, but the kitchen was deserted, the staff evidently having decided on discretion as the better part of valour. Tom and I paused on either side of the swing doors, both realising that beyond them might wait a surprise or two, arranged by West especially for our benefit.

I crouched down, gun at the ready, then gave a nod to Tom, who flung the doors open and leapt out of the way. The rat-a-tat report of machine gun fire greeted us. Bullets chewed up the door jamb inches above my head and played a percussive refrain on pots and pans in the kitchen behind me. I fired back, seeing one man fall.

An elaborate forward roll – definitely one for the cameras, had there been any – and I was in the restaurant, crouching behind a vacant table and chair for cover. Unarmed, Tom stayed where he was, leaving this to me.

There were two more of them, both waiters and both sporting the sort of round-magazined machine guns that would have made Al Capone proud. The tabletop in front of me bucked and danced under the barrage. The slim-stemmed wine glasses it had supported shattered in a myriad of crystal shards. Ducking down lower, I aimed under the table and shot at the nearest waiter's legs, hitting him in the ankle. With a yell of pain, he went down.

The chair I had taken cover behind was thrown backwards, to tumble over me, its back completely chewed up by the hail of bullets.

There was only one of them left and the clock was still ticking. I decided that desperate measures were needed, and rolled out into the open, between the tables, where I could get a clear shot at him. Once, twice, three times I fired. One of them hit home. The shooting ceased and the man crumpled.

After a second's pause, waiting to hear if another gun open up, I risked getting to my feet. To my amazement, people started to clap. Immediately around me the tables were empty, but patrons had remained in other parts of the restaurant, presumably thinking this was all just part of the entertainment, or perhaps not caring whether it was or not. The applause swelled, until it seemed that everyone present was joining in.

Then came the sound I'd been dreading. Machine gun fire recommenced. There was a sudden, sharp pain in my right hand as a bullet struck it. The gun went spiralling away.

I cursed myself for a fool. The guy I'd shot in the foot was still in the game, and now he had a gun and I didn't. Suddenly, a figure reared up behind him, bringing a wine bottle crashing down on his head.

I recognised her immediately: the beautiful flapper who had spoken to me at the Hub.

I studied her across the goon's unconscious body, and found myself walking across to her, grabbing a napkin from a nearby table in passing and using it to bandage my injured hand. "You followed me?" There could be no other explanation.

"Sure. Thought it might be fun."

"Why?"

She shrugged. "All this unrelenting debauchery is entertaining enough at first, but after a while you reach stimulation over-load; it gets boring. Everyone here's the same – drunk on pleasure. Then I see you, standing still as a statue, not in a hurry to go nowhere like everyone else. You stuck out like a sore thumb. Focussed, sober and obviously different: a man with a mission. I was intrigued, so I followed you."

Tom had strolled out from the kitchen as the girl spoke. He retrieved my gun from where it had fallen and examined it carefully, presumably to check that it was still functional.

"I'm certainly glad you did," I assured her.

That brought a smile. "I'm Ellen."

Tom now turned the business end of the gun towards us.

"Tom! No!"

But it was too late. He fired.

Not at me, though, as it turned out. With an 'oh' of surprise etched upon her face, Ellen toppled backwards, straight onto one of the dining tables, which gave way on the side she struck as she tumbled to the ground. The white linen tablecloth slid off to cover her body like a shroud. A single blood-red rose started to bloom in the material, where it must have been resting directly on the wound.

I stared at him, aghast.

"It was too convenient," he explained casually. "Her turning up to save us like that, I mean. She has to be a plant, has to be working for West."

"We'll never know now," I pointed out, a little petulantly.

"Look at it this way: if I'm wrong, then all I've done is sent her home a few minutes early. She was just through telling you how bored she was. I've probably done her a favour. And if I'm right, then I've just saved us a load of grief."

He had a point.

I flicked a glance at the digits in the periphery of my vision: 02.05

"Come on, where's West? We've got to move," I urged.

"Why, has the countdown started?"

I nodded, and told him how much time was left.

He went pale. "Shit!"

"I take it West really is up to something major, then?" I asked. It was that suspicion which had prompted the A.I. to dispatch Tom to The End of Time pocket in the first place.

"Yeah. This whole pocket is booby-trapped. A replicating virus; all the while the pocket's been in existence, West has been preparing it, refining it in readiness for shut-down."

"Go on."

He took a deep breath. "Shutting down the pocket will trigger the virus…"

"Why wait for the pocket to shut down?" I interrupted. "Why not just launch it anyway?"

He shrugged. "To give it time to replicate, to appeal to West's sense of the dramatic, just to be perverse – who knows? The point is that by now the virus must have been replicated a million-fold. It's designed to hunt down and infect all other pockets, which West insists are indeed simulations."

He threw my gun back to me as he spoke. I caught it in my good left hand.

If anyone could pull off such a crazy idea, it would be Aaron West. Assuming he succeeded, it would mean the end of the pockets, but was that such a bad thing? Many argued that the pockets were a cancer, that an increasingly large percentage of humanity was becoming obsessed with what was, ultimately, a sedentary and non-productive pastime. Maybe they were right.

I grinned. "Well, I guess that would be us out of a job." It was hardly the end of the world.

So why did Tom's sour expression suggest otherwise? "That's not all," he continued, snatching up one of the dropped machine guns. "You know how everything in life seems ordered, seems to have a mathematical explanation, how cosmologists and physicists have come up with equations to explain just about everything? Well according to West, that's no coincidence. He claims that our universe, our reality, is itself just an incredibly complex simulation, mathematically mapped out, down to the finest detail."

"An idea that's been put forward before," I pointed out, "more than once."

"Yes, but in an abstract, theoretical way. West claims to have come up with the mathematical proof. And this 'End of Time' virus of his isn't designed to hit just the pockets, it's designed to hit *all* simulations. It's specifically intended to unravel the formulae that underpin reality... *our* reality."

Now that's what I call raising the stakes.

"One minute until the end of time," said a voice I was going to be glad to lose, whatever happened.

"Which way?" I asked, reckoning we could walk and talk.

He led me to the far side of the restaurant, diners and waiters scattering from our path. We reached a door which declared itself 'Private'. It was locked but flimsy, and gave way to a solid kick.

00.39 said the digits, which seemed suddenly larger.

"Why would anyone want to do that? Destroy reality, I mean." We were charging up the stairs beyond the door at this point, with Tom in front.

"To see what lies beyond, to find out what's really real," he suggested.

His machine gun chattered as he ran. A figure at the top collapsed and started to tumble down the stairs. Tom hurdled him, and I did the same a fraction later.

"But would West or anybody else be around to find out?"

"Probably not, but I think he's beyond caring."

As we reached the top of the stairs a figure erupted from hiding, slamming Tom against the wall, but in doing so he left himself open to me. A kidney punch, then I gripped him by the collar, hauled him off of Tom and threw him down the stairs after his friend.

00.20, the digits informed me.

We paused for a second to catch our breath.

00.19

It didn't honestly matter whether West's theories were right or not, we couldn't take the risk that they might be. We had to stop him.

"If we take West out, that's not going to trigger the virus, right?" We were moving again now, towards the only door that led off from this landing – a solid oak job.

"Right; from what he said to me, it's the pocket itself that's the key."

"And with him out of the way, there's every chance that we'll be able to open communications with the A.I. again and stop the countdown."

"Sounds as good a bet as any."

Tom fired on the run, shooting all around the door's lock and handle as we approached it. He fired until the magazine was empty and then flung the gun away. We were at the door. I kicked it open and we strode inside.

00.10

West sat behind a desk, waiting for us. That sincere, kindly face, remembered from a hundred chat shows, smiled at us in welcome.

00.09

"Mr. Bryce, and you've brought a friend, I see. You're too late, you know."

Without further ceremony, I lifted my gun and shot him. It might have been with the wrong hand but my aim was true, and I still hit him dead centre of the forehead. His head jerked back and then the body collapsed forward to sprawl across the desk.

00.08

"Can you reach the A.I.?"

00.07

I shook my head. "You?"

He did the same.

00.06

"Damn."

00.05

That was it, our final play. There was no time to try anything else.

00.04

"What do you think?" I asked.

00.03

"I think West was mad, that he's completely lost it."

"Obviously, but was he right?"

00.02

"Maybe," he said, grudgingly.

"Yeah, that's what I thought too."

00.01

"We'll soon know, I guess. It's been nice knowing you."

"Likewise."

00.00

PROGRAM TERMINATES.

***

I wrote this for an anthology called *the End of Time*, theme suggested by the title. It wasn't accepted, but that didn't greatly bother me — I'd enjoyed the experience of pitting characters against a critical deadline.

Darkchild

Jus was glad to be leaving Mars. Man's presence here was too new, the domes and huts too Spartan. Everything suffered from a disconcerting sense of impermanence, as if Earth's precarious toehold on this near-neighbour was transitional and might crumble away at any moment.

He had imagined that Mars would feel much like Luna, just a little fresher, but he'd been wrong. Man was so well established on the Earth's moon that it now felt as if he belonged there. They even had rats and cockroaches for goodness sake, not to mention graffiti. If *that* wasn't proof positive of mankind having arrived and put its collective feet firmly under the proverbial table, nothing was.

Mars felt entirely different. The place suffered from an almost siege-like claustrophobia. Jus, able to sense the resultant stress in everyone around him, had been counting down first the hours and then the minutes to his departure.

He only wished that Luna was his current destination. Instead, he was on his way to a place that promised to be even less reassuring than Mars – a station at the very edge of the territory humanity might claim as its own: the asteroid belt.

Man had settled Mars and then moved outward, arriving at the inner belt... where he'd stopped. Oh, there were plenty of reasons – fiscal, political, logistical – many of them all too plausible when spun out silkily by those whose job it was to spin, but they still smacked of justification.

Rumours persisted. *Something* had been found in the asteroid belt; something which had given the powers-that-be reason to pause.

Jus was about to find out what.

*

Darkchild sat alone.

Her only stimulus, a methodical, unrelenting chink of repetitive sound: water dripping somewhere. Otherwise, there was silence. No breeze, no scent fractured the absolute stillness. Stygian darkness enveloped her.

Deprived of light, of vision, she focused inward, concentrating on herself – touch the only sense that could be relied on – her hands clasped about her knees, her knees drawn up against her chin. She could *feel* that they were there, but that was all. Her eyes registered nothing.

After a while she started to rock; gently backwards and forwards, clasped knees acting as a counter-balance to her upper torso. She found the sensation soothing, so continued....

*

"That's her?"

Jus stared through a plate-glass window at a small, sterile-looking room suggestive of hospitals and laboratories. The room was clearly built around a single bed, which supported the supine figure of a woman. Young, he noted, and attractive, or she would have been without the plethora of tubes and attachments that sprouted from her body and temples.

McCreedy came up to stand beside him. As always, Jus found his eyes drawn involuntarily to the unruly shock of ginger hair that crowned the man's head, like the crest of some strutting cockerel. A brief glance only, then his gaze returned to the motionless girl.

"That's her," McCreedy confirmed softly.

"And the artefact?"

"It's right there, on the table beside her."

Having been told where to look, he wondered how he could ever have missed the small, metallic sphere. "It seems so innocent, like a trinket or something."

McCreedy gave a truncated laugh, which emerged as a grunt. "Some trinket."

"You're sure it's a weapon?"

"No, but that's our best guess." They stood for a moment longer, each lost in their own thoughts, before McCreedy took a deep breath and said, "Come on, let's get you properly briefed."

Jus lingered to steal a further look at the girl and then followed, being led past the window to a small office where Johnson was already waiting.

McCreedy did most of the talking. "The wreckage was found on one of the larger asteroids. Pure luck it was found at all. It appears to have been a building of some sort – a small station is our best guess. At least, there's no sign of a propulsion system or anything that might indicate it was a ship.

"By analysing the surrounding rock, we've ascertained that the damage was sustained about 2,500 years ago, but we don't know how old the structure itself is. The material is completely new to us and we're still trying to find an accurate method of dating it."

"Any idea what happened to the structure, what destroyed it?"

"Not as yet." Jus sensed that the words were a half-truth, but clearly McCreedy had no intention of sharing anything further.

"The only undamaged item we found – at least it appears to be undamaged – is the artefact."

Jus had studied images of the sphere at length: a dull metallic surface, etched with a series of fine markings, clearly a deliberate design, though whether they represented language or were purely decorative remained a mystery.

"As you've seen, apart from its origins, there's nothing overtly impressive about the thing. It's just an engraved metal sphere. We know it's hollow, but the composition of the metal is new to us and obtaining images of what lies within has proved…

well, difficult. About all we've been able to determine is that it's a mechanism of some sort."

"Durable too," Johnson cut in. "I can't imagine anything that we've built will still be functioning after two and a half thousand years."

"Assuming it is functioning," Jus observed.

"Well it's doing something," McCreedy pointed out. "Dr. Lees' condition testifies to that. Of course, whether that represents it functioning or *mal*functioning, we have no way of knowing."

"Have you tried to break it open?"

"No."

Despite the instant denial, Jus found that hard to believe.

"You must understand that it was very early in our investigations when Dr. Lees…."

"Succumbed," Johnson finished as McCreedy searched for a more delicate phrasing. "She just keeled over while examining the object."

"This might sound like a stupid question, but are you certain beyond any doubt that the sphere's responsible?" Jus wondered aloud.

"Positive. The only reaction she's shown since the collapse was when we moved the sphere away from her, at which point her body went into violent spasms akin to an epileptic fit. No question there's some link, we simply don't understand what. We might yet be forced to break into the damned thing, but we're trying to avoid doing so for three reasons. One, the possibility that anything we do could kill Dr. Lees."

A touching sentiment, but somehow Jus couldn't see the authorities halting research into the first functioning alien artefact ever discovered over concerns for the health of a single comatose individual.

"Two, the consensus is that we're dealing with a weapon here, a means of isolating and entrapping the mind of an opponent, enemy, criminal, or whatever. The military are worried that if we attempt to force the thing open, we might damage whatever mechanism is inside."

Ah, the military. That at least had the ring of truth about it.

"Three, if the artefact *is* a weapon, it might not take too kindly to being tampered with and we've no idea what defence mechanisms it could have. So while we haven't completely ruled out a bit of controlled vandalism, that's being kept as a last resort."

*

Jus digested that, giving the second two explanations more credence than the first. "And Dr. Lees' condition since her collapse?"

"Stable, so far. There's some brain activity but it's all at the autonomic level. Enough to keep her body breathing and the blood circulating but that's about all. The rest of her is simply… somewhere else."

*

Jus stretched out on a bed beside the corpse-like form, with the artefact on the opposite side of her. At his request, it had been moved a little further away. Maybe it would make no difference whatsoever, but distance appeared to be a factor to some degree, so he reasoned that this might weaken its hold over her a fraction. He wanted every possible advantage here, however tenuous.

Since arriving at the station he had been thoroughly prepped and was now as ready as he was ever likely to be.

So why did memory desert him just as the procedure was about to begin? Why, when he was lying beside the comatose woman and about to go under, could he not remember the most important detail of all?

"Her name," he said urgently, "what's her first name?"

"Sara," somebody answered.

Yes, of course, Sara. He slotted that into the appropriate

place within the model he had built in his mind, the mental image of a personality that he held before him.

"*Sara.*" It became the focus, the word uppermost in his thoughts as he reached out...

Jus was a telepath. Almost. He was the closest thing to that mythical mental superman humanity was ever likely to produce. Despite frequent false hopes, true telepathy had continued to be elusive, but a more passive psionic ability had been confirmed: empathy. There were certain individuals who were highly sensitive and reactive to the emotions and moods of others – a process that went beyond simple response to physical and visual clues, but was instead shown to involve a mental reaction to more intangible thoughts and emotions.

The group of genes responsible had been identified and isolated, then manipulated and bred for. At the same time, genes that were thought to act as natural blocks and inhibitors to the ability were eradicated.

Jus was the result.

In certain very rare cases he *was* capable of more proactive mental contact, of a limited form of telepathy, but only with those who carried two or more of the all-important genes he himself was packed with.

Hopes of reaching Dr. Sara Lees now rested on this ability. She carried within her several of the tell-tale genes. In fact, it had been conjectured that this might explain why she succumbed to the artefact when no one else associated with the project had.

Of course, since her collapse, the sphere had been handled with kid gloves and few had gone near it, which might also have been a factor.

As Jus slipped into the trance-like state of focus, he concentrated on her name, repeating it in his mind like a mantra:

Sara...
Sara...

Sara...

Splinters of light. He seemed to be drifting within a sea of fractured vision – moving in a previously inconceivable fashion through jagged, bright, blinding shards of discontinuity. Impossible to gaze upon; impossible to look away from.

Sara...
Sara...

Then he was through the dazzle and the eye-burning glare into what waited beyond: complete and utter darkness.

Sara...

*

Darkchild sat alone.

Until, impossibly, something changed where nothing conceivably could. At first it confused her; this disturbance, this disruption in the harmony, the blankness that was her world. Sound, so faint that initially she was able to ignore it. But the sound grew steadily louder, forcing her to acknowledge its existence, to accept this new thing and embrace it as an element of her world, a new facet of the darkness. But still the sound grew; insistent... demanding... unavoidable.

"Sara..."

She stopped rocking. "Go away," she hurled into the darkness.

"Sara." The sound now hung menacingly close. It had found her.

"What are you?"

"A friend."

She turned the word over in her mind, examining it. 'Friend'.

It seemed vaguely familiar. "What is 'friend'?"

"Someone to talk to, someone to share with, someone who stops you from being alone."

Sluggishly, long unused mental processes began to come to her aid, bringing with them memory, causing her to counter with, "Someone to talk about you, someone to betray you."

"Who to?"

That gave her pause. She turned the question around, grappling with ideas that were not so much new, as long-forgotten. Still she came back to the reality that she was alone. "Friend?"

"Here."

She could sense it now: a nebulous presence, the shadow of a personality. "Where are you from?"

"Home."

Another word with overtones of the familiar; a word that brought with it a sense of warmth and comfort. She tried to think, to reach beyond the darkness, beyond being alone... but failed. And when she turned her attention outward again, Friend had gone.

*

Jus pulled himself upright. A smile creased the corners of his mouth for no apparent reason, perhaps a manifestation of the relief he felt at being back. The first thing he focused on was a curly mop of ginger hair.

"Well, were you able to reach her?" McCreedy wanted to know.

Jus nodded, "After a fashion."

"How do you mean?"

He sighed, pausing to find the right words, words that would convey some sense of what he had just experienced. "She's locked away in a place of total darkness," he said at last. "Mentally, I mean. Nothing else there, nothing at all – there's no light and no sound except for this..." What was it? What had he heard at the fringe of awareness?

"Water," he realised. "The sound of dripping water. That's the only stimulus." He gave an involuntary shudder. "She's completely isolated, and yet *something* pushed me out."

He remembered again the irresistible force that had gripped his mind and ejected him, thrusting him swiftly towards consciousness just as he was starting to make progress. What had done that: Sara? Or the sphere itself?

"But you reached her," McCreedy persisted, oblivious to all else.

"Yes, I reached her."

"Can you bring her out?"

Again Jus paused, considering his answer. "I think so. There was a definite reaction from her; awareness and even a limited dialogue."

He stood up. "Give me half an hour. I need to grab some food and I'll take the opportunity to go through her file again. I'll pick a strong image to focus on, probably from amongst her parent's reminiscences – a memory from her childhood or some other likely trigger. I need to draw her back into herself."

"So soon? You're really that hopeful?"

"Yes. We made progress. I want to build on that rather than let it slip away."

"It's your funeral."

That from Johnson. Jus gave the man a long, cold stare before leaving.

He was tired, but came back as promised. He sensed the importance of a quick return. There was something in that darkness that sapped the will, eating away at the very soul. The longer Sara spent there, the more difficult it would be to retrieve her – Jus felt it instinctively. He was determined to re-establish the link before it faded from her mind.

As he settled down beside her recumbent form, he found his eyes drawn to the artefact, resting so innocently on the far side of her bed. Despite McCreedy's assurances that they had not yet tried to break it open, he wondered whether in fact they *had* made the attempt and failed.

Not that it really mattered. Now was hardly the time for such distractions. Now was the time to concentrate, to reach out and make contact with Sara Lees once more.

Sara...
Sara...

Again he was surrounded by dazzling, fractured light, before slipping into dark, soul-sapping emptiness.

Sara...

As before, he pushed her name out in front of him, questing, straining for a response, the slight tug, the twitch that would herald contact.

Sara...
Sara...

Nothing. Despite all his efforts the dark remained bleak and unyielding, the emptiness unbroken.

Eventually he ceased calling and paused to collect his thoughts and gather his energies. Either Sara was unable to sense him this time or she chose not to hear....

Sara...

Determined not to give up, he sent the ripple of thought ghosting through the darkness again. For what seemed an age he called, at first with increasing desperation and then with growing resignation, as he came to accept his failure. He never once caught a hint of another human soul.

At length he stopped, defeated, and set about returning from the inner to the outer world. He very deliberately allowed his concentration to dissolve, waiting for the familiar relief, expecting to slip back to consciousness... Only to fail at this as well.

There was no glare of lights, no McCreedy and Johnson hovering anxiously... just the all-pervading darkness.

Panic swept over him. He calmed himself, surmising that it was tiredness and lack of concentration that prevented his return. Once more in control he tried again, but failed as thoroughly as before.

And then he sensed something, at the very edge of his mind's perception. Not Sara, but something ghostly, tenuous and intrinsically strange. It was gone before he could be certain of anything. Despite his every effort, nothing else encroached on the emptiness.

Then came the sound. So faint at first that it barely registered, seemingly more the echo of a noise than the noise itself; but once he was aware of it, once his attention became attuned to its presence, there could be no mistake: the monotonous, unrelenting plink of dripping water. Jus had never heard anything more terrifying in his life.

He clasped his knees, drawing a crumb of reassurance from that small human contact, even though it was only with himself. After a while he proceeded to rock, gently backwards and forwards. He found the sensation soothing, so continued.

Darkchild sat alone.

*

It was an older McCreedy who stood by the bedside, his crown of ginger hair now shot through with grey, though it remained as unkempt as ever.

He was talking to Carlton – the latest in an apparently endless line of bureaucrats whose questions were always the same, or at best variations on a theme. By McCreedy's side stood

Henke: a diminutive, frighteningly efficient woman who had joined the project after Johnson left acrimoniously more than a year ago.

The project had become a very different affair, scaled down as events superseded its prominence. A second alien facility had been discovered, one in better condition than their own, and Mankind had finally shaken off the paralysis caused by stumbling across the presence of an ancient alien intelligence within the Solar System. He had moved beyond the asteroid belt, reaching the moons of Jupiter.

Funding had been systematically cut and McCreedy accepted that it was only a matter of time before they were closed down completely.

There was only one bed now. Sara had slipped away one day, the monitors showing that all brain activity had ceased. Perhaps, in a sense, that marked some sort of victory for her; perhaps it had been a deliberate step – an escape from that dark, isolated hell.

The monitors showed that, in Jus at least, life remained. Sanity was another matter; the monitors had no means of judging that.

"You're sure this will work?" Carlton asked.

McCreedy's eyes flicked to Henke, knowing what his answer would have been but hoping that she might offer greater reassurance.

"No," she replied curtly. So much for reassurance. "But we have little choice. He's dying."

"It *should* work," McCreedy muttered.

"It should," she confirmed. "But this is alien technology." A reminder intended purely for Carlton's benefit. "We *think* we now know enough to bring him out, but the only way we can ever be certain is by making the attempt."

"Do it," Carlton instructed after a pause.

McCreedy sighed with relief. It was the authorisation they

had been waiting for.

Ironically, the breakthrough had not come as a result of their own efforts, but through the work being carried out on the second station. Its far less damaged computer system enabled the other team to avoid many of the frustrations and dead-ends that he and his people had blundered into here.

Somehow, the aliens had adapted the asteroid they built upon to supplement their computing capacity, realigning the molecular structure of the very rock around them to provide increased storage and processing capabilities. The experts were still struggling to come to grips with the concept; McCreedy had no intention of even trying to.

Some of the alien language had been deciphered and the ancient systems had begun to yield scraps of the secrets they held. Most of the big questions remained unanswered – who were these ancient visitors to the Solar System, where had they come from, what had destroyed their stations and, most important of all, were they still around? However, amongst the fragments of information that had been recovered was what appeared to be a reference to their artefact.

McCreedy and his team finally had a clue to the sphere's true nature.

"So it's not a weapon, after all," McCreedy murmured, mostly to himself.

"No," Henke agreed, oblivious to the rhetorical nature of the comment.

She spoke in such a calm, neutral manner. Was he the only one who found the truth so very humbling? "A game," she continued in the same matter-of-fact tone, "a mental puzzle – how to escape from the dark."

"An executive toy," McCreedy sighed. "Something to break up the monotony of a routine day – whatever that might mean for *Them* – intended to be no more than a few moments diversion."

He could not suppress an involuntary shudder, causing both Henke and Carlton to look at him sharply.

"I was just thinking," he said by way of explanation, his own gaze fixed upon the figure in the bed before them. "If this is what one of their toys can do to us, to two such fine minds, what would happen if we ever *did* stumble across something they actually designed to be a weapon?"

Neither of them seemed to have an answer to that; nor, McCreedy felt certain, did anyone else.

***

The original version of this one was written way back in the mid-1980s – the closing scene featured a comparison to a Rubik's Cube; that's how long ago! But I was never entirely satisfied with the result and shelved it. For some reason I remembered the piece and dug it out again in 2008, rewriting it extensively. This time around, it seemed to work okay.

As I remember, the original intention was to write a story in which an alien artefact was completely misunderstood due to the limited imagination of its human discoverers; further, I wanted events to demonstrate just how trivial our own intellects might prove to be in galactic terms. The near solar system seemed the natural setting for the story, with the asteroid belt still a potential source of surprises.

A Piratical Sabbatical

You're good, you know that? Well yes, I do realise that's what you're paid to be.

No, really, I wasn't being a smart-ass... sorry. I just never realised it was going to be *this* realistic.

How it all started? At college; the usual vacation-time question: 'what do I do now?' *Everybody's* doing something; even my kid sister's gallivanting around the galaxy with her boyfriend. I wasn't going to sit around kicking my heels now, was I? Then I saw this ad on campus...

What; my parents? They're off on some pampered luxury cruise: auto-masseuse, stimulants-on-tap – the works.

Anyway, so I see this ad: Pirate Experience, the chance to be a buccaneer for a few weeks, how cool is that?

I took the virtual tour and I was hooked!

It was so well put together. We were all taken to this deserted corner of the old space port. Darkness, flickering lights – it already felt brimming over with skulduggery, even before we were in the air.

I didn't know any of the others, which was part of the adventure.

No, I didn't bother asking anyone. Pointless – I knew all my friends were already fixed up. I would have been too, if Marcy hadn't dumped me; the two-faced....

Okay, sorry. We boarded this rickety shuttle, and guess what they piped over the sound system as we took off? Old sea shanties: 'yo-ho-ho and a bottle of rum'. Stewards even came round with mugs of grog. It was all *so* authentic.

We docked with a larger craft waiting in orbit – *The Queen Anne's Revenge*. What kind of crazy name for a ship is that?

Sorry, haven't a clue. I'm not very good with ships... a frigate maybe?

Anyway, we boarded *the Queen Anne* and were each allocated a bunk – not hammocks thank goodness, but still pretty crude.

Oh, I'd say twenty-five, maybe thirty of us. I never bothered counting.

We were divided into groups of four or five and given a rota of duties. One morning it would be minor patch-work and repairs – plenty of those were needed – the next it might be swabbing the decks... I kid you not. If that ship ever had auto-clean, it had broken down long ago, or been switched off especially for our benefit.

The mornings were spent on chores, while the afternoons were reserved for more fun things: gunnery lessons in the simulator – I was particularly good at that – target practice with pistols in the ship's range, even sword-fighting and some hand-to-hand stuff. Never realised there was so much involved in being a pirate, to be honest. It was exhausting but exhilarating.

In the evenings, after dinner, the lights would dim and we'd sit around a holo-fire sipping grog and bumboo from our black-jacks – that's a sort of cup – while members of the regular crew told tales of famous pirates and their exploits.

The crew were great; they had all the jargon and would roar at us to 'avast' and say 'ahoy' instead of hello, stuff like that. There was even the odd 'shiver me timbers'.

And then, to cap it all, they 'discovered' a ship – a big liner, ripe for plundering. We knew what that meant: time for some real piracy. Sirens sounded and everyone ran around. I was assigned to gunnery, since I'd done so well on the simulators.

To be honest, the piracy bit wasn't as much fun as I'd hoped. It was mainly just waiting around. I wasn't involved in actually breaching the cruise-ship's hull – I hadn't done *that* well at the simulators, apparently – but was given the job of mopping up. So when two shuttles launched from the target after it had been breached, I shot them down.

Three shots, that's all it took, and I hit them both. Big explosions. Wham!

Of course I'm proud. It was some shit-hot shooting and it's not as if anyone actually died, after all.

That's ridiculous. What reason would I have for *really* plundering an ocean liner?

Money? Come on, have you any idea how rich my parents are?

Ha, ha, that's a good one – no, of course I'm not trying to bribe you.

Really, Officer, I'm *not* trying to bribe you.

After the raid? Well, the crew were in fine spirits – extra grog all round and lots of singing.

Next morning there were a few sore heads and dodgy stomachs, I can tell you. But instead of our chores we were given these two sealed chests....

Yes, the ones you found us with. We were put ashore at some backwater planet and told to wait, that someone would be along shortly to show us where to bury the treasure.

Well, we waited and waited, until you lot showed up and took us all into custody. I have to say, the way you came screaming down in that cruiser with all those flashing lights and gleaming insignia was quite something – very convincing. The most authentic part so far.

I realise you've done it many times before, this is just another part of the Experience, but even so....

That's ridiculous. My folks are major wealthy. I've no motive for pulling something like this in the real world.

What do you mean 'inheritance'?

The ship we hit? I can't remember. If they told us the name, I missed it.

Golden Star? Sorry, means nothing to me.

My parents' cruise ship? Oh that's good, that's really good. You had me going there for a minute.

Lucky for me I *know* this is all part of the package. None of this is real, right?

Right?

***

This was my second sale to *Nature*, a year after the first. I had never before attempted a piece which was in effect a monologue, or rather one side of a conversation. In this case it was actually an interrogation as told from the victim's point of view.

Ideas that can be effectively condensed into a story of between 850 and 950 words don't occur to me all that often, and I was not in the least certain how a comedy about pirates in space hoodwinking gullible thrill-seekers would be received. Thankfully, Henry Gee again took the story, telling me that to him this read like a Bob Newhart sketch, which was very flattering.

Glitch in the System

The village of Barton Bridge is one of those idyllic little hamlets tucked away in a hidden wrinkle of rural Kent. Those of us who live there have always considered ourselves fortunate to do so, perhaps a little smugly, truth be told. At least, we did; before the eighteen wheelers arrived.

I wouldn't mind if their coming this way made any sense at all, but it doesn't. The whole thing is one hi-tech screw-up.

Yes, I know we're the first village you arrive at when you exit the motorway at junction 9, and I realise we're not a million miles from Cropley – the biggest industrial park in the south east – but if you stay on the motorway until junction 10, there's a dual carriageway that takes you all the way into the site itself.

Until recently, Barton Bridge was a quiet, unassuming village; the sort of place where life pauses and draws a sweet breath before continuing on its way at a calmer, more leisurely pace. The village boasts an excellent family-run butchers' shop, a newsagent which doubles as a grocery store, a particularly impressive Norman church, and two pubs – though only one worth mentioning, the Cock and Bull, which always has a welcoming fire in the winter and an open door to the beer garden in the summer.

Our only claim to fame is a decrepit stone circle on the crown of the hill just to the north, overlooking the church. Every summer, this 'ancient monument' is worth a coach-load of tourists or two, though in truth it's a pretty sorry excuse of an attraction – nothing like Stonehenge or Avebury. *Our* stone circle is so worn away that it more closely resembles the stubs of rotted teeth protruding through the gums of the Earth than anything to be proud of. Why anyone should want to see it, I have no idea. I doubt if many do twice.

Other than the summer coaches, the only non-local traffic we used to see was the occasional tourist who had turned off the motorway on a whimsical impulse, or those who were hopelessly lost. Not any more. Now it's eighteen wheelers rumbling through the village the whole day long. I blame the EU. Until recently, vehicles of this size were not even allowed on British roads. The government took a firm stand over the issue; briefly.

So now these lumbering multi-wheeled behemoths are everywhere, clogging up Britain's already crowded thoroughfares. But why, you may wonder, once they reach our neck of the woods, do they insist on ducking off the motorway early in order to make their way cross-country on roads better suited to a horse and cart?

Sat-Nav, that's why.

The same wonder of modern technology that leads unsuspecting travellers to the edge of precipices and has processions of cars trundling lemming-like across private farm land. Oh yes, I watch the news.

When it's a case of some rich city exec getting mud on the paintwork of his brand new Merc, that's cause for a wry smile, but when it's a stream of juggernauts being misdirected past my own front door, that's another matter entirely.

Five o'clock every morning they start, regular as clockwork. You would think they'd learn; that after coming this way once or twice the drivers would realise there is a better, easier route. Doubtless some do, but not enough.

The problem is that they come from all over Europe, not just this country. In fact, we see more from France, Holland, Germany and beyond than we do from the UK. Presumably that's because the British drivers *do* learn, while their continental counterparts are forced to rely on Sat-Nav for guidance in an unfamiliar country. There is one, mind you, who is definitely British, and he never seems to catch on. Every Monday morning he's the first one through, 5.00 a.m. without fail.

Nobody in the village is immune. In a place this size it's impossible to escape the intrusion. Brenda and Alan, two doors away, have taken to hanging a big banner out of their bedroom window saying "TAKE JUNCTION 10" but it doesn't seem to have made much difference. The Women's Institute have even started up a petition.

Fat lot of good that will do.

The ultimate insult came last week, when one of these warehouses-on-wheels knocked down the sign at the Cock and Bull, which is the very heart of the village. The vicar at St. Thomas's might disagree with me there, but few others in Barton Bridge would.

The sign was one of those hanging ones – the sort that swings from a gibbet-like arrangement, as if to celebrate the fate meted out to the highwaymen of old. All right, so I know the post supporting it has been leaning towards the road for years, and I realise that Jerry, the landlord, has been meaning to get a new sign in any case, but that's hardly the point.

Barton Bridge is simply not the same anymore.

The powers-that-be are aware of the 'glitch' – such a small, neat and inoffensive word for such a major pain in the ass – and have even sent experts to examine the problem onsite. I know, because I've spoken to one of them. It was a few weeks ago. There were these two men wandering around the village with clipboards and the sort of tripods that seem ubiquitous with surveyors and civil engineers. One of them even had a laptop which he perched precariously on the low stone wall that encloses the Cock and Bull's car park.

I sauntered over to wish them a good morning and ask what the hell they were doing – politely, of course. They explained that they were there because of the eighteen wheelers and the 'glitch' with the Sat-Nav. To be honest, I was surprised they needed to come to the village at all. I mean, I'd have thought this was the sort of thing that could be fixed by reprogramming their systems, adjusting the set up or whatever. Apparently not. According to the guy I was talking to, it's not just one company's system that is affected, but all of them; and they've tried adjusting, tweaking, recalibrating, reprogramming and every other 'ing' you can think of, all to no avail.

Then, while investigating the problem, they discovered a peculiar local irregularity, a previously unrecorded natural phenomenon, and some bright spark at head office thought the two things might be related. My new friend muttered something about a "localised aberration in the Earth's magnetic field'."

This sounded like bullshit to me, and I said as much, in a jovial way, adding that I didn't see how any small aberration could affect a system built around satellite triangulation.

He agreed, saying, "Nor does anyone else, to be honest, but something's affecting it, and it's not in the software or the hardware, because all the manufacturers are suffering, and this magnetic peculiarity is the only thing anyone can find that makes this place unusual." He shrugged. "I guess there might be a connection…."

I walked away feeling more disgruntled than ever. If this was the best they could do, we were never going to be free of the eighteen wheelers.

I repeated the conversation to Jerry that evening when I popped into the Cock for a swift beer.

He nodded sagely, as if none of this was news to him. "Well, it's not the first time strange things have happened around here."

This was news to me, but then I'm a comparative newcomer to the village, having only moved here eight years ago. Such a brief residence by no means qualifies me as 'local'. That requires a generation or two at the very least.

"The village is on the Greenwich Meridian, you know," Jerry

told me, as if that explained everything.

I later discovered that he was quite right, but that it explained absolutely nothing. Barton Bridge is situated on the Meridian, or zero longitude, the universally recognised starting point for modern navigation. However, the Meridian is a more or less arbitrary line running between the north and south poles, and it was only agreed upon in 1864, at an international conference in Washington DC. I looked it up on the internet. The Meridian only exists as a convenience, a way of unifying international map references for navigation purposes. So what does that have to do with a natural phenomenon, with a 'localised aberration in the Earth's magnetic field'?

To my surprise, Gwyneth agreed with Jerry. Gwyneth is our local Pagan. She dresses as a Goth, wears scary makeup and runs an online occult store, selling everything from organic herbs and tinctures to hand-crafted jewellery and books with mysterious-sounding titles.

When I mentioned Jerry's assertions and the Meridian's fairly recent historical origins, she smiled and asked, "But why do you think they placed the world's Prime Meridian where they did?"

"Well, because it passes through the main telescope at Greenwich observatory," I replied, remembering what I'd read. "We were a great naval power then, and so…" I began, before realising that I had no idea where my own argument was leading.

"It's because of the ley lines," she said quietly; "the lines of power that criss-cross the country, that underpin the whole world."

I stared at her blankly. I had heard of ley lines, of course, but knew little about them.

"You *did* know that Barton Bridge sits on a major ley line, didn't you — one which follows the same course as the Prime Meridian?"

I shook my head, mutely.

"It runs form the Barton circle all the way to Calmore Abbey, and it's one of the most powerful lines in Britain. Surely you must have known that?"

I shook my head again, wondering why no one had ever mentioned the fact in the eight years I'd been here. Not the sort of thing that crops up in general conversation, I suppose; unless you happen to be chatting with Gwyneth, of course.

"That's why they elected to place the Meridian where they did," she continued. "Not that anyone realised as much at the time, of course. It was all done by instinct, at the direction of their subconscious."

"And you think this is what's causing the aberration that's playing havoc with the Sat-Nav systems and has everyone so baffled?"

"Of course."

Gwyneth speaks with such authority, with such a sense of knowing, that I always find it impossible to doubt her. Even when I subsequently discovered that the whole concept of ley lines – mysterious currents of natural energy thought by some to link historic sites and ancient holy places – was first mooted as recently as 1921, I never doubted her for a minute. I just felt that a little more clarification was in order.

When I mentioned this trivial detail to the lady herself over a neighbourly drink the following evening, she dismissed it with a shake of her head. "No. That might be when we rediscovered the Earth's power, but our ancestors knew all about it centuries ago. Why else would they build so many spiritual buildings on the ley lines?"

This seemed a somewhat circular argument to me, but I wasn't about to voice any dissent.

"Besides," she continued, "the power of the wind didn't suddenly spring into existence when man first built a windmill. A wildflower growing on a mountainside is there whether anybody sees it or not, and the power of the Earth was manifest in ley lines long before we ever thought to look for it. You can't blame the ley lines for modern man being a little slow on the uptake."

This particular man was definitely slow on the uptake: it had only just begun to dawn on me how attractive Gwyneth is.

The conversation gave me plenty to ponder, but it didn't take me any nearer finding a way to banish the eighteen wheelers from the village. It seemed that every time I tried to get to the bottom of what was going on, I just ended up with more questions and possibilities.

Take the haulage companies, for example. As already mentioned, most of the trucks that come our way are from other countries, but a few of them *are* British, including my friend Mr. Five O'clock Mondays.

It's now reached the point where I'm awake by a quarter to five most mornings, in anticipation of that first ground-shaking rumble. I can look out of the bedroom window and watch them go by, so close that it's tempting to open the window and lean out to see if I can touch them.

I've seen the face of the man driving that first lorry of the week: dark haired, moustached, in his thirties, features rigoured by a look of intense concentration. Always the same lorry, always the same driver, first thing every Monday. I finally thought to take down the licence and the company's phone number – emblazoned white-on-green, part of the livery.

The first few times I rang I kept hitting a corporate brick wall. A variety of polite young men and sweet voiced ladies told me on innumerable occasions how sorry they were for the inconvenience caused by the unfortunate routing of commercial vehicles through the village and promised to look into the matter. But nothing seemed to be done and nobody would comment on the specific vehicle I kept giving them the registration for.

That all changed a couple of days ago.

I guess I did raise my voice a little, but under the circumstances, who could blame me? Finally I created enough fuss to be put through to somebody a little more senior than the telephonists: a Mr. Johnston, who proved to be a lot less polite than the staff working under him.

"What the hell do you think you're playing at?" he demanded by way of greeting. "Are you some kind of sicko?"

"What?" I asked, taken aback.

"Coming on the phone and upsetting my girls by constantly throwing the number of Bob's truck in their faces — is this your way of trying to get your own back?"

"I'm not trying to do anything except get a message through to you people to tell the driver of your bloody truck to keep on the motorway until junction 10!" I yelled back indignantly.

"Which is all well and good, except that you and I both know that we no longer have a truck with that registration number."

"Of course you do! It comes charging past my house every Monday..."

"Ever since that particular vehicle was involved in a fatal accident just north-east of Cropley two months ago," Johnston continued, shouting over me. "The driver, Bob Stokes, died on the way to hospital. But then you already know that, don't you!"

No, I didn't, but his words did ring a bell. I remembered seeing pictures of the wreck on the news at the time and thinking that this one had probably come past my house. But it couldn't have been the same one I was phoning about.

"No, you're wrong," I began, but Mr. Johnston had already hung up.

It's now Monday morning, and Jerry should be here soon. I check my watch for the umpteenth time: 4.30. Any minute, in fact.

I'm fed up with finding yet another question every way I turn. The Prime Meridian, ley lines, aberrations, glitches... I still have no idea which of these has led to which others and whether any of them are responsible for the arrival of the eighteen wheelers in Barton Bridge but I do intend to find out, and there is one question I'm going to get an answer to right now; with a little help.

You see, I met up with Gwyneth again at the Cock last night. I was hoping it might be a sort of a date, but we ended up talking about my conversation with this Johnston fellow and Jerry somehow became involved. He'd always wanted to be a policeman before he became a landlord, and still has a few friends who are. He pulled a favour with one, who confirmed that the number I'd jotted down did belong to the truck written off in the fatal accident.

Gwyneth is in no doubt as to what all of this means. It turns out that the place where the crash happened is on the same ley line as Barton Bridge.

Granted that there appear to be some weird forces at play, and that our innocent little village seems to be at the confluence of some pretty strange coincidences, could what I see every Monday morning really be the ghost of a man driving the ghost of a truck along the same route that led to both their deaths? Impossible, surely. It's like some old legend about ghost trains come to life in our sleepy little corner of England.

Gwyneth used the word spirit rather than ghost when talking about the driver, but it's all the same to me.

I had a fair few last night – must have done, because I can't even remember Gwyneth leaving. But I was sober enough to arrange for Jerry to come around this morning. We're going to start getting some answers, aided and abetted by a little item that he showed me in the boot of his car before I went home. He says he bought it off the internet. Maybe he did, though you can never be certain with Jerry.

This was the first time I'd seen a Stinger. American, of course, but it's now the favourite method of stopping a fleeing vehicle for police forces in this country as well. It looks like a concertinaed rubber mat bristling with long metal spikes. Jerry assures me it will stop even an eighteen wheeler. Apparently you just toss it out across the road and wait.

So, no more questions. The answers start here. If Mr Five O'clock Monday is a spirit, presumably his ghost truck will just roll right over the Stinger without stopping and without triggering it. On the other hand, if he isn't, if there is a more mundane explanation and the Stinger brings him grinding to a halt, then we'll have struck the first blow for Barton Bridge in the fight against the eighteen wheelers. In that case, we'll be heroes, with our picture in the local paper. Probably even make it onto the TV.

Either way, it's a start.

I know what you're thinking: do I really believe in ghosts?

Well, if you were to ask me right now, I would have to say… No comment.

You'd probably be better off asking me again in half an hour or so. I should have an answer for you by then.

***

Not so long ago there seemed to be a spate of stories about Sat Navs leading people into ponds or across bemused farmers' land and to the edge of precipices, and that set me jotting down a few snatches of dialogue which then grew into scenes. Somewhere along the line, a few bits and pieces about the Greenwich Meridian filtered forward from the hinterbrain and were caught up in the mix, and the story flowed from there. The result was a quirky little piece difficult to categorise, which makes it difficult to market, so I held it back thinking I'd put this one into my first short story collection… and here it is.

The Battle for Paradise

Lee eased forward, peering ahead and being careful to make no sound. Beside him, Carter did the same. It was early morning. The sun slanted down through sporadic gaps in the cloud cover – arrows of brilliance that illuminated the ground beneath like celestial spotlights, one of which fell conveniently on the glen before them. They crawled with stomachs pressed flat, presenting as low a profile as possible, trusting that any slight movement would be lost against the tree-line.

Trees bracketed their position. Hardy evergreens – green-skirted sentinels of these upper highlands, their spear-straight trunks initially devoid of branches until erupting in frond-laden boughs at about head height. They provided an impressive backdrop to the intended targets.

Lee had always loved the highland landscape, with its impatient brooks and impetuous waterfalls, its rugged patchwork of conifer forest and heather-laden moors that draped haphazardly around rocky knolls and were stitched together by gorse and fern.

This was said to be the last stronghold of the cylathine and was certainly the only place where the legendary beast might still survive, though none had been seen in nearly a decade. There were plenty of pictures of Holmes World's most successful carnivore available on the datanet and a convincing animated model had even been built – convincing to anyone who had never seen the real thing – but the last known specimen had died in a preserve near Poltown. A year before its death, Lee had been taken to see it as a birthday treat by his parents. He marvelled at the ridge of quill-like bristles which could be raised to terrifying effect when needed, and learned that the cylathine was named – or rather misnamed – after a long-dead terrestrial carnivore because of the pattern of faint stripes saddling its back.

As the young boy stood watching, the great wolf-like creature had stared back at him for an instant and he had glimpsed something both majestic and terrifying in its eyes: defiance, wholly alien intelligence, and an enduring anger. Mankind may have captured this beast, but it remained unbowed. The image was one that haunted Lee's dreams for many nights and had remained with him ever since.

Now he was here, in what was said to be the cylathine's last bastion, crawling on his belly over ground still damp with dew. The parts of his body that remained exposed – hands and face – were at the mercy of the bitterly cold wind which whipped across the peaks to scour rocks and cheeks alike, while his own body heat kept his well-insulated torso warm. The pungent aroma of wild flowers and crushed, damp grass struggled to make an impression against the stench of sweat and sodden clothing.

They endured all this in the hope, the expectation, of catching something more than a brief glimpse of the cylathine's preferred prey.

With the decline and probable demise of their only serious predator, the fleet-footed yal were expected to grow less timid and undergo something of a population explosion. Not so. The lithe herbivore remained stubbornly scarce and frustratingly elusive, and no-one really knew why. Some claimed this as proof positive of the cylathine's continued existence; though, as evidence, it struck Lee as circumstantial at best.

By necessity their approach was agonisingly slow, since their quarry was notoriously skittish and nervous. In three days of tracking they had caught no more than distant glimpses and knew this current situation was the best chance they were ever likely to get. Lee prayed that the wind didn't change direction, or his and

Carter's over-ripe bodies would stand out like olfactory beacons to the yals' keen senses.

Slowly, ever so slowly, the pair edged forward.

Patience gained its reward. Grazing not more than fifty paces from them was a herd of yal a dozen strong. At any given moment one or more of the animals would look up, slender ears twitching and nostrils flared, as if aware of the two stalkers, but Lee knew that it was just natural paranoia – a survival instinct that had served them well over the centuries. He was fascinated by the apparently haphazard way the duty of lookout rotated throughout the group. Never were all necks bent to feed at once, yet there seemed to be no formal pattern to the process.

He spared a sideways glance at Carter, to find the older man totally engrossed, the digital binos glued to his face. To be granted this close a view of so many yal together was a documentary maker's dream, particularly one as dedicated as Carter.

Which reminded him of his own responsibilities. He flipped his binos down and started filming, zooming in to pick up ever-greater detail, focusing on an individual animal, watching the delicate, almost prehensile lips as it bent to feel out the tenderest shoots, noting the almost circular jaw movements as it chewed, then catching the blink of a long-lashed eye. He slowly panned out until the whole herd was brought into the field of view; an image which he held, taking the time to simply bask in the wonder of it all.

He was aware at the time of being moved by the scene, of it touching some corner of his inner self, but its impact was to be slow-burning and many years would pass before he fully appreciated its effect.

This world was called Paradise with good reason. Official documents might still call it Holmes World – originally Holme's after the captain of the survey ship which first discovered it – but in conversation, people invariably referred to it as Paradise. It was an unspoiled, idyllic world which boasted tropical rain forests, swathes of tall-grassed pampas and broad-leafed woodland, snow-capped mountain ranges and oceans sprinkled liberally with volcanic atolls and small, sandy-beached islands. But it was the highlands that truly claimed Lee's heart, which perhaps explained why this moment proved to be so much more than just another beautiful memory.

Unfortunately, the moment had little chance to linger, but was instead snatched away even as it arose.

Suddenly the yal raised their heads in concert and froze, all staring in the same direction – off somewhere to Lee's right. For a split second the tableau held before disintegrating, as the animals all broke at once, darting towards the trees and melting into the pine forest. In the blink of an eye the glade stood empty, with no clue that the yal had ever grazed there.

Lee's first reaction was an electric thrill of hope. He started scanning in the direction that had so concerned the yal, praying for a glimpse of tawny striped fur or the suggestion of a powerful form. But no matter how hard he scoured the area, he could find nothing. It was ears rather than eyes that provided the clue. Movement within the trees – something large was in there, just out of sight. Whatever it was, it seemed far too clumsy to be a predator.

Seconds later Carter's heart-felt curse brought confirmation that this was definitely not a cylathine. The older man was already clambering to his feet when Lee saw it. A figure emerged from the trees... no, more than one, a whole squad. Soldiers; infantry on manoeuvres. Chameleonware had masked them at first, making them impossible to spot amongst the foliage. Once they were out in the open they shut down the eye-foxing camouflage, presumably at some unheard command, because all of them shimmered into focus at once and were revealed in full battle armour.

Lee flipped up his binos and stared at them with naked eyes:

metallic silver warriors, their burnished bodysuits glinting in the sun. To Lee they seemed just as magnificent as any cylathine and he could only imagine how terrifying it would be to face such apparitions across a battle field.

Carter apparently failed to view them in quite the same light.

"Hey!" He yelled, moving towards them. "What do you think you're doing? This is a planetary reserve."

If the soldiers heard him they gave no sign but instead continued on their way, heading down the slope in the opposite direction. Without hurrying, they were already out-pacing the fuming Carter, leaving him to trail hopelessly in their wake, powered battle suits propelling them at a rate which no man on foot could hope to match. After a dozen or more futile paces he gave up and came back, still livid and still complaining.

"Why do they have to drill here?"

Because of the open space, the rugged and varied terrain, the unlikelihood of disturbing any people... there were a dozen reasons, all of which Carter undoubtedly knew, so all Lee actually said was, "There is a war on."

Not an easy thing to remember here on Paradise, where the ongoing conflict remained little more than a distant source of gossip – something to pass comment on along with the weather, the latest scandal, and the sports results.

"I know there's a war on," Carter snapped, "but it's a hell of a long way from here, thank goodness. Aren't there enough ugly chunks of rock and swathes of wilderness between here and there for them to march up and down on and blast chunks out of with their macho-weapons, without them bringing it all here?"

Lee was not really paying attention, but instead was straining to watch the infantrymen as they disappeared in the distance, a stray ray of sunshine occasionally striking a silvered suit, causing it to sparkle like some fallen star. He was itching to flip down his binos again but resisted the temptation, knowing it would only anger Carter all the more.

He found his mentor watching him, blue-grey eyes staring with an intensity normally reserved for the wildlife. Perhaps he had seen in Lee's face some echo of the fervour he himself felt in the presence of the yal. Irrationally, Lee felt suddenly embarrassed, even a little guilty, as if caught in the act of doing something illicit.

"Lee, don't be seduced by all of that – the glamour, the adventure…" He had rarely seen the older man so serious. "You and I, we were both born here on Paradise and it's easy to take all this for granted." As he spoke he gestured, encompassing the whole world. "You've no idea how lucky we are, no idea what a ruin our kind has made of just about every other planet we've settled on.

"Why do you think I chose this career?"

Lee shook his head, resigning himself to being lectured at.

"So that I can keep showing people, everyone out there," now he gestured at the skies "what a world *can* be like, what it should be like, so nobody has an excuse for forgetting just how wonderful nature is when she's given the chance.

"There are millions of people ready to go to war, but who's going to fight for Paradise when the time comes?"

Despite himself Lee's eyes strayed down the slope, trying to catch one last surreptitious glimpse of the distant soldiers. He tuned out Carter's voice, no longer paying attention to the words and letting the lecture wash over him, his thoughts and dreams elsewhere.

*

History would remember it as the Great War. Brady would wonder afterwards where the 'Great' had come from; to him it was pure Hell.

Zarnussi Landing had always looked like a tricky operation, but he'd fought through many of those. The plan had been straightforward enough, if unoriginal – *if it ain't broke, don't bother trying to fix it* – the army's unofficial maxim. They landed in three

waves at a carefully selected site, with the shock troops first down
– heavy infantry whose job it was to secure a perimeter and dig
in, establishing a beach-head (a term still commonly used despite
its antiquated meaning). Hot on their heels were the second wave
– more troops and vital equipment: field lasers, small cannon,
rocket launchers and some light armour. The final wave, sent in
only when the landing area was considered secure, consisted of
the heavy armour, the iron fist of the expedition which would
enable them to punch forward and conquer.

Text book stuff. Of course, Brady had never yet come across
a text book which had been written under fire.

The first two stages followed the script. They met some
resistance but it was neither markedly heavier nor lighter than
expected. The troops had dug in, the artillery and light armour
deployed and the third wave given the go-ahead to land.

Word of the disaster reached Brady aboard the orbiting
transport just as the first shuttles were returning to their berths.
The enemy had come up with something new: a pulse weapon of
some kind. It was unleashed to devastating effect just as the third
wave descended. Every piece of equipment above personal field
suits had abruptly ceased to function. The shuttles bearing 'the
iron fist' had dropped like stones. No-one had any casualty
figures as yet, but Brady knew that you could scratch the whole
of the heavy armoured division and he tried not to think about
those poor troops already in situ beneath.

The enemy's counter-attack was entirely predictable. The
landing area quickly developed into a killing field.

He lost his temper with the shuttlebay sergeant and had to
relieve the man of duty before getting the just-docked shuttles
refuelled and ready to go out again.

"I'm sorry, Sir, we have to carry out maintenance…"

"Screw maintenance and get them ready to launch."

"Sir, regulations state…"

Which was when he really swore.

The behemoth-like transport carried three further shuttles which had not been used in the landings. None of them were designed for this sort of job but he was hardly in a position to be fussy. Unfortunately, all pilots *were* already committed to the operation. A quick appeal identified five people onboard with some shuttle-piloting experience. They included Brady himself, which explained why he was now in the co-pilot's seat of an unarmoured craft hurtling into the battle zone, in defiance of at least a dozen different regulations and all dictates of common sense.

"Sunbeam's gonna kill you when he finds out about this," said the diminutive corporal occupying the pilot's seat beside him.

General Augustus Summers had retired to his quarters as soon as the first wave of landings was successfully accomplished, to 'save' himself for later in the campaign when his presence would be more needed. The derivation of his nickname was self-evident. It certainly had nothing to do with the man's disposition or popularity.

"Sunbeam is welcome to do whatever he likes with whichever bits of me make it back, assuming any do."

"Hey, quit being the fazzing optimist, will you. It's my ass on the line as well... Sir."

Brady had to grin at the honorific, so clearly an afterthought. "Corporal Sullah, consider yourself on report for use of inappropriate language."

"Again?"

He glanced across at the corporal, her brow furrowed in concentration as she manually piloted the shuttle, calculating trajectories and dragging every ounce of acceleration out of the press-ganged craft. They had been through a lot together and there was nobody in the army he trusted more.

A piercing siren filled the small cabin. Sullah stabbed a button and silenced it.

"Wasn't that the navigation alarm?" he asked into the

resultant silence.

"Uh-huh. We're about to hit atmosphere and I'm pushing every safety margin anyone ever thought to fit an alarm for."

Exactly as he would have expected. He checked the scanners and saw the other two utility shuttles following in their wake, one with just a single pilot, which was stretching the term 'skeleton crew' to the point where the skeleton was minus a rib-cage and short of a limb or two, but they had no choice. Every second that ticked past represented more lives lost.

Suddenly the going got rough, as they were buffeted by the first traces of the thermosphere. The craft shuddered, stilled for a second and then started to shake more violently and unrelentingly. He knew they were now knifing through the layers of atmosphere – a scalpel slicing an incision into the planet's protective outer skin. The whine of tortured metal and displaced air was audible, even through the insulation, and the cabin grew increasingly hot and oppressive – or was that just his over-active imagination? Another glance at Sullah showed him that the corporal's scowl of concentration had become a grimace and her close-cropped auburn hair glistened with sweat, as her fingers deftly flew across the control board to make constant, minute adjustments.

"I'm taking us in for a high-speed drop," Sullah explained unnecessarily. "So brace yourself for some heavy decel at the bottom." It was a sign of her nervousness – the need to vocalise the obvious. Even veterans were human.

As they came closer the in-atmosphere radio sprang to life, bringing them the chatter of suit-radios, the bark of orders, snatches of up-dates on troop displacement and casualties, desperate appeals for support, the distant hiss and staccato drumming of automatic weapons, the muffled thump of explosions and the heart-wrenching screams of the casualties... the sound of battle, the sound of people dying. His people.

The more robust military shuttles were well ahead, capable of entry speeds that would have been suicidal for them. Going in first, they would hopefully draw the enemy's fire from their own highly vulnerable craft. That was the theory, at least.

They tore through the lowest levels of cloud cover and the site of the battle became obvious. An area that boasted its own spectacular and lethal ground-hugging fireworks display. No sooner had he registered the scene than they were upon it, dropping fast and looking for a likely landing spot.

A light started to flash urgently and persistently – the proximity alarm. A klaxon would undoubtedly be wailing had Sullah not already killed it. They were coming down amidst military shuttles taking off. He glanced at the monitors; too few, way too few. Goodness only knew how many soldiers would never make it back, how many shuttle crews had answered his order to return, only to join the ranks of the dead.

He started trying to second-guess Sullah, searching the monitors for a landing spot.

"There!" But she had already seen it; a patch of ground currently vacant and relatively un-cratered.

They plummeted towards it, Sullah slowing at the last possible second – though not by much, or so it seemed to Brady as they came to a jarring halt. He was unbuckled and out of his seat even before the hatch was blown. The atmosphere was near enough to Earth-normal as to make no difference: a nitrogen oxygen mix with traces of inert gasses, argon predominant.

In passing, he grabbed a snub-nosed 340 from the weapons rack. Pointless really – if the enemy were close enough for him to shoot at, they really were in trouble – but he was infantry and found the familiar presence of a gun in his hand comforting.

Neither radio feeds nor screen image had come close to conveying the reality. They never do. The flash of lasers and blinding flare of explosions, the trail of missiles and counter-missiles lit up the night; a stuttering stroboscope of death. But it was sound that really grabbed your attention – the relentless report of weapons of every calibre and design, punctuated by the earth-trembling thud of explosion.

The one thing eerily absent was the sound of the human voice. Suit-radios carried essential communication, but for the most part the soldier on the ground had enough to do simply trying to stay alive.

A figure materialised out of the night, the faceplate of his body-armour raised so that he could shout, "How many can you take?"

"Forty." The calculation had been made prior to departure, as Brady galvanised engineers into ripping out seating and every other superfluous fitting from the shuttle's interior. The actual figure had been thirty eight.

A ripple of movement in the darkness coalesced into a rag-tag group of hunched and running figures, made almost sinister in the flickering light cast by explosion and flame. Some were stumbling or had to be supported by their fellows.

Brady jumped down to help. The initial soldier, a lieutenant, suddenly stiffened. "Sir, I'm sorry, I didn't recognise…"

"Forget it," Brady interrupted, "let's just hurry these men aboard."

That didn't take long. Fear, shock, pain, anger and resignation were all represented in the parade of faces that flowed past, some of whom he recognised.

"That's forty-one," said the Lieutenant, as they lifted a final pair of wounded aboard. He nodded acceptance of the tally, which agreed with his own.

"We can manage forty-two," Brady said.

"No, Sir. I'll stay with my men."

They both knew what that meant.

The hatch was already dilating. Brady squeezed his way through the packed craft to the cockpit, clambering over and around the wounded and the exhausted.

"Grab hold of anything you can," he called out, realising

even as he said it that there was probably very little left for anyone to hold on to. "This might get bumpy."

Sullah had started to take off even before he reached the seat. The shuttle rose ponderously, over-laden as it was. He buckled in and scanned the screens, freezing at the sight of one of them.

"Missile lock!" he yelled.

Sullah swore under her breath, adding a more audible, "Hang on."

Whatever she had been about to attempt remained an unborn notion, too late to be effected. Afterwards he could never say for certain which awareness had arrived first – the violent, jarring vibration of metal fragmenting around him or the blinding flash of explosion. Then came the pain.

*

He was in a bed, lying supine, with a vague sense that time had passed but no concept of how much. Part of him was surprised to be waking up at all, but the thought was detached and nebulous, the irresistible lure of sleep a blessed relief.

The next time he felt a little more focused. White; everything was white. Fragments of memory, unwelcome and bitter, nagged for attention at the corners of awareness. Assuming this was a hospital, whose hospital was it? Had he been rescued or was he now a prisoner of war? The latter seemed more likely.

His nose itched. He reached up to scratch with his left hand only to discover that no hand was there, nor arm for that matter.

He knew there should be more of a reaction – shock, dismay… but both emotions were as absent as pain. Drugs, presumably. Sleep welcomed him back like an old friend.

His third awakening was apparently induced. A face peered down at him; round, with kindly eyes of darkest brown, framed by a burst of laughter lines. A woman, middle-aged, who introduced herself as Dr. Something-or-other. A second unfocussed figure, white against the white, proved to be a younger woman once his eyes adjusted. She was concentrating on a hand-held diagnostic pad as the doctor spoke. Pretty – the nurse – with sparkling blue eyes and hair tied back beneath a cap, out of sight.

The doctor was speaking to him in calm, clear tones, explaining about his injuries and the treatments he had undergone, but all he could think about was what colour the nurse's hair might be.

Only on the fourth return to consciousness did Brady discover that he had in fact been rescued. Someone he felt he should know occupied a bed beside him. A long, chisel-chinned face that ought to mean something... "Black, isn't it?" he said at last, dredging the name from the recesses of memory. "Captain Black." One of his own officers.

"Yes, Sir, welcome back."

He slowly pieced together what had happened, in part from bits and pieces that the medical staff told him, but largely thanks to Black. He had been brought away from Zarnussi on the final shuttle, pulled from the wreckage by an anonymous soldier and loaded aboard the ship being piloted by the crew of one. Amazingly, a lowly engine-room 'tech with a smattering of flying time had single-handedly flown a shuttle into a battle zone and brought it back in one piece. To her, Brady owed his life.

Mind you, by all accounts it had been touch-and-go for a while. He suffered broken ribs, multiple fractures to the left leg and severe head injuries – the doctors had feared for his right eye. As for his left arm, it had been crushed and burnt beyond any hope of saving.

He could never remember afterwards whether it was Black or one of the staff who first told him about Sullah, that she had failed to make it back.

"We're going to lose, aren't we, Sir," Black said at one point. He meant the war, of course.

"Not because of that pulse weapon we're not."

"No?"

"No. We'll fall back, lose ground – until we either figure out how to block the pulse-weapon or we steal its secrets, at which point the balance will be restored again. Then at some stage we'll come up with a new weapon or tactic and regain the ground we've lost and maybe a little more… until they come up with a countermeasure for *our* advantage, which will mean stalemate again… And so on."

"Will it ever end, Sir?" Black asked on another occasion. Or perhaps it was the same conversation. He was still sedated much of the time and everything tended to blur and merge.

"One day. One day the politicians will patch-up their differences, or perhaps like the rest of us they'll find themselves unable to remember what we're actually fighting about in any case. One day it has to end."

Eventually the time came when he woke up and recognised his thoughts as being at least part-way sane. He found himself alone in a private room and wondered whether Black had existed at all, or whether he had dreamt the entire sequence.

Not long afterwards he was discharged, both from the hospital and from military service – the latter honourably, with commendations and a shiny new medal. The medal had been presented amidst much hoo-hah and public interest at a ceremony the previous day. He attended in a hover-chair, a touch which struck him as ridiculous – it was his arm that was missing, not his legs – but this was a media circus and the powers-that-be insisted. He was permitted to stand, to great applause, only for the presentation itself.

Later, much later, he was to learn that the top brass had been divided over whether to honour him for his bravery or court-martial him for abandoning his post aboard the transport. In the end it was decided they needed a hero more than they needed another disgraced ex-officer.

For reasons that were explained but which he failed to absorb, regrowth was not an option; something to do with the nature of the injury to his shoulder, the damage to nerve and muscle. Of course, he could have been patched up with prosthetics and pressed back into service in some capacity or other, but the simple truth was that such measures made little sense economically. Prosthetics cost, and the authorities had plenty of more pressing fiscal needs.

On the day he left, Sullah's ghost appeared in the mirror as he was dressing.

"So what are you going to do now?"

He shrugged, "Go home, I suppose."

"I thought you said you didn't even remember where home was anymore."

"I didn't. But lately… I've started to remember again."

The image faded and he was left staring at his own reflection. Then, just as he turned to go, a familiar voice whispered, "Brown doesn't suit you, by the way."

He lapsed back into the private world of his own thoughts, reluctantly emerging some time later when drawn out by an uninvited conversation.

"Where are you headed?" asked a fellow passenger in the shuttle seat beside him – a jovial lady of more-than-middle-age and expanded waistline.

"Holmes World."

"Holmes World…" She frowned as if trying to recall an illusive detail. "They call it Paradise, don't they?"

"Yes, yes they do. It's where I'm from." Why had he volunteered that piece of information? It just invited further comment, which was the last thing he wanted.

"Did you lose that in the war?" Her eyes took in the absence of his arm.

"Yes," he said without elaboration, hoping she would refrain from asking anything else.

Suddenly it was Sullah beside him, her image supplanting the over-curious woman. "Poor you; having to leave Paradise to go to war."

"Yes," he agreed a little wistfully. "Poor me."

*

Colonel Lee Brady (retired) found Paradise greatly changed in his absence.

To his complete embarrassment, he arrived home to a hero's welcome – dignitaries, crowds, massed-ranks of media and even a live band playing uplifting and patriotic tunes. Having decided to brand him a hero, the authorities were clearly determined to ensure his celebrity status.

No sooner had he set foot on the planet than offers came flooding in, from after-dinner speeches to exclusive rights to his life story, though most of the latter were only really interested in dramatising his experiences in the war, particularly at Zarnussi.

In many instances the financial inducements were staggering.

His first few days back were a whirlwind of receptions and functions. It took him several days to gather the confidence to say 'no', or even to realise that he could. Only then did he have a chance to catch his breath and reflect. Only then did he have the opportunity to really look at the world he had come home to and appreciate quite how much it had altered.

When he left, the war had seemed far away from Holmes World. Now its shadow loomed ever closer. Not simply due to the increased media coverage but also in people's conversation and general attitude, as well as more obvious physical signs. Lee was appalled by how many of the planet's wilderness regions had shrunk or completely disappeared, being swallowed-up by the expansion of towns and fast-track industrialisation.

The glen where a wet-behind-the-ears youth had once watched a herd of timid herbivores feed was now off-limits, part of an infantry firing range, while the yal themselves were listed as an endangered species and the cylathine had long since been officially consigned to history.

All around there was a far more robust military presence.

Paradise felt like a planet that was gearing-up for war, if not yet under siege.

Lee recalled words said to him an age ago, which at the time had seemed empty and irrelevant. They were spoken by a man whose wisdom he was only now learning to fully appreciate: *who's going to fight for Paradise when the time comes?*

Since waking up in the hospital, Lee had felt trapped in a strange half-life, going through the motions expected of him, existing rather than living. Now that started to change, as the stirrings of new purpose began to germinate deep inside him.

For the first time since Zarnussi, he felt truly alive again.

It was not too late for Paradise. There was still much of the world worth saving, if only people would wake up to what was going on around them. Who better to set the ball rolling than a man whom the whole world seemed desperate to hear from? Of course, the money would also come in handy. He called up the list of latest offers and realised that, potentially, he was a wealthy man. He glanced at the list more closely. Correction: a *very* wealthy man.

Sullah appeared to him again that night. This was the first time he had seen her since arriving home, which he had taken to be a promising sign of progress, but there she was in the mirror again.

"So, you're off to fight another war, are you?"

"Looks like it. Who knows, maybe this one will even have some point to it."

"That *would* be novel," she quipped. "Still, you know what they say: there's always a first time."

Her voice and presence faded, leaving Lee alone with his reflection, which showed an expression he hadn't seen on his face in quite a while.

He was smiling.

***

Ian Whates

Science Fiction is often accused of not being sufficiently optimistic. So I determined to write a story that was. Of course, the best way of making something seem particularly uplifting is to contrast it with something which clearly isn't, and few things are more distressing than war.

The story allowed me to play around with space opera and do a few things which are, hopefully, a little unexpected.

It's About Time!

There were four of us in the briefing room: one doing the talking and the rest being talked at. The man making all the noise was Jansen, although he preferred to be called 'Colonel' or 'Sir'. We had other names for him.

"There are three nexi!" he barked, using the sort of volume most would reserve for cavernous halls in which entire regiments were seated.

Beside me, Reynolds leant across a fraction and whispered, "What's a nexi?"

Unfortunately, there was not an entire regiment present; just myself, Reynolds and Sondra Neergard on his other side. In such circumstances it's pretty hard for *any* communication to go unnoticed.

"What was that, Reynolds? Speak up so we can all hear!"

"Nothing, sir..." he said instinctively, before realising that denial was never going to get him off the hook. "I was just..." Self-consciously, he began again. "Isn't the plural of nexus nexuses?"

Jansen fixed him with a glare that could have toasted marshmallows at thirty paces. "Is it now?" If the look were fire, the voice was pure ice. "How gratifying to discover you can get *something* right. Almost makes me proud to have you in my unit... almost."

The comment was a bit uncalled for, I felt. It was a reference to Reynolds' last mission, which had been less than successful – not through any fault of his, but since when had the keepers of military records allowed a minor detail like that to trouble them?

"It's vital that we take out all three of the *nexi.*" Was the emphasis on that last word just my imagination? The quick glare towards the occupant of the seat beside me suggested otherwise. "Two won't do. Strategy insists this is an all-or-nothing gambit. If one of you fails, all three of you might as well have stayed at home." At least this time he had the good grace not to stare directly at Reynolds.

Any sympathy I might have felt for my unfortunate colleague evaporated as soon as the briefing ended, to be replaced by a sense of envy. Not that he would have noticed. He was too busy being consoled by the voluptuous Neergard, who really ought to have had better taste. I feigned indifference and headed for Supply.

The place was its usual chaotic self – an incomprehensible jumble of equipment and clothing, apparently arranged in accordance with the whim of some deranged eccentric. Costumes and outfits of every imaginable colour, material and style overflowed from rails and peeked around the edges of bulging cupboard doors. There was an entire wall racked with hand bags, shopping bags, briefcases, attaché cases and suitcases, many crammed into slots too small to accommodate them. A table just inside the door held the dismantled parts of at least four guns from as many different eras and an amorphous pile of dark material heaped beside the reception desk proved to contain an assortment of crumpled black and brown business suits, presumably discarded following some mission or other. A suit of full armour stood behind reception, staring at me with blankly.

Supply always reminded me of a strange amalgam between a major film studio's costume department and a spoilt brat's play room.

"We're a bit short on 17th century clothing," the insipid clerk explained once I succeeded in dragging his attention away from a tray of wrist watches that were apparently the most fascinating thing in the world. Now there was a surprise; I had yet to discover an era for which they were *not* short. Though, in truth, I reckon that all they were ever really short of was an organised system.

In the end I settled for an all-concealing overcoat – black, since I was scheduled to be dropped at night. This time out it was just a quick hit and run, so there would be no need for detailed authenticity... I hoped.

The clerk flipped the seal on a small container and I took the proffered infochip, reaching round to the back of my neck to press it into a vacant portal. The module was a half-sensed presence at the back of my mind, a reservoir of knowledge eager for release. A whispering trickle threatened to leach out, but with a conscious effort I suppressed it until needed.

Just as I was preparing to leave, Reynolds and the fickle Neergard sauntered in to be kitted out, laughing.

"Hey, what's the rush?" Reynolds asked, sociably.

"The Colonel said immediate departure, remember?" I snapped, more peevishly than intended, but what the hell? Before he could reply, I was gone.

Kleb was on duty at the gate; his tall, thin frame folded into the operations chair. A raised eyebrow was the closest he came to a greeting. By his standards that was almost a show of affection. Other figures hovered in the background, absorbed in their work and ignoring me completely. In stepping onto the plate I was subjected to a scan, which read my mission chip and automatically calibrated the gate. The operator passed his spread palm over the trigger sensor and I was on my way.

One thing you could always count on with Kleb was a quick departure – no chance of being delayed with any frivolous banter when he was on duty.

1675. The 17th century is not really my bag. To be honest, any period that is PDS (Pre-Decent Sanitation) I could happily live without. Even at night, the place stank. I checked my watch: right place, right time. Well done the Tech boys. They never had let me down yet but I always felt a huge sense of relief at arriving safely. Now for that infochip.

The town 'Northampton' was first referred to by the Anglo Saxons, circa 913. In 1086 the Domesday Book records 300 houses and as many as 2,000 inhabitants. National Parliament was first held in Northampton in 1131...

For Time's sake! There was enough background here for a years-long deep cover mission. This was supposed to be hit-and-run, a quick in and out, not an educational excursion. Someone in Tech must have been bored, or perhaps this was their idea of a laugh – 'let's see how much irrelevant garbage we can cram onto a single mission chip.'

While rifling through the mass of information for the bits that were actually useful, I silently vowed a variety of slow and painful tortures on the culprit upon my return.

It was pitch-dark. There were no street lights in this period; not that I had a problem seeing into the infra-red. The streets were incredibly narrow. That, combined with the over-ripe stench, created a genuine sense of oppressive claustrophobia. The streets were also completely deserted. I wondered if some sort of curfew might be in force and consulted the infochip. It had nothing on the subject, predictably.

At least it gave me the right address: St. Mary's Street. The drop had been calculated perfectly, depositing me almost on top of the target. I let myself into the cottage. The room was empty, the open fire untended. It sputtered listlessly, as if preparing to go out, which would never do. This sorry excuse for a conflagration seemed an unlikely source for the Great Fire of Northampton. Of course, that was where I came in.

The equipment this time around was unsubtle and fairly brutal, which suited me just fine. I unshouldered the gun, held it level and squeezed the trigger. The backwash of heat as the jet of flame shot forth was glorious. I played it over the fire and surrounding wall: dry and timber-built, so it caught nicely.

I strolled back down St. Mary's Street, the gun slung nonchalantly over one shoulder. There was no indication of an alarm being raised as yet. According to the infochip the fire was destined to spread quickly and dramatically, causing widespread devastation – killing eleven people and destroying two-thirds of the town. Looking again at the way the houses were crammed so closely together, it was no wonder.

I paused to take my bearings, the chip providing me with a remembered map that had never been seen by my own eyes. There seemed to be churches everywhere. That would be St Mary's closest to me… While over to the left, that could only be the Church of the Holy Sepulchre: a round church – even from here the curve of its walls apparent. I needed to be heading right.

As promised by my augmented memory, All Saints Church stood close by and came quickly into view. History stated that the church would be ravaged by the fire, but I never had a problem with giving history a helping hand. This time I used the widest setting, playing the jet of flame across the front of the church. It caught nicely.

Satisfied, I turned and strode away.

The satisfaction lasted only until I arrived back at Central, where things were decidedly tense. Jansen scowled at me as if I were personally responsible for whatever was amiss. "It looks as if your friend Reynolds is determined to be a screw-up all his life."

He indicated the swirling and ever-changing dance of holographic figures and equations that occupied the centre of the room: the TARDIS.

Quite why it was called the TARDIS I have no idea. Its operators are a breed apart – bio-enhanced intellectual freaks, genetically bred for their role and universally referred to as Strategy. I once asked one of them about the name TARDIS.

"It's always been called that. The name goes back centuries. It's an acronym," he assured me.

"An acronym for what?" I persisted; rather logically, I felt.

"Time something-or-other," he said. It was at that point I became convinced that *nobody* knew where the name had originally come from or what it actually meant.

Now Jansen pointed at the high-tech mystical swirl and said, "See!"

No, I did not, as he well knew. I had never been able to interpret anything displayed by the TARDIS. I was aware of what it was supposed to be – a computer-generated model of the ever-changing consequences and developments resulting from our tinkering with events up and down the time lines – but reading it was another matter. The only thing I had ever gained by staring at that pulsing column of light was a headache.

So quite why he was now directing my attention to the display was anyone's guess.

"No change," he growled. "No sign of Reynolds, either, and he should have been back by now."

That was worrying. "Do you think he met with some Opposition, sir?"

There was Opposition, you see. Nobody knew who, what or when from, but missions had been interfered with and on occasion foiled. The most popular theory was that they were from our future, determined to balk specific missions which they deemed detrimental or undesirable. I was far from convinced. The interference seemed too disorganised and not effective enough for that. Dissidents seemed a far more likely explanation; some sort of temporal terrorists.

"How the hell should I know?" Jansen answered my question. "You can tell me when *you* get back."

"Me?"

"Who else do you think I'm talking too?"

Back-to-back jumps were unusual but not unheard of.

Neergard had trained as a Tech before choosing active service and she once told me that back-to-backs were not a good idea, that they screwed you up both mentally and physically. A cheerful thought to take with me as I headed towards the gate for a second time.

2175; five hundred years after my last visit to Northampton. The place had changed a bit.

I took no chances going through, sending two disks ahead of me; one set for sonics and the other loaded with a quick acting gas. Disks are a bit like grenades but more sophisticated – less messy and reusable apart from anything else. I counted down the seconds and then stepped into 2175.

Nobody lay comatose at my feet, but a little way off two figures, a man and a woman, were clambering onto some sort of hover-bike. As I looked more closely it was obvious that the girl was unconscious, or virtually so, and was being helped on by her companion. They were dressed in similar fashion to me, though a little less conservatively. For once Supply had come up trumps and I was properly kitted out. This was a really cool era for clothes, though I could have done without the tubing attached to my head and was less than convinced about the haircut.

Even as I watched the man leapt onto the bike, which swept away at impressive speed, carrying the pair around a corner and out of sight.

They had obviously been caught by the disks, or at least the girl had been. Were they waiting for me, lying in ambush, or just in the wrong place at the wrong time? Difficult to say and not something I could afford to waste any time worrying over. The incident just made me all the more determined to complete the mission and be gone as quickly as possible.

The streets seemed as deserted as they had been 500 years earlier. This time the mission chip *was* able to confirm a curfew, which spoke volumes about the prevailing political climate. It also made the presence of two casual bystanders all the more unlikely.

I retrieved the two disks and strode on towards my target, which loomed in front of me.

Northampton's Guildhall is a magnificent building; not that I was there to admire the architecture. Thankfully, *this* mission chip had been more efficiently programmed than the last and refrained from attempting to tell me what the architect might have had for breakfast.

I carried a gun – I *always* carry a gun – but this was going to take a little more than a simple hosing down with flames; the Guildhall would need to be hit from the inside. They had security, of course, but our counter systems were from an age they hadn't even dreamed of yet. I entered without a problem.

The place was even more impressive when viewed from the inside, but I refused to be distracted.

The incendiary devices we use are real beauties. They spray fire everywhere in no time at all, yet when they go off, the sound *im*plodes. They're not completely silent, but they are oh-so quiet. Three were needed here. The chip supplied me with precise delivery points.

As I walked away I half heard, half felt, the muffled whumpf of their implosion. Flames were licking out of the doomed building even before I vanished.

Things seemed no less tense back at Central, despite my success.

"No sign of Reynolds?" was the sum total of my greeting from the Colonel. Not that I had expected a pat on the back or anything.

"No, sir." It had never crossed my mind to try looking for him. For one thing I had no idea where to start and for another the mission took first priority. To go off searching for a missing comrade was liable to get me court-martialled. I told Jansen about the pair who had probably been waiting for me. He grunted but made no direct comment.

"We need to hit all three nexi," he growled. "Neergard's also gone awol. You're gonna have to complete her hit as well."

Hardly a surprise, but not exactly welcome news either. Two jumps on the trot were irregular; three would be breaking just about every rule in the book, which was unlikely to bother Jansen under the circumstances. But after two I was already a bit disorientated; a third would be just begging for a bad case of time lag.

"September 30th 2015," he said. "Here's your target." Unusual: he normally left this sort of detail to the mission chip.

The image of a building materialised in the air before him and I understood his decision to employ the personal touch. It was a surreal moment. "That's the Guildhall," I blurted, wondering whether I was already time lagged. "I've already hit it."

Jansen knew exactly what I meant. If something had still existed to be destroyed in 2175, how could any mission to take out the same object in 2015 possibly succeed?

"They rebuilt it."

"Rebuilt it?" Was parrot-like repetition a symptom of time lag?

"Why not? It's a glorious building. Of course they'd want to restore the thing. Assuming the 2015 mission succeeds, that is. And it *must* succeed."

"Why is it so important?" Time lag, definitely. Nothing else would prompt me to question a mission, or forget to call Jansen 'sir'.

He glared at me. "You're supposed to be a soldier, aren't you?"

"Yes, sir!"

"What do soldiers do?"

"Obey orders, sir."

"Right." He turned away, dismissing me in the process.

Except that this proved to be one order which I failed to obey. Oh, the intention was there when I left Jansen, but on the way to Supply it was hijacked by sudden realisation.

I headed straight back to the gate, bypassing Supply. Kleb looked up, clearly surprised to see me yet again.

"I need to arrive on location an hour before the time designated on the chip," I told him, stepping up onto the plate. In my haste to report to Jansen I had neglected to return the previous mission chip, which still whispered at the base of my skull.

"Not a good idea," Kleb assured me as he read the codes and realised I was intent on jumping back on myself. "Time paradox." From him, this amounted to a major speech.

"Don't worry; I'll be careful not to get too close when my earlier self comes through."

He hesitated but then shrugged. "It's your funeral." With that he turned back to his screen and made some minor adjustments before sending me on my way.

Nobody was in sight on this occasion. The Guildhall stood ahead, as imposing as ever, but the two on the hover-bike had yet to appear. I walked forward towards the corner which memory told me the bike would vanish round. Sheets of thin paper that might have been newsprint or perhaps wrapping-material blew across the road, bisecting my path. The wind buffeted me – its intermittent howl and my footsteps the only sound. Whoever enforced the curfew did so vigorously enough to ensure results. There was not a soul about. It was eerie, unsettling, as if I were treading through some ghost town; a world cleansed of all life.

Once around the corner I started to look for somewhere to wait, to hide, finding this in a stairwell that led down to a door at basement level. At last, a sound; a low hum that seemed to emanate from behind the door. Changes in pitch and modulation were almost rhythmic and suggested this might be somebody's excuse for music. I accessed the mission chip but its parameters didn't stretch to information on anything so esoteric. Forget the curfew; if this *was* what passed for music, then the citizens of the 22nd century had my sympathy.

I crouched lower, making sure my head was below street level as a light swept the pavements. Impressive: the beam ranged into both infrared and uv. It emanated from a broad, wedge-shaped car that cruised down the street, ominous in its near-silence. I didn't need to see the black and white insignia to realise that this was either a police or military patrol.

It was the only vehicle that disturbed the night until the appearance of the hover-bike. Even the droning from behind the basement door ceased, mercifully, leaving emptiness in its wake.

Finally, with a low-pitched hum and the gentle swish of displaced air, the bike shot past me. I waited until it was out of sight before leaving my hidey-hole and edging up to the corner.

The couple were already off the bike and standing close to the spot where I would appear. There were no weapons in sight, which was reassuring. Right on cue a shimmer reminiscent of a heat haze manifested in the air directly in front of them. Then my two disks came sailing through.

"Shit," I heard the man exclaim.

My augmentations blanked out the sonics and the gas from the other disk was odourless and invisible, so there was nothing dramatic, just the sight of the girl suddenly wilting.

He caught her as she fell and started to half-drag, half-support her as they stumbled back towards the bike. Time for me to retreat to back to the stairwell.

I reached it bare seconds before they came tearing back round the corner, at which point I stepped out into the road. The bike juddered to a halt a few paces from me.

"Hi, Reynolds. Is Sondra okay?"

He blinked but to his credit took my sudden appearance in his stride. "She'll be fine. Just caught a whiff of the gas."

I glanced over his shoulder. "We'd better move away from here. I'll be emerging to take care of the Guildhall any second. Then you've got some explaining to do."

With Neergard semi-conscious and slumped on the bike, we

walked rapidly away, turning the first corner we came to so that both concrete and distance lay between us and the Guildhall. As we walked we talked, or rather he did. Sondra was threatening to throw up, so I gave her a snort of something to counteract the gas.

It turned out they had rented a place not far away.

"We wanted to be as near to the entry node as possible," Reynolds explained. "Didn't want to be in the open at night longer than necessary – there are patrols out, enforcing the curfew."

"I know. I saw one."

We made it back to theirs without incident, with Sondra more or less fully recovered by the time we arrived.

"So you're *eloping*?" I still could not quite believe it.

They nodded gleefully. Sondra was perched beside him, clinging to his arm, and the pair of them grinned at each other like love-struck teenagers.

"You know how it works, Jansen would have had one of us transferred out if we'd let on that this was anything more than just casual." She was right. Relationships were not exactly encouraged but they were tolerated, as long as there was nothing serious… as long as it was just sex.

"We've wanted a way out for a long time," Reynolds explained. "We're sick of it – all the tampering and tinkering with the past, being sent here and there without explanation, without knowing why or even what we're supposed to be achieving. I know you feel the same, we've talked about it." True, but I had never considered deserting.

"And you were coming to intercept me just to say goodbye?"

"To ask you to join us. We knew that when I failed Jansen would send back-up and, with things as stretched as they are, it was going to have to be you. Then the disks came through and we thought that maybe we'd guessed that bit wrong."

"So you panicked and ran."

"Yeah."

When I came through the first time and saw the pair escaping, Sondra had been facing away from me as she was helped onto the bike, while the elaborate collars and tube-attachments this era favoured had obscured Reynolds' face. Besides, my mind had been on other things and I would have expected to see him alone if at all, not with a woman. Only later, back at central, did the pieces fall into place and the small clues of familiarity crystallise into recognition.

"We had an arrangement with Kleb," Sondra explained.

What? "You bribed him, you mean."

She shrugged, "If you like." Kleb was bribeable? Life was just full of surprises. "We had to wait until we were both assigned missions during his shift."

"So you got him to send you to 2175 after Reynolds instead of to 2015."

She nodded. "We were desperate to vanish, to find a time and just disappear together." Again the shared, goofy grin. "This is as good a time as any. We've dummied up some IDs and are working at getting something more permanent."

"They'll come after you, you know. When things at Central have calmed down a bit, they'll come to see what happened."

Reynolds laughed. "We've a whole world to hide in."

"But they'll still find you."

Sondra shook her head. "Not without the mission chips — that's how they keep tabs on us and we destroyed ours as soon as we came through."

Cold realisation stabbed at me. "I've still got mine."

Which is when it hit us.

The idea is that jumps should be initiated at specific points, or nodes, but people can be grabbed from almost anywhere, just with less reliability and greater discomfort than at a proper node. I don't pretend to understand the technicalities. You want specifics? Ask Neergard — she's the one with the Tech training.

This was a real doozie. A wave of agony washed over me, as if I were being pulled apart or maybe turned inside-out. I knew what it meant. Central had found us through my mission chip and were now pulling all three of us in to face the consequences of desertion. How could I plead innocent? After all, I was supposed to have gone to 2175. Idiot.

By the time it ended I was beyond caring where or when I was. Accumulated time lag and the effects of an off-node jump left me praying for a swift death to escape the agony. Somebody took my arm and pumped it with a subcutaneous micro-spray. I started to feel better almost at once and was able to focus, finding Neergard grinning down at me.

"Now we're even."

"Thanks."

Grass; I was lying on grass. I sat up to see ferns, huge ferns all around and beyond them... trees. The place smelt of damp earth and there was the background buzz of life – the sounds of insects and maybe birds. Okay, so perhaps I was not at my sharpest, but even so, this did not look like Central.

"Kleb must be tidying up, shunting us off to some forgotten corner of time in an effort to hide his tracks," Reynolds concluded.

"When are we?"

He frowned, thoughtfully. "Paleolithic. Probably Middle Palelolithic, I'd say."

"Oh, great. Thanks, Kleb."

Then he laughed and beamed a big grin in Neergard's direction. "Well, we wanted to hide away somewhen they'd never find us."

The role of gooseberry has never greatly appealed to me, and the prospect of playing it to love's young dream when the only other females on the planet are Neanderthals would have been enough to drive anyone to despair. Except that Sondra had not responded to Reynolds' enthusiasm by going all doe-eyed and moon-faced, far from it. Instead she was efficiency-in-action, unclipping a small compartment on her belt and taking out a familiar-looking flat container.

"I thought you said you both ditched your mission chips."

"We did." She batted her eyelids at me in mock-innocence. Bad move; it brought back memories and I felt the jealousy start to stir again. Then she was grinning a conspirator's smile. "I trained as a Tech, remember? This is a pirated chip, one of several we smuggled out."

"We've been planning this for a while," Reynolds added.

Neergard took out the infochip and was already reaching behind to try and insert it into her neck portal. "Help me with this, would you?"

I smoothed down a ruffed collar and pulled away a tube that had been so essential in 2175 but looked ridiculous now. It clung stubbornly to her skull, abandoning its hold with a reluctant 'pop'.

"Ow!"

"Sorry."

The chip was finally in.

"We didn't want to be stranded if things went wrong in a particular era," Reynolds explained, "so we came prepared."

I stared first at him, then at her. Sondra's eyes now sported the unfocused glaze of somebody who has accessed a chip and is assimilating a lot of information, fast.

"I don't believe it," I murmured. "You've brought the full specs for a gate, haven't you?"

Reynolds winked. "Yes, among other things... A few essential parts, for example"

"Of course, I remember now," Sondra muttered, half to herself. "The only tricky bit will be coming up with a power source."

I began to smile as realisation dawned. No wonder the Opposition had always seemed so fragmented and disorganised.

After all, there were only three of us… so far.

***

In 2005 Ian Watson and I, along with some other members of the Northampton SF Writers Group, organised NewCon 3, a science fiction convention in Northampton. The event was themed on 'Time' and while preparing for it, I rattled off a story of around 2,000 words. This was intended as a deliberate homage to the old time travel stories I used to love, by the likes of Isaac Asimov, Poul Anderson and Fritz Leiber. I also threw in nods towards a couple of TV shows and a more recent author of such stories, Connie Willis.

The piece appeared on the NewCon 3 website, with a staged ending thrown in to promote the convention.

Later, I revisited the story, rewrote it, ditched the ending and continued the tale, more than doubling its length in the process. The result was "It's About Time", which appeared in the first NewCon Press anthology *Time Pieces*, a volume published as a fund raiser to cover the debt left by NewCon 3, which, ehem, far too many people failed to attend, missing out on a treat!

The Laughter of Ghosts

Everybody had forgotten about the Ghurkhas; everybody except Anthony.

Perfectly understandable, of course. The British government had wanted them withdrawn and disbanded years ago – too expensive. Besides, what was the point in maintaining a military presence in Brunei these days? Well, there was always the oil, but apart from that?

It was the Sultan who wanted them to remain. He trusted them more than his own troops and for some reason being so closely linked to Britain and Her Majesty's forces still carried a lot of prestige in that part of the world. So he offered to pay for them out of his own pocket.

How could anyone refuse an offer like that?

So there they were. A highly efficient and lethal military force, part of the British army, recruited from one foreign country and paid for by another. Now that is bizarre. Hardly surprising they were overlooked.

Britain had recalled most of her troops in an effort to defend the sovereign Isle, but everything had happened so fast and some units had simply not been able to respond in time. The Americans' first priority had been to mop up such far-flung forces. There had been some heavy fighting but weight of numbers and superior hardware told in the end. There were still rumours of British troops continuing to fight a guerrilla action here and there, but most had quickly capitulated or been taken out.

To all intents and purposes, the war was over. Britain had

fallen in a little over two weeks. The French were already submitting tenders for a share of the rebuilding work.

Only in Brunei had any sizable force escaped attention. The Americans relied on intelligence provided by the CIA, which proved to be a God-send. The Ghurkhas did not appear on many of the regular military lists – payroll for example – and it seemed that someone at Central Intelligence had skimped on their homework.

Anthony, who had been responsible for liaison with the Ghurkhas during his posting to Brunei, thought of them as soon as news of the invasion broke. He had watched everything closely from afar – no war could be fought in privacy anymore, every move was monitored and reported by the media, every decision discussed and dissected. He used his own position and contacts to fill in the occasional blanks that the media missed.

Nobody had remembered the Ghurkhas in Brunei.

He determined to act independently and made a point of avoiding all official channels, having no idea which might be compromised and no way of knowing whether any of them at all were still valid for that matter.

He slipped out of Singapore just ahead of the world-wide sweep to round up every senior British diplomat and place them under armed guard for their 'own protection'.

His wife and two children, one little more than a babe-in-arms, had already gone to stay with her mother. She was Malayan and they would be as safe with her as anywhere.

While waiting at the airport he caught a glimpse of a newscast by the US President. Anthony was too far away to hear individual words but could make a reasonable guess at the message in any case. Doubtless the propaganda would be delivered with all the conviction and heart-felt sincerity for which the man was famous.

*

It was odd coming back to Brunei. Like stepping into another world; a tranquil paradise where the upheavals of the outside were no longer relevant, could not possibly be real. The temptation to stay here and simply vanish was seductive and had to be consciously set to one side. He could probably do it, too. He still had many friends here, locals and expats. He could pick up the threads of his past life and disappear, leaving the world to go hang itself.

For how long, though? Only until reality came crashing in – which it would, eventually.

No, there was little point in playing ostrich by ignoring what was going on. Anthony headed straight for the town of Seria, just outside the Bruneian capital, where the 700 or so Ghurkhas were stationed. With him he carried his kukri, the wickedly curved fighting knife which had earned such a fearsome reputation in operations around the globe. His had never seen service. It had been a gift from the officers of the Ghurkha battalion, a sign of friendship and respect – both of which he was fully prepared to call upon if needed.

In the event, they were not. He was escorted directly to a Ghurkha in colonel's uniform. Instant recognition and smiles all round. Prakash, someone he knew well, thank the Lord.

It emerged that the Ghurkhas had been left here in a vacuum for weeks. No orders, no direction and no ideas. Some had deserted, heading back to their native Nepal when it became clear the British cause was lost, but most had stayed on. These were a fiercely loyal and honourable race.

Impotent and frustrated, they watched developments with dismay, not knowing how to respond. They were as pleased to see Anthony as he was to see them and no one chose to dispute his authority. They were also ready to leave at a moment's notice.

Quite why they should be so patriotic to a country not their own was a mystery to anyone who took the trouble to wonder about it. After all, the British had used Ghurkhas as front line troops for decades, throwing them into one hot-spot after another, all the while proud to count them as part of the British army. Until they were either injured or retired.

A former Ghurkha received a pittance, somehow falling outside the normal benefit package available for regular soldiers. Of course, ministers would quote you the reasons for this if pressed. As far as Anthony could recall, they boiled down to two:

1. The British government could not afford the enormous cost involved.

2. The standard of living is completely different in Nepal, so the usual benefits package is neither required nor appropriate.

While granting there was some validity to the second argument, it still smacked of convenient rationalisation to Anthony, who considered their subsequent loyalty a miracle.

The first moment of tension arose at the airport, as they were boarding to leave. A Bruneian official raced up in an open-top jeep with a handful of regular soldiers, demanding they should stop. Two trucks tore up behind them, disgorging more troops.

It was a surreal tableau. On the one side, a hastily gathered squad of visibly nervous soldiers, doubtless wishing they were anywhere else but here. Facing them: a brigade of Ghurkhas, bristling with weapons and itching for a fight.

The ironic part, of course, was that both sides were paid from the same purse.

In the end Anthony and his men were allowed to leave without needing to resort to violence. Frothing at the mouth he may have been, but even the Bruneian official was forced to concede that there was very little he could do to stop them. Just as there was little Anthony could do to stop the Bruneians reporting everything to the Americans. He could only hope they would choose not to – relations between Britain and Brunei had always been pretty good... Mind you, no British official had ever turned up unannounced and walked off with their Ghurkhas before.

That only left the American spy satellites to worry about.

Anthony knew full-well how effective they could be. He also knew their limitations. The Yanks could not be watching every inch of the planet's surface every second of the day, and right now there were plenty of other things going on around the world to occupy their attention. He hoped.

Nor did it seem an unreasonable hope when you considered that, for all their technology and much-vaunted resources, the Americans had failed to notice a whole force of Ghurkhas. God bless the CIA.

Once they were airborne, Anthony had a chance to stop and reflect on what he was doing, to ponder exactly what had prompted him to take such a direct course of action. After all, he was a diplomat, not a soldier. The only battles he had ever taken part in were fought with words and wits rather than bullets and missiles: potent in their own sphere, but hardly credentials for this sort of undertaking.

It had been a news report – the proverbial straw wreaking mischief on the back of an over-stressed camel – a live broadcast direct from London. Even now he could clearly recall the image of General Weiskopf straddling the steps of St. Blair's, eyes invisible behind designer shades, which themselves were shadowed by his pristine camouflage helmet, the unbuckled straps of which fell down each side of his face and bounced disconcertingly as his jowls worked. The General was announcing to the free world that he and his boys were "proud to be instrumental in liberating the oppressed peoples of Great Britain."

He made a great deal out of his having personally witnessed men and women weeping in the streets as American soldiers sauntered past. An unequivocal display of joy and gratitude, or so the General maintained.

Of course, strictly speaking it was only England and Wales that had been 'liberated', but the Americans had even more trouble differentiating between England and Britain-as-a-whole than the English did.

The horrifying images of kilted highland regiments leading the charge against the barricades at the Houses of Parliament, like berserkers of old, were etched indelibly on his memory.

Anthony had always liked the Scots. Why, some of his best friends were Scottish.

He never had grasped the depth of resentment that some Scots nursed towards the English. He knew it was there, but had always thought it little more than good-natured rivalry, given lip-service without actually being adhered to. It was a shock to discover how much more it meant to some.

Conversely, while Scotland declared for the Americans, Wales stood firmly by her ties to England within the United Kingdom, suffering some of the heaviest bombing as a consequence. Northern Ireland stayed out of it, but then they had their own problems, what with the emergence of the New Irish Republican Army.

Despite their name, the NIRA had little in common with the old IRA, but since when had such details ever troubled the opportunist?

Rumours of funding from the States had yet to be substantiated.

Anthony's thoughts ricocheted back to the present. If someone in Brunei did contact the Americans, so be it. He was taking his Ghurkhas to the one place the Americans would never dream of looking. He intended for them to attempt the unthinkable and achieve the impossible. Someone had to strike a blow for Britain. He wondered whether history would remember him as a hero or as a ruthless terrorist. That would all depend on who got to write the history in question, presumably.

When he first set out Anthony had no definite objective in mind beyond reaching the Ghurkhas before someone else remembered them, giving little thought as to what he actually intended to do with them. But during the flight from Singapore a course of action had begun to suggest itself. By the time he landed in Brunei, this had become a fully crystallised agenda.

This whole situation was monstrous; something had to be done. If he remembered his fables correctly, the best way to kill a monster was to strike off its head.

In this instance, that meant killing the President of the United States of America.

*

Air traffic in and out of the USA had continued to build throughout the new millennium. Of course, with all the uncertainty of war it had tailed off a little recently, but not by much. After all, the war itself was such a long way away.

US air defences were on full alert, but with such a high volume of traffic it was a hopeless task attempting to distinguish the innocent from the potentially threatening. Mistakes were likely to happen. Only two days ago a civil airliner had come down off the coast of Florida, with no survivors. The official line was that it was due to a mechanical problem, but there were persistent rumours that it had been brought down by American air defence systems.

That old familiar phrase 'friendly fire' had been swiftly dusted down for yet another cruise through the tabloid headlines.

Yes, America was vigilant... after a fashion. The problem was, there was something in the American psyche that just couldn't accept the reality of any threat. After all, the war was over, wasn't it? The Brits were beaten. Anyway, who in their right mind was going to invade America?

Okay, so there was Pearl Harbour, but that had been a hit-and-run raid and when you came down to it, that had been Hawaii. Granted, Hawaii was part of the United States, but it was not *really* America as such, was it?

Then there was 9-11. A lot fresher in the memory, but time remains a great healer and though America would never forget, the passing of decades had soothed the resultant trauma. It still ached like an old, ever-present wound, but it no longer burned with righteous fire.

No one had ever actually invaded the USA.

Until now.

After discussing alternatives with his officers, Anthony decided the best option was to land in Canada, within reach of the US border. The choice was made that much easier by the location of their objective.

The President was spending time at one of his favourite retreats. Not Camp David, but a sprawling lodge in Aroostook County, Maine, New England.

They moved mainly at night, infiltrating the border in small units and regrouping once they were on US soil. During the day they would hide out in deep woods. The greatest threat was from tourists and sight-seers, but they were careful and had a lot of country to hide in.

There was only one incident – a family of hikers: mother, father, teenage daughter and younger son. Their dog escaped, which was regrettable but there was no point in fretting about it. The people were dispatched quickly and efficiently, in accordance with Anthony's standing orders. He was no monster, but knew that surprise was everything. They could not afford the slightest risk of discovery. Still, the executions troubled him despite their necessity. He consoled himself with the thought that on a mission like this collateral damage was inevitable…and besides, how many innocents had died in the UK during the last few weeks? Even so, he was relieved that it was another unit that encountered them, glad that he only heard about the killings after the event.

They lived off the land, not easy with such a sizeable group, but if anyone could do it, the Ghurkhas could. Anthony had once spent four days deep in the Bruneian rain forest with a unit of Ghurkhas on a training exercise. They had brought rations, but on the second night out had prepared a meal solely from roots, shoots and leaves gathered from the forest, flavoured with spices from their ration belts.

Remarkably, it was one of the best meals Anthony had ever eaten.

Maine was a long way from Brunei, but the Ghurkhas seemed to have an instinct for ferreting out the edible and nutritious.

The attack was launched two nights after they crossed the border. The President's retreat lay deep in forest and was surrounded by a wooded compound. The US military were there in force but appeared to be pretty relaxed. There were holes in the security all over the place – partly because this was not the easiest of places to secure but mostly because no-one was seriously expecting any trouble.

In their accustomed small units the Ghurkhas drifted through the defensive perimeter like ghosts.

Anthony was with a squad commanded by a Corporal, Pala, whom he had grown to know over the past few days. Pala and his men were assigned to him as bodyguards. Whether they saw this as an honour or a chore, Anthony was never entirely certain.

He did his best, but he was simply not as adept at this sort of thing as his escort. Inevitably, it was *his* clumsiness that drew the attention of a sentry. Even so, it was not him that the trooper actually discovered but one of the Ghurkhas, who deliberately left himself exposed so that the rest of the party could find cover.

The sentry came toward the crouching Ghurkha, night goggles down and gun levelled. "Hey Sarge, look what we've got here," he called over his shoulder in a loud stage whisper. "A little guy playing at being a soldier." He was still smiling as the Ghurkha disembowelled him. For his part, the sergeant said nothing; principally because he was busy having his throat cut at the time. Neither of the sentries had noticed the second Ghurkha creeping up behind them.

It was the first time Anthony had ever seen the kukri used in anger, the first opportunity he had to fully appreciate quite how it had earned its fearsome reputation.

They moved on, with Ghurkhas going on ahead to clear the way and avoid any more surprises. The further they went, the more concentrated the security presence. Twice Anthony had to step over the motionless forms of US soldiers before the bulky outline of the lodge itself loomed out from the darkness and the sheltering trees.

Oddly, it seemed at first that the front door was unguarded. An illusion that lasted only until it was opened by their own men. Several bodies had been heaped unceremoniously inside, some in uniform and some not – the missing sentries; both military and secret service.

He looked away, concentrating on the house around him, which was impressive to say the least. The entrance opened into a vast high-ceilinged hallway, dimly illuminated by occasional pairs of lamps spaced along the walls. An ornate crystal chandelier hung from the ceiling's centre like some grotesque earring. It remained unlit. His eye was inexorably drawn to the sweeping staircase, which split gracefully to meet with landings that bracketed his position to either side. Several doors led off from the hall to right and left, all closed.

From behind him, somewhere in the night, came the sound of automatic gunfire. It was what he had been half-expecting, half-listening for throughout the mission. The real surprise was that they had managed to come this far without being discovered. In a strange way this long-anticipated sound came as a relief now that it was finally heard, while making everything that much tauter and more urgent.

Muffled noise came from behind one of the doors, almost certainly a reaction to the gunfire. A Ghurkha instantly slipped across to stand beside the door in question, moving to grab the figure who stepped through as it opened.

A maid: pretty, slender and young. She wore full maid's dress, complete with white bib-apron and small frilled hat, looking bizarrely out of place next to the Ghurkha in his dappled combat uniform, like some extra who had just stepped from the set of a Miss Marple mystery and found herself in the wrong movie.

Even as that thought crossed Anthony's mind, a hand clamped over the girl's mouth and a kukri flashed.

Perhaps it was the tension of the situation or perhaps just a growing familiarity with violence, but he felt less regret about her than he had on being told about the family of hikers. She was probably secret service in any case.

The gunfire sounded nearer. Corporal Pala and his men went back outside to take up defensive positions, guarding the entrance.

Another Ghurkha gestured him over to a particular closed door, holding up one finger emphatically and pointing to indicate that there was a solitary man inside. Anthony risked opening the door a fraction and peered in. It was the President. He was pacing up and down with obvious impatience.

After some furious signalling, the Ghurkhas reluctantly agreed to wait in the hall. He opened the door and stepped inside; alone.

It was a long room. The far end accommodated a dark wood table, encircled by several high-backed chairs. A log fire, embers aglow, graced an impressive stone hearth to his left.

The only things to adorn the walls were an irregular series of paintings. Preserved in oils, the faces of long-dead men gazed down from formal portraits.

The President turned towards him, perhaps alerted by the sound of the door despite his care.

"About god-damn time!" he exclaimed, before resuming his pacing.

Uncertain who he was being mistaken for, Anthony took a moment to assess the man before him. Slight – far shorter than he looked in newscasts – with a furrowed brow and thinning hair peppered with just the right amount of grey to look distinguished. He wore a suit that might once have been expensive, classy, but now just looked lived-in, as if it had been worn continuously for days.

"Sorry to keep you waiting, Mr. President," Anthony temporised.

"You people really have a fucking nerve! Don't you know I've got a country to run?" He reached the end of the room, swivelled and paced back again, gesticulating wildly.

"Now don't get me wrong, the food here's great and it's good to get away once in a while. I know you're busy men yourselves, what with your corporate empires to oversee and everything, but that doesn't give you the right to treat me like this. A month! I've been late for meetings myself in my time. I could have excused a few hours, a day even... but a month?" He stopped and jabbed a finger at Anthony's chest. "I'm not irrelevant you know, not yet."

An assertion which seemed highly questionable under the circumstances.

A month? That meant that the President had been here since before everything kicked off.

Anthony thought about the newscasts; that wise, reassuring face addressing the American populace and, by extension, the people of the world, explaining in earnest tones why the invasion of Great Britain was such a regrettable necessity.

Fake, all of them. Were they computer-generated, an actor, or a combination of both? Not that it mattered, he was just fleetingly curious.

All the while, the man whose face had been thus plagiarised – the President of the United States, believed by many to be the most powerful man on the planet – had been here in this remote wilderness, waiting for a meeting that was never going to take place. The poor schmuck clearly had no idea of the situation, might not even be aware that there had been a war at all.

Anthony was abruptly conscious of the unaccustomed weight at his belt, where a borrowed pistol rested. He had come here determined to cut off the beast's head. Unfortunately all that was available was its figurehead. But he had to go through with it, didn't he? Some sort of blow had to be struck for Britain, for all the right-minded people of the world, and for the Ghurkhas who were even now sacrificing their lives to give him this opportunity.

"Mr. President, I'm sorry."

The instant his finger tightened on the trigger it occurred to Anthony that he might actually be doing the real powers-that-be a favour – creating a martyr out of a puppet who had already served his purpose.

The man's face showed puzzlement, then shock and complete disbelief. Even at the very end, he never understood.

All along the walls the eyes of dead Presidents stared down at Anthony from their heavy-framed portraits, as if in judgement. Anthony allowed the gun to drop to the floor, his arm suddenly heavy and too weak to hold it up any longer. He gazed at the crumpled body for a moment, trying to make sense of all this. While he did so, the sounds of gunfire drew ever closer and then abruptly louder, suggesting that the fighting had reached the house itself.

It would not be long now.

Somewhere, he felt certain, the ghost of Bin Laden was laughing.

***

My brother-in-Law, Philip, works for the Foreign Office. When I first met him he had just returned from a four year posting in Brunei, where his duties included being the official liaison with the Ghurkhas stationed there. He was a great source of both information and anecdotes about the Ghurkhas, which I filed away, certain that they would prove useful for a story at some point without having any idea how or when.

A few years later, in 2003, Tony Blair's government took Britain into an invasion of Iraq on America's coat tails. I was incensed, feeling at a gut-level that this was wrong and ill-advised in all sorts of ways. An idea for a story started to form in reaction, which married perfectly with all the Ghurkha-related bits and pieces at the back of my mind. The indignity and frustration I felt boiled out as "The Laughter of Ghosts".

Written in anger, the story contains a fair bit of anti-American sentiment and I had no real expectation that it would ever find a market. Then, Farah Mendlesohn issued a call for submissions for an anthology to be called *Glorifying Terrorism*, intended as a protest against the potential implications of certain clauses within the recently passed anti-terrorism laws… This seemed a possible home for the story, and so it proved.

A Bit About Ian

Ian Whates lives in a comfortable home down a quiet cul-de-sac in an idyllic Cambridgeshire village, which he shares with his partner Helen and their pets – Honey the golden cocker spaniel, Calvin the tailless black cat and Inky the goldfish (sadly, Binky died).

Ian's love of science fiction began while he was still at school, manifesting itself when he produced an SF murder mystery as homework after being set the essay title "The Language of Shakespeare", much to the bemusement of his English teacher.

His first published stories appeared in the late 1980s, but it was not until the early 2000s that he began to pursue writing with any seriousness, joining the Northampton SF Writers Group in 2004 after being introduced to its chairman, Ian Watson.

In 2006 Ian launched independent publisher NewCon Press, quite by accident (buy him a pint sometime and he'll tell you about it). That same year he also resumed submitting short stories, selling some 25 to various venues by the time May 2008 arrived. One of these even found its way onto the shortlist for the BSFA Awards in 2008... and it didn't come last!

This success surprised the author even more than the awards and accolades accumulated by his various NewCon Press anthologies, but he's certainly not complaining.

Ian is currently a director of both the Science Fiction Writers of America (SFWA) and the British Science Fiction Association (BSFA), editing *Matrix*, the online news and media reviews magazine, for the latter.

In September 2008 Ian completed his first novel, *City of Dreams and Nightmare*, on the strength of which respected literary agent John Jarrold agreed to represent his work; and a month later Solaris books commissioned Ian to write two space opera novels, which he is currently beavering away at... honest!

THE BRITISH SCIENCE FICTION ASSOCIATION

Don't just *read* about British science fiction… be a part of it.

Proud of our history and excited by the future.

The British Science Fiction Association: over 50 years of providing a focus for the people who love to read, watch, learn about and talk about science fiction.

Why join the BSFA? Well…

1. **The Community of Fans**

2. **Exclusive Magazines**

3. **Exclusive Discounts on Books**

4. **Support and Advice for New Writers**

5. **The Very Best of Reviews and Informed Opinion**

6. **Keeping Up to Date With News and Events**

7. **The Ability to Vote in the BSFA Awards**

8. **Affordable Membership Fees**

WHY MISS OUT?

To discover more, visit our website and forums at
www.bsfa.co.uk/bsfa/website/default.aspx